Blood Curse

Blood Curse

Waves of Darkness
Book 1

Tamara A. Lowery

Steele Rose Publishing

Blood Curse
Waves of Darkness Book 1
By
Tamara A. Lowery

1st Edition, Gypsy Shadow Publishing, March 2011 eBook, November 2013 print

2nd Edition, Tamara A. Lowery DBA Steele Rose Publishing, 2021

Cover art, © 2021 Fatima Saddiqa
Interior art, © 2021 Tamara A. Lowery

talowery.wordpress.com

Published in the United States of America

Print ISBN 978-1-956849-00-4
Ebook ISBN 978-1-956849-01-1

Foreword, Warnings, and Acknowledgements

Welcome aboard! Before we set sail, a few words about this series of books as well as a few warnings.

My husband and I first conceived the basic premise for the Waves of Darkness series in 2005. We thought it would be a good idea to combine pirates and vampires into a single series. At first, we thought it a completely novel idea. That notion was quickly proven wrong as I came across other books and even a comic book series with such a combination. Still, there is plenty of room for expansion in the niche, and Waves of Darkness takes a sufficiently different approach so as not to step on other creators' toes.

Although we came up with three core characters together, the rest of the crew and the course I set them are entirely my own.

The books were first published by Gypsy Shadow Publishing, and the first 7 books were originally published through them from 2011 to 2017.

I parted ways with them in 2018, and all rights reverted to me. After failing to secure a new publisher, I decided to put them through revisions and release a 2nd edition of each of the first 7 books. These 7 books complete the Sisters of Power story arc.

As of this writing, I have already drafted the 8th book in the series, which is the start of the Daughters of the Dragon story arc. This second arc is planned to take place over 7 books, as well, and will be the end of the series.

Now for the warnings: if you are easily offended, this is probably NOT the book for you. My pirates are not nice. My vampires do not sparkle. The story takes place during the American Revolutionary era, although it only gets passing mention. That being said, I do include activities which took place during that era, as well as use prevalent gender role attitudes of the time. This means, males are often condescending and/or violent toward females. Human trafficking, whether the trade of African slaves, or of women and children as sex workers, were often activities carried out by pirates. After all, why kill or drown what you could sell?

There are also instances of rape.

Although I include such in the book, it does NOT mean I condone such behavior. It merely reflects some of the brutality of a pirate's lifestyle. I DO include strong female characters throughout the series.

There is a human sacrifice detailed in the book.

Vampires, by definition, are serial killers.

If I haven't scared you off by now, I hope you truly enjoy the story.

I would like to thank Charlotte Holley and Denise Bartlett at Gypsy Shadow for giving me my break a decade ago.

I would like to thank Stephanie Osborn, Dave Schroeder, HP Holo, William Joseph Roberts and numerous other authors who are convention friends or members of the Facebook writing/author groups I subscribe to for their help and advice in bringing this book back to light.

You guys are the BEST!

Dedication

To my pirate
My husband Derik
Without whom Viktor Brandewyne would never have been

Once Upon a Tide...

On a pleasant summer afternoon in 1750, a young boy drifted lazily among the salt marshes which inundated coastal Georgia. He'd fished for a while that morning without any luck. Having grown bored with the activity, he'd allowed his punt to drift where it would in the maze-like channels between the marshlands, tidal flats, and small islands formed from the oyster shell ballast dumped by merchant ships preparing to take on cargo in port.

He had no worry of getting lost. He'd navigated these waters for as long as he could remember. The boy knew he was currently about three miles south of Savannah.

The warm sun and cool breeze lent themselves to napping. Soon, the boy dozed off. The sound of other boys chattering and laughing woke him. They sounded nearby. As quietly as possible, he rowed toward the voices. The high tide influenced his decision to take the little flat-bottomed punt into the marsh grass before getting too close. His black hair and bronzed skin marked him as different from most of the inhabitants of the colony and occasionally made him a target of other children. Many of the more superstitious adults thought his vivid green eyes marked him as possibly mad or possessed. No telling what mood these strangers might be in.

Peering through the grasses, he saw two boys around his age busy pulling up their crab traps. The wooden tub seated in the middle of their boat brimmed with their catch. Three empty traps sat stacked in the back of their boat. Crabs practically stuffed the current trap they worked; several of the crabs quite large.

The boy was very fond of the sweet meat of the sought-after blue crabs. He knew old Mother would be glad of the treat, as well.

Although, she'll probably grumble that I didn't net her some shrimp to go with them, he thought to himself. His decision made; he nudged his boat through the flooded marsh to join the other boys.

"Those are some mighty fine-lookin' crabs," he told them by way of greeting. "I'll have them."

The younger of the boys, brothers, smiled at him. "You want to buy them?"

The lone boy smiled back and calmly stated, "No. I'll take them. Now."

The older brother scowled at him, ready to defend their catch from the young interloper. "You can't just take them," he countered. "You have to buy them, if you want them. We worked hard for these crabs, and we're going to take them back to town to sell them."

The boy said matter-of-factly, "My waters, my crabs. Hand them over. I won't tell you again."

Rather than comply, the older brother shouted, "I said, you can't have them!"

Taking his oar, the boy nimbly jumped into the brothers' boat and promptly used it to knock the older of the two into the water. He brandished the oar at the younger boy. The lad quickly decided the water a better place to be than in the same boat with the mad young bully. The victor then began tying their boat to his punt, to tow it back with him and ensure they didn't try to give chase to reclaim their catch.

The older brother looked a bit panicked at this. His sibling wept in fear.

"Hey! You can't just leave us out here! We could drown trying to get back home," he pled.

He looked at them, almost expressionless, and said, "You should have given me the crabs when I told you to." He rowed away, not caring if they made it back or not. "Whatever fate the tide and marsh have for you is your lot now."

Of course, the lads made it back to Savannah. Otherwise, the legend would never have been born of how, in the summer of 1750, an eleven-year-old Viktor Brandewyne committed his first act of piracy.

And the rest, as you soon will read, is history.

Chapter 1

On August 18, 1771, the pirate ship, *Redfish*, limped madly across the choppy waters twenty miles northeast of Hispañola, the *HMS Bonnie Mae* closing rapidly. The Navy ship pursuing her started the chase almost five hours earlier, after exchanging fire just north of Tortuga Harbor.

The *Redfish* ran towards a strong storm on the horizon, hoping to lose her pursuer in the heavy rains. What had looked like a mere storm five hours ago now revealed its true nature; hurricane. A wall of clouds stretched from horizon to horizon. Gusts of wind played hell with the surviving rigging, and the seas grew heavier; waves soon towering above the masts.

The pirate ship had not fared well in her exchange with the *Bonnie Mae*. Her topmast and mizzenmast hung snapped and splintered, destroyed by chain shot. The bodies of the dead or mortally wounded scattered the quarter deck and gun deck. To add insult to injury, a stray cannonball had blasted a good-sized hole at her waterline. Before he bled to death from a leg wound, the ship's carpenter at least managed to get a makeshift patch in place. The rough waters hammered away at it, though, forcing bits of oakum loose around the plug. Clearly it wouldn't hold much longer.

Already, the *Redfish* was taking on water. Her captain, Viktor Brandewyne, known more commonly as Bloody Vik Brandee, knew the ship was doomed. But he was determined they'd not be taken to experience the King's "kind" mercies.

"Aft lookout report!" Viktor bellowed.

"Aft lookout, aye," the pirate in the rigging called back. "She be closing with us, Cap'n. Pro'ly be on us in another hour. She's atwixt us and the nearest land."

"Understood, aft lookout. Forward lookout report!"

"Forward lookout, aye. That be a bad 'un, Cap'n. Definitely a hurricane. Heavy seas ahead. We be in no shape to tangle with that bitch," the lookout answered.

Viktor mulled his predicament: Navy at his back; monstrous hurricane before him; no apparent escape. He made his decision.

"Mr. Rigger," he addressed the helmsman, "steer me a course due east."

"Aye, Cap'n. Um, Cap'n, that'll take us straight into the hurricane," Rigger pointed out.

He smiled darkly. "Aye, Jim. It will." Shouting loud enough for the remains of his crew to hear, he announced, "Listen up lads! We're taking the *Redfish* right down the gullet of that storm afore us! If the King wants our ship, he'll have to follow us into the mouth of Hell itself to catch us! What say ye?"

A unanimous roar of agreement rose from the crew. Each man knew the only alternative was dangling from a gibbet in Port Royal or at Wapping, on Execution Dock.

"Then step to it, ye scurrilous dregs!" he ordered. "We've a hurricane to catch!" Turning, he faced the storm and their certain doom. "Don't fear, Jim. I've a few tricks left. We'll cheat ol' Cob same as we'll cheat the King of his prey."

"Aye, Cap'n."

Aboard the *Bonnie Mae*, the Royal Navy captain muttered to himself, "You think you're clever, Brandee, but your wiles have finally failed you. Your ship cannot withstand that tempest." Aloud, he ordered, "Helmsman, follow our pirate prey at a good distance.

We'll not go into the storm ourselves, but I do not want the *Redfish* to escape it. What we started; the good Lord is about to finish for us."

"Aye, sir."

As the light faded, the storm and sunset darkening the sky, the captain of the *Bonnie Mae* watched through the glass, until the fury of the storm swept the *Redfish* away.

Days later, when the storm was spent, the *Bonnie* Mae surveyed the area. A good deal of flotsam littered the waves. The busted hulls of a couple of small boats drifted among the wreckage. A few bloated or dismembered bodies floated among the debris. More shark activity than usual deterred any thoughts of salvage. They found no survivors to rescue for hanging.

At the end of her cruise, the captain of the *HMS Bonnie Mae* had Viktor Brandewyne removed from the lists of wanted pirates. He reported the pirate ship *Redfish* lost at sea with all hands.

Three days after the *Redfish* sailed into oblivion, two small boats landed at dusk in a sandy little cove just west of the seaside village of Terra Beau, on the north shore of Hispañola. Ten men scrambled out and proceeded to drag the boats up into the nearby vegetation, where they could easily be hidden.

Vik Brandee ran a speculative eye over the remains of his crew. Just a week ago, they'd been forty strong, the whole sea theirs to roam, plundering and pillaging where they would. Now, he'd lost over half his crew to the Royal Navy's guns. The angry sea and storm swallowed another seven.

The mortally wounded and the poor bastards unlucky enough to draw the short straws to stay with the ship and take her into the storm comprised the last few.

Vik and the nine men with him had lowered their boats, once the seas had gotten rough enough to hide the activity. As added insurance, they had pulled dark painted sailcloth taut over them.

These made the boats almost impossible to distinguish from the surrounding waves.

Still, only luck allowed them to escape the storm. Nearly swamped the first night, the found themselves forced to spend almost as much time bailing seawater as rowing.

Now, the ten of them were ashore and in relatively good shape. Brandee's and his first mate, Rigger's, foresight made sure each man brought provisions enough for a week, as well as plenty of coin for when they made landfall.

"Good news, Cap'n," Jim Rigger grinned. "I know this shore. That village just down the coast is Terra Beau. It's about an hour's walk from this cove, and she has a fine tavern and inn; good food, fine spirits for such an out of the way spot, and saucy wenches."

Viktor let out a hearty laugh. "Trust you to know where the whores are, Jim. Probably know 'em each by name, too."

"Not all, Cap'n," Rigger grinned. "Been a few years. Probably some fresh 'uns been added since."

"Then we should go see. Wouldn't want you to miss out on any new experiences." Viktor clapped the man on the back, hefted his sea bag, and headed up into the jungle, looking for a footpath to the town in question.

The Dead Wolf Tavern was a favorite haunt of the less-than-sterling members of society. Fights among patrons were frequent and often ignored, save by those who wished to join in or were wagering on the outcome. Vik Brandee and his men caused no more of a stir than was usual for the place.

Rum and other spirits flowed freely, the tavern keeper enterprising to part the pirates from as much of their coin as possible, before they decided to leave port. He'd instructed his girls to do so, as well. He kept an eye out to make sure none of them were too roughly handled, though. If one was injured or scarred, she'd be of no use to him.

Brandee and his men took full advantage of the services. Two girls, one perched on either knee, hand-fed Jim Rigger bits of meat and fruit. One pirate's snores emanated from under a table, a half-full bottle clutched in a meaty hand and two more empties nestled against his side. Three others tossed knives at a much-abused cork target. The rest engaged in eating, drinking, or wenching upstairs or in back.

A few local men were present, as well, eating or drinking. One dark-skinned youth sat at the end of the bar nursing a bottle of rum and glaring around sullenly. When not shooting evil glances at the pirates, his eyes kept gravitating to a particularly buxom mullato girl.

One of the few girls serving food rather than one of the men, she drew one's eye. She possessed fine features, full lips, and eyes blacker than night. Tendrils of glossy black hair, which escaped her braid and cap to form a wispy dark halo around her face, offset the warm, golden-brown tone of her skin. The old tavern keeper charged much more for her services than any other of his stable of wenches.

Viktor decided to find out if she was worth the coin.

A couple of hours later, Viktor and the wench lay resting from a rousing round of sex. He rolled to his side, facing her, and propped himself up on his elbow to gaze admiringly at the young woman's nude form. The lamplight gave his coppery skin a ruddy hue, but it made her golden skin seem to glow. Vik used his free hand to brush a sweat-soaked, raven tendril of hair from her face.

"So beautiful, so young, and amazingly skilled," he complimented her and gave her a gentle smile. "Carmella, pet, what led you to this life?"

She returned his smile, her body still relaxed from their lovemaking. "My parents are dead, and I like men," she answered.

"I can tell you do." He laughed. "I much prefer an experienced woman to one who barely knows her own body. It makes things so much easier and enjoyable." He stroked a finger lightly down her arm, raising chill bumps and causing her to shiver a bit. "Have you always lived in this port, pet?"

"*Oui*," she sighed. "A young sailor once offered to smuggle me aboard his ship, so we could sail away and be married."

He continued to caress her as she spoke, fingertips moving skillfully across her bare skin. "I am glad you did not go with him." His voice was warm and deep. "It would have deprived me of enjoying your exquisite company. May I ask why you stayed?" A shadow of distant horror crossed her face, as she replied, "Our cook, Edmina, told me once of going off with a sailor, when she was young. When her lover's captain discovered her on board, he had both of them beaten and let the crew use her in front of her lover. When all the men were through with her, she was torn and bleeding; her hips were crushed. They put her ashore, not caring if she lived or died. She healed enough to walk again, but her womb is dead, and she goes into hysterics if any man so much as touches her. Henri keeps her around to discourage us from leaving his service —and she is a good cook."

Viktor leaned down and kissed Carmella on the forehead. He didn't care for this new direction of the conversation or how the girl tensed up because of it. He did not want her dwelling on a subject that would inhibit her ability to pleasure him.

"It is sad that your friend fell in with such a sorry crew of pirates," he whispered into her hair. "We are not all such blackguards, pet."

"Pirates? Ha!" She gave a bitter laugh. "No, the bastards who took Edmina were His Majesty's finest." Barely contained venom filled her voice.

Viktor smiled to himself at her response. He knew exactly which British Navy captain she spoke of. Only the man's reputation for cruelty could keep his crew in line. His frequent drunkenness made him a piss-poor commander. Viktor remembered the cheers which went up when he gutted the wretch in a tavern brawl in the Bahamas seven months previous. The battle had hardly been worth the effort.

He waited for the full import of what he'd said to register with her. He didn't have to wait for long.

"You are a pirate, *Capitan*?" she smiled.

"Aye. Have you been with many pirates?"

"*Non*, but I've always wanted to try one."

"And why have you not?"

"There is little here to draw a pirate's attention," she answered him. "There is no treasure, only small local trade, and the harbor is shallow, I've been told."

"Oh?" he prompted.

"*Oui*. It is rare for anything larger than a small, shallow-water sloop or the coastal ketches to make port here. Warships and merchant ships have to anchor out nearly a mile away and come ashore in launches or canoes. Few captains feel it worth the effort, since our village has nothing special to offer."

Viktor trailed kisses along her collarbone, murmuring. "Ah, but that is only because they do not know of your presence, my pet." His hand became a bit more insistent in its caresses.

She writhed in response, her own hands exploring his body. "*Mon Capitan*! Ready again, and so quickly! I am impressed," she giggled.

"You will find that my appetites are insatiable, pet." He softly growled, as his kisses turned to playful nips. "And skilled though you are, I believe there are some new tricks I can teach you yet."

Wrapping her legs around him, she purred, "Then take me, *mon Capitan*."

He wasted no time in doing so.

The next morning, Viktor found the tavern keeper, Henrí, and procured Carmella's services until further notice.

"There are some things I do not share with my crew, old man. My wench is one of them. She is not to accept a consignment with anyone, until I decide I am through with her. Honor this arrangement, and I will pay double her fee. Dishonor it, and you will lose your best whore."

"Understood, Cap'n," the greedy pimp readily agreed. "Carmella's yours exclusively, as long as you like." The man's avarice would see to it.

The pirate captain strode to one of the brothel shanties behind the tavern and rapped on the door. "Rigger, on deck now!" he ordered.

His first mate stumbled out the door sans shirt. Feminine hands grasped at his arms, and at least three voices protested his leaving. Laughing, he shooed them off. "No worry, ladies. I'll return — and I want you fully rested, when I do." Finally, he managed to get out the door, pulling his shirt over his head as he did so.

Viktor chuckled, "Greedy bastard. One day, you'll learn that sometimes quality overrides quantity."

"Aye, Cap'n," Rigger nodded, grinning, "but why not enjoy both?"

"Greedy bastard." Vik shook his head. "Roust Jon-Jon and meet me at the docks."

Rigger nodded and left to find the pirate in question. He located the man snoring away beneath the same table he'd drunk himself under the night before. Jim kicked the sole of the man's boot. He was rewarded with an incoherent grunt. He kicked harder. "Get up, Jon-Jon, ya great heap o' shit."

"Bugger off!" Jon-Jon curled into a ball, cradling his head.

Jim bent over and grabbed a handful of shirt. He then proceeded to haul the man out. "Get on yer feet, Jon-Jon."

"All right, leggo!" he protested. "I'm up, already. Why am I up?"

Rigger clapped him on the shoulder and grinned. "Cap'n wants us to go shoppin'."

That day yielded no profit. They had mingled among the fishermen, porters, and the few men hoping to gain a berth on the next merchantman to come through. Most of the latter were youngsters or young men bored with island life. After all, who wanted to spend their life in some backwater fishing village, when there was an entire ocean out there?

The problem: there was no ship to get on. Disappointed, but not really surprised, Viktor and his two mates returned to the tavern. The pirate knew a ship would be along, probably within the next two days. At least he gained a little more information to compliment what Carmella had given him. The village supported a small trade of local fish and produce for fabric and raw metals. He understood why the wench wouldn't know much of that. Respectable masters did not permit their apprentices or indentured men to frequent taverns or brothels.

The next day, fortunes turned for the better. Two sloops and a brigantine made port. The brigantine rode too low in the water to come up to the docks but lay at anchor out in the harbor. She sent several small boats in to give her crew liberty.

At their captain's behest, Rigger and Jon-Jon joined Viktor in his room to discuss their plans. "Well, lads?" He sat back and looked at his mates expectantly.

Jon-Jon went first. "Both the sloops are coastal traders. All I've seen all day are bales of cloth comin' off and barrels of bananas, papayas, and salted fish goin' on, Cap'n. Word is they make this port every fortnight with another pair of boats comin' the week between."

"What arms?" Brandee asked curtly.

"No more'n four guns apiece, Cap'n," he said with a sneer. "Buggers are right dull about our sort. Figure no one'd bother with 'em, since all they do are local trade. They got a couple more fishing villages atween here and the port they do business with. Milk runs; very borin'."

Viktor looked at Jim. "And the brigantine in the harbor?"

"She be fat and ripe for the taking, Cap'n. She won't be easy, though. Fifteen guns, ten of 'em are twelve-pounders. But," he paused for effect, "my lovelies have been busy among the crew she sent ashore."

Viktor gave a predatory smile. "I take it they've brought you some interesting news."

"Aye," Rigger looked smug. "Seems her master's not too popular. He put in here to take on provisions and replace those of the crew too sick to go on, but only after the threat of a mutiny."

The pirate captain leaned forward and tented his fingers. "How fortuitous; I do not believe we could have asked for a better opportunity. Mr. Rigger, see to it that her captain meets with an unfortunate accident this evening. Eliminate the more loyal of his mates, as well. Mr. Jon, tell the men to be at the docks by eight bells of the middle watch. They're to double up on their pleasures tonight, you two as well. We sail at dawn."

Once his mates left to carry out their orders, Viktor went down to the tavern for food and drink. He requested Carmella attend him while he ate, intending to return upstairs with her afterwards to take his full pleasure.

About halfway through his meal, a shadow loomed over his table. He looked up to see a local youth glaring down at him. Viktor recognized the boy as the same one who'd been shooting evil glances at him and his crew from the end of the bar for the past two nights.

"You're in my light, boy. Go away," he dismissed him, and went back to eating.

"Goddam pirate bastard," the lad slurred, his breath reeking of the cheap rum he'd been drinking all day. The tavern noises grew muted, ears and eyes straining expectantly at the brewing confrontation. Some of the pirates quietly made bets about how long before the local boy died.

The tavern keeper started to hustle over. "David, go home," Henrí told him. "You're drunk, and you know *Mamaan* Juma doesn't want you sniffing around my girls. Scat, boy."

"Get back behind your bar, old man," Viktor ordered in a tone that brooked no argument. He turned his full attention to the drunken youth. As he addressed him, his voice turned calm and soft; a reasonable smile graced his face. "You have a quarrel with me, boy, or just a general dislike of pirates?"

Needing no further encouragement, David launched into a loud tirade. "All you pirates are stinking pigs! You take, always take! You take the best of everything! And you're the worst of all! You take my sweet Carmella! I see how she looks at you and no one else. I want to marry her, free her from this life, but you come and turn her heart from me. Bastard!" The boy was almost in tears from anger and alcohol.

Viktor's smile became one of pity. "Poor boy, I did you a favor," he sighed. "Only an idiot falls in love with a whore. Why should she give you something for free, when she can get good coin for it?" He reached over and pulled Carmella to his side, an arm around her waist, his hand dipping lower and caressing suggestively. "And she is worth every piece, I must say. You may be stupid, but I have to admit you have good taste."

He released her waist and stood, coming around the table to tower over the boy. The hand the boy held a bottle with trembled, as a sense of the true danger to himself began to seep through his alcohol-soaked brain. Viktor placed a hand on the boy's shoulder and gave him an almost kindly smile.

"Get yer stinkin' hand off me, you pirate pig!" David shrieked, trying to shake loose without success.

Viktor brushed his free hand slowly back through his shoulder-length raven hair in a practiced gesture his men recognized immediately. He sighed. "You realize you have taken things past the point of no return, David, was it?"

The boy nodded, eyes starting to show too much white.

"I'm glad you understand. It has to be this way. And David, you really should know a man's name, if you're going to insult him." He tightened his grip on the youth's shoulder and buried the long dagger he'd retrieved from its sheath, hidden at his nape, deep between the boy's ribs, until he found the heart. "Viktor Brandewyne, at your service, sir."

He let the boy drop to the floor and watched, until the knife in his chest stopped quivering with each heartbeat. "Lads, clear this flotsam out of here. I'd like to enjoy the rest of my meal in peace."

As a couple of pirates moved to drag the body out, one asked, "What of yer dagger, Cap'n?"

"Leave it. He's earned it for having the balls to even confront me. Carmella, pet, my mug is empty."

She got a fresh bottle from the bar and refilled his cup. "Be careful, *Capitan*," she whispered. "That boy was a favorite of *Mamaan* Juma. She's a powerful bad witch. Black magic."

"Bah, nothing but islander superstitions," he waved the warning off as nothing.

Chapter 2

Brandee finished his meal without further interruption. "Carmella, pet, join me in my room in about half an hour, he instructed her. "I've some business to attend to before tonight's festivities." He gave her a wink and a slap on the rear that made her giggle. On his way to his room, he tapped one of his crew and motioned for the man to follow.

Once in the room, Brandee scrawled a quick note then handed it to the pirate. "See that Mr. Rigger gets this as soon as possible. You should find him somewhere near the docks."

The quantity of drink he'd had with his meal had its natural effect. The idea of being in the throes of animal lust in a room perfumed by a chamber pot full of his rum-rich piss did not appeal to him. So, he made his way back downstairs and out the back to use the public ditch.

Just as Carmella left the tavern's public room to go up to Viktor's room, a muffled shout and the sounds of a struggle distracted her. The noise came from the back alley. She thought she recognized Viktor's voice. Curiosity prompted her to investigate. She held no doubt that her *Capitan* could handle himself in a fight, but she would like to watch. The quiet ferocity of the man excited her and ignited her desire like no other man had since she'd taken up her profession. The murder of her would-be suitor thrilled rather than saddened her. That her current lover killed a man for possession of her filled her with a heady sense of empowerment. Had she truly known Viktor Brandewyne, she would have felt fear rather than flattery.

She reached the scene of the scuffle and verified she'd indeed heard Viktor. The scene before her, however, proved far different from her expectations. Two attackers beset the pirate captain. Their slow, shambling motions should've made them easy to defeat; yet they seemed to be winning. Viktor cut the hand off one attacker and ran the second one through, and still they kept coming. Even the severed hand crawled over and managed to attach itself to the pirate's leg.

Carmella screamed. She realized *Mamaan* Juma had sent her zombies to fetch the pirate who had dared to kill one of her favorites. The sudden noise distracted Viktor for a moment and gave the zombies the opening they needed. With Viktor's sword still in its chest, one of the zombies brought a fist crashing down on the pirate's head with superhuman strength. Viktor dropped to the ground, limp and unconscious. The impaled dead man grabbed his shoulders, the other reached for his legs. The zombie's hand reattached as soon as it came in contact with its arm. The two creatures melted into the darkness with their prize.

Carmella ran back inside, fleeing up to Viktor's room, terrified that the zombies would return for her. David's death had been indirectly because of her, after all.

The pirate Viktor assigned as messenger found Jim Rigger as he climbed up to the dock from the small dugout he had "borrowed" for his deadly errand.

"Mr. Rigger, Cap'n told me to find ye and give ye this note."

"Thank you, Murph," Rigger took the scrap of paper and moved closer to one of the lanterns hanging along the dock to read it.

Viktor wrote, "The old man has seen too much. Dispose of him." Rigger folded the note and shoved it in his pocket.

"Murph, go tell Jon-Jon the ship is ready for boarding," he ordered the messenger. He headed back to the tavern to deal with the innkeeper.

He found Henrí asleep on his cot in his storeroom with one of his wenches curled up naked next to him. As quietly as possible, Rigger slit both their throats. Standing and looking at the bodies, he shook his head. "Waste of a good wench."

He turned and made his way towards his captain's room to give a brief report before finding a wench or two to spend what was left of the night with.

Carmella gave a startled shriek when a knock came on the door. She realized it wasn't *Mamaan* Juma's zombies come for her when a muffled male voice said, "Oh, sorry, Cap'n. I'll not disturb you." Gathering her wits, she went to the door and out into the passageway.

Jim Rigger was almost to the stairs, when she called out to him, "*M'sieur*, the *Capitan* has been taken."

Rigger whirled on her, grasping her arms, a fierce look on his face. "Talk fast, bitch. Who took him? Where? Answer me!" He punctuated each demand with a rough shake.

Carmella whimpered, fear of *Mamaan* Juma battling with the more immediate fear of the angry pirate whose clutches she was in. Rigger drew back a hand to strike her, and the fear of him won out.

"*Mamaan* Juma, sh-she sent her monster demons to bring the *Capitan* to her," she stammered.

"Talk sense, woman," Rigger ordered. "Who is this *Mamaan* Juma, and what business does she have with Captain Brandee?"

"She *beau coup mal* witch, *m'sieur*," Carmella explained. "The *Capitan*, he killed one of her favorites tonight for challenging him. The boy, David Reneau, came in and told the *Capitan* he want me. He call the *Capitan* names."

Rigger knew his captain well. Brandewyne would brook no insult to himself from some islander pup, especially not over a tavern whore. That Carmella still drew breath spoke of how talented a lover she must be. Ordinarily, in a similar situation, Viktor would have killed the whore, as well, for inconveniencing him.

"Do you know where this witch took him?" Jim asked. "Can you take me there?"

She nodded, but terror showed in her eyes. Fear of what the witch would do, if she caught her almost paralyzed her. Rigger saw this but found her unreasoning superstition irritating. "I am not leaving without my captain, wench. Now take me to him!"

Carmella took a shuddering breath and made her decision. "I will take you there, and hopefully we can rescue the *Capitan*. But I cannot stay here anymore. *Mamaan* Juma will kill me, or worse, if I do. I help you in exchange for safe passage away from this island," she bargained.

"Fair enough," Rigger agreed.

Viktor woke with a splitting headache and numb hands. It took him a few minutes to be able to think clearly past the pain. He realized he was suspended by his wrists. Strong cord was tied around them then run through an iron ring near the top of a tall post. Yet, he faced outward rather than toward the post, so he did not believe his captors planned to flog him. It puzzled him as to why he had been taken. The fact he was obviously outdoors rather than in whatever pathetic jail this little port might boast told him whoever had him was not any sort of official.

A strong blaze flared to life before him, temporarily blinding him. An ominous, deep female voice addressed him from beyond the flames, "De time has come to pay for your sins, white man."

Viktor's arrogance came to the forefront. "I am Viktor Brandewyne. I do what I will and suffer no man to call me to task for it."

"I am no man, pirate," the voice stated. Its owner made her appearance. An old, fat, black woman stepped through the bonfire. She did not jump or run through, rather she walked through at an unhurried pace. The flames spread away from her feet and body with each step, never touching her. Her bare, flaccid breasts hung to her waist, having long ago lost the plump fullness of youth and motherhood. A coating of some white paste covered her arms, torso, face and dreadlocks. She wore reddish brown patterns painted on this pale background; her face decorated with a skull design. Various herbs, bones and shells hung about on her person.

"I am *Mamaan* Juma," she proclaimed. "I know who you are, white man. I know what you are, and I know what you did."

Viktor curled his lip in disdain at this crazy old woman, who apparently fancied herself a witch. His mind explained away the zombie attack and her fire walking as the result of some hallucinogenic herb being slipped into his food or drink. He'd heard of such things before.

"I'm no more a white man than you are, and I've done many things, old woman," he sneered. "What is your grievance?"

She gave him a bone-chilling, soulless glare, then ignored him and began gyrating around; a slow, strange, deliberate dance. The steps took her close to the fire again. She grabbed a string of herbs from her waist and tossed them into the fire, producing a green flash. Viktor found her swaying dance both repulsive and mesmerizing. She murmured in some sing-song language as she continued to dance, alternately seeming to pray to the blaze and gesticulating at him. The latter moves were both ominous and obscene.

She danced around to the other side of the fire, out of his line of sight.

When she returned to his side of the blaze, she was no longer dancing. Instead, she led a goat and carried an earthenware bowl devoid of any design or decoration. Speaking again in the unfamiliar tongue, she took a stone blade from the band of her skirt and used it to slit the goat's throat. She laid the animal down to bleed out into the bowl, then took the same knife and cut away Viktor's shirt.

His mind screamed at him to lash out at the witch, but he felt paralyzed. Apparently, her spell rendered him mute, as well. He wanted to yell and rant at her. He wanted to get loose and slit her throat and gut her. How dare she insult and humiliate him like this?!

She dipped a brush made of palm frond into the bowl of goat blood and started painting designs on his chest, speaking some unknown incantation with the completion of each brush stroke. Finally, she stood back from him, examined her handiwork, and nodded.

"You pirate; you a killer; white man." Her voice carried pure, scalding hatred as she emphasized the last bit, clearly intending it as an insult. "I know you. I know your kind. You kill easily, freely. You kill many men and never pay, but you killed my child, my David. You spill his blood; you spill my blood. For that, you gonna pay, white man!"

The witch took a gray powder in her palm and blew it onto him, causing it to adhere to the sticky blood drawings. Again, she muttered in some language he couldn't understand. This time, it caused his skin to crawl with unreasoning fear. He despised the sensation, and he vowed to kill her — slowly.

She dipped her hand in the blood, then held it up in front of his face, palm toward him. The sight and scent of the blood held his full attention. The witch spoke, the words seeming to seep into his very pores. "I curse you, white man. You lust for gold? No more. What you spilled so freely, without a thought, now will become more precious than any treasure. You will pass by an entire mountain of gold for a single drop. Food will not satisfy your hunger. Wine will not quench your thirst. What you drink now is redder than any wine. You will forego a bountiful feast for just a taste of blood. You spill blood; now you live for it. You will take it from even those you do not wish to, because without it, you will die."

"Then you will know my pain, my loss. Blood will make you strong, but with me you will be weak." She touched three fingers to his forehead, and he was immediately seized with a gut-wrenching hunger. If he hadn't already been hanging by his wrists, his legs would have buckled from the intensity of it. *Mamaan* Juma's bloody hand held his entire attention. So concentrated on it was he, that he didn't really comprehend her parting words, although he would remember them much later.

"We will meet again, pirate, and when we do, it will not be pleasant. Even now, those who think of you as friend are nearby. They will see you on your way, but your way leads back to me."

She stepped back into the fire. It swirled around her, hiding her from view, then it belched a huge ball of flames straight up. All that was left to see was a spiral of smoke rising from the embers and the dead goat. The earthen bowl had shattered from the heat of the fire's death, and what was left of the blood rapidly soaked into the ground.

Rigger and Carmella saw the entire exchange and *Mamaan* Juma's performance. They'd arrived at the edge of the clearing just as the witch had made her entrance. Jim had the devil's own time, first keeping Carmella quiet, then keeping her from running off. He had not wanted to draw *Mamaan* Juma's attention. He hadn't believed the girl's story of zombies, but he knew the old woman must have very strong allies for them to have overpowered his captain.

He waited for a few moments after the old witch vanished, both to let his eyes readjust and to make sure she really was gone. He couldn't explain the dread she'd engendered in him.

Once he was sure it was safe, Jim went over to Viktor. He took his dagger and went to work on the captain's bonds. They proved very difficult. The way Viktor was hanging, Jim thought he would probably be out for a while.

"Carmella, get over here. I'm going to need your help getting him back to the docks," he called.

"Rigger, is that you?" Viktor found his voice. He felt so weak and hungry. His vision blurred. He could only make out vague shapes and movement.

The cord finally gave way, and Rigger had to act fast to keep his captain from collapsing into a graceless heap on the ground. "Aye, Cap'n," he confirmed, relieved that Viktor was awake. "I took care of our problems. The men have the ship by now."

"Good. How did you find me, man?" Vik asked.

"Carmella led me here. She saw them take you. The wench is positively terrified of that old hag; thought I was going to have to knock her senseless to keep her quiet."

Viktor sighed, "She has good reason to be afraid, Jim. I am cursed."

"The bitch must have drugged you, Cap'n," Rigger scoffed. "There's no such thing as curses."

"Perhaps, perhaps not, but this is no drug-induced phantasm. I think I may need to go see old Mother."

"We're going to Savannah?" Rigger brightened. It was one of his favorite ports.

Viktor chuckled. "I thought you might like the idea."

"Just wish it was under better conditions, Cap'n."

Viktor managed to stand on his own. "How much of what took place here did you and the wench see?"

"All of it, Cap'n. From the moment the hag appeared until she vanished, although I couldn't make much sense out of any of it."

Viktor looked at his first mate, and Jim could have sworn his captain's eyes glowed faintly. He got a sense of overwhelming hunger, and it unnerved him a bit. "Cap'n?"

The reality of this "curse" already began to make itself known to Viktor. He needed blood, human blood. The man in front of him was full of the vital fluid. But no, he would not feed on Rigger. His mate was of more use to him alive than as a meal. But there was another source nearby.

"The wench must still be frightened," he commented. "I see her cowering over there on the edge of the clearing."

Jim could barely see the girl, himself. She must've moved, for the captain to have spotted her so easily.

"I trust you to keep your silence, Jim. Some of our crewmen are too superstitious for their own good. I imagine this little adventure might spook a few of them. Go. Wait for me in the jungle a ways. I need to speak with Carmella a moment."

"Aye, Cap'n." Rigger walked away to give Viktor the privacy he required.

She'd watched them talk, apprehensively. Their conversation had been too low for her to overhear, but *Mamaan* Juma's had not, and Carmella had understood a great deal of what the old witch had said. Not all of it, but more than either of the pirates had. She was truly surprised, when Viktor let Rigger walk away. Maybe she hadn't heard correctly, or, even more amazing, maybe the witch wasn't as powerful as everyone feared.

Viktor started walking toward her. His steps were unsteady, more of a stumble than a stride. There was nothing wrong with his voice, however. "Carmella, pet." His voice held pure enticement. "There is no longer any need for you to be afraid. The witch is gone, and I still stand."

The tavern wench didn't question her sudden absence of fear. Her *Capitan* was with her now. When he staggered just as he reached her, she was quick to catch and support him about the waist. She thought her heart would burst with joy, when he smiled down at her. She also believed she had never seen anything so lovely as the dim, emerald glow of his eyes. Strange, how she'd never noticed them before.

"Thank you for your help, my lovely Carmella." He continued to smile at her, brushing fingertips across her cheek and into her raven curls.

She returned his smile with a look of pure adoration. "I would do anything for you, *mon Capitan*."

"Anything?"

"My life for you," she avowed.

"I am glad you said that, Carmella. Thank you." He tightened his fingers in her hair. "I'll take it." With a strength and speed he'd never dreamed he could possess, he clutched her to him and sank unexpectedly long, sharp teeth deep into her throat. She managed one feeble squeak and struggled against him. In reaction he growled and clutched her tighter. Oh, but she tasted sweet, her returning fear adding a spicy tang to her blood.

Gradually, her struggles became weaker. Soon, she lay limp in his arms. And still, he fed.

Rigger waited patiently in the jungle for Viktor to join him. He knew his captain well enough to know that he probably intended to kill the wench. She had seen too much to leave her here, and she would be nothing but a burden aboard a ship. Plus, unlike Jim, Carmella probably couldn't be trusted to not talk to the crew about this evening's events.

Besides, the murder that had sparked this inconvenient disruption of their plans had stemmed from a dispute over the pretty whore. This entire fiasco had been a delay they could ill afford.

He nearly jumped out of his skin when Viktor suddenly just stood there placing a hand on his shoulder. The captain appeared to have recovered his strength.

"Make sure everyone's on board. As soon as I've gathered my effects, I will join you. We sail immediately. Set course for Savannah."

"Aye, Cap'n."

"Oh, and Jim, I feel some better now, but I'm still not fully recovered. I will be spending most of the trip in my cabin. You will bring me my meals. See to it I am not disturbed otherwise."

"Aye, Cap'n."

The two zombies *Mamaan* Juma had sent earlier to fetch Brandee now emerged from the jungle silently. They collected the bloodless body of Carmella and melted back into the darkness.

Chapter 3

The old woman sat on a stump, tending the fire in front of her tabby hut. The ancient oaks, with their beards of Spanish moss, obscured the stars overhead. The sparks of her fire made their own dancing constellations. She gave the coals a poke with her stick and stared into the fresh swirl of flame and embers, reading what she could there.

After what seemed like ages, she cackled to herself and shook her head. "The devil, himself." She smiled.

She gave the fire another poke.

Rigger stood, holding a tray of food, at the door to the captain's cabin. "Cap'n, dinner," he called softly.

"Enter."

He shouldered the door open and carried the food in. He set it down and traded out the fresh dishes for the ones from the previous meal. He glanced at Viktor with surreptitious worry.

The captain's appetite was positively voracious, yet he seemed to be wasting. His face seemed thinner, and his skin was growing unhealthily pale. Rigger feared the man had picked up some strange tropical illness.

"We just passed Sapelo, Cap'n," Jim reported. "We should make Savannah before midnight."

Viktor sat brooding, not really looking at his mate. "Good. I need to visit Mother Celie. Jim, I may need your help getting there."

"Of course, Cap'n; you think the Thunderbolt Witch can help you?"

"Aye. Never took much stock of witchcraft, but the old hag is a good doctor as well as witch, and she's the closest thing to a mother I've ever had. She may have a cure for what that bitch did to me."

Once they were tied up, Rigger relayed to Jon-Jon that Viktor was putting him in charge of disposing of the stolen cargo. Then, he procured a flat boat to get them from the docks at River Street to Skidaway Island. The ferry wouldn't be operating this late at night. It had been full dark for at least three hours.

Mother Celie's tiny tabby house was surrounded by moss-draped oaks; trees that had been ancient long before the first white man ever touched Georgia soil. The thick branches interlaced so closely they rendered the sky invisible. The dark felt like something alive and, for now, menacing.

Viktor remained perfectly calm, almost to the point of seeming to be in a daze. Jim, on the other hand, grew more and more apprehensive and agitated with every step. He'd been to visit Mother with Viktor a few times before, but never after dark.

The old woman perched on a stump, tending a small fire. She spoke to them before they even reached the little cave of light formed by the fire's glow, never looking away from the dancing flames. "About time you got here, boys. You almost didn't make it on time," she chided.

"You know why I've come?" Viktor didn't sound as if he'd been as surprised by her greeting as Jim was.

"Old Mother knows, boy. Better than you do, yourself, Viktor Brandewyne. Jimbo, you a might too jumpy; you best stay out here and tend the fire for old Mother Celie. I got to take Viktor inside and have me a talk with him." She fixed the young pirate with a gimlet eye. "Mind you, Jimbo, don't you let that fire die out, or I'll take a switch to your backside."

"Don't worry, Mother, I won't let it go out," Rigger smiled. He felt great relief that she excluded him from the proceedings. Memories of *Mamaan* Juma had been causing restless, troubled dreams for him the entire voyage.

Celie went into her hut. When Viktor didn't move fast enough to suit her, she banged the floor with her stick. "Get yourself in here, boy! You ain't got all night," she scolded.

He went in and closed the door behind him, before she could fuss at him about that as well. The old woman had somewhat raised him, when he'd permitted. Even as a child, he'd been willful. He always viewed visits to Mother Celie with a combination of fondness, amusement and a touch of fear. He'd felt the sting of her hand or a switch often enough. She was, perhaps, the only person he would permit to speak to him in such a commanding tone without being tempted to kill or beat them for such insolence.

She was Mother Celie, and she commanded his respect.

The old woman sat down at the table in the small, one-room hut. Viktor hooked a stool with his foot and started to sit with her. "No!" she snapped. She pointed to the far end of the room with her stick. "You sit over there."

He did as she said, but the fact that it both irritated and, on some deeper level, hurt him showed in the stiffness of his shoulders. "I came to you for help, Mother." There was a slightly sullen tone to his words.

"Already said I know why you came, boy; been expecting you for nigh on a week. When you was little, I always got the feelin' you was the One, 'course I been wrong before. But that was long before you was even born." She seemed to be rambling to herself.

Celie sharpened her gaze on the pirate. "But your run in with Juma proved you're the One."

Viktor snarled at the mention of the witch. His curiosity was sparked, as well as his ire, however. "How do you know of that bitch, Mother?" he demanded.

Celie rapped on the table with her stick, then, shook it at him. "Don't you take that tone of voice with me, boy!" She softened her voice and continued, "First, I need to find out what you know and understand about what's happened to you, then, I'll know what I need to tell you about it; and about what comes next. Now, best as you can remember, tell me what happened."

Viktor started at the interruption of his meal by David, but Mother Celie stopped him. "The why ain't important, boy. All you need to tell me is what she did."

He started over, this time only recounting the actual encounter with *Mamaan* Juma. When Mother pressed him for what he did afterward, he told of Rigger freeing him and of feeding on Carmella.

Celie nodded, as if he'd confirmed something she already knew. "Yep. She done worked a good 'un on you, boy. But I think she mighta just killed you instead, if she really knew you like she thought she did." She smiled cryptically. "I know you're not feeling too good right now, Vik. We'll take care of that soon enough."

She took a deep breath, stared at the pirate before her, then spoke, "Viktor, there are creatures of darkness that feed on blood. All they know is darkness and Hunger. They be clever hunters. They look like mortal men, but they ain't. They're a heap stronger and faster, and they can do things normal people can't. But they have to have blood. Without it, they just whither up like an old, dried toad-frog."

"That witch tried to make you into one of those things, but she didn't finish the job."

"What do you mean, she didn't finish?"

"Those things are called vampires back in the Old World," Celie explained. "That's what you've become, in a way. But you're a vampire by curse, not by blood. You're not a true, full vampire. She couldn't make you that, because the only way to make you that is for a real vampire to bite you."

"Talk sense, Mother."

She pursed her lips, thinking how best to explain things to Viktor in a way he'd understand. Finally, she decided on her course. "You're still alive, boy. That, more'n anything proves you're not a full vampire. Y'see, a vampire is dead, yet it ain't dead. I believe the word for it is undead. An undead vampire can't go into the daylight. They'll burn like fatlighter, if they do. They can't even be by an open window during the day. No, they're of the darkness. But you can bear the sun's touch, can't you, boy?"

He nodded. "Yes, I didn't go on deck during the voyage here, because I didn't desire the company of the crew. But I found great pleasure in standing by the open window of my cabin, especially in the morning; the sounds and smells of the ship coming to life seemed so much sharper this voyage."

Celie cackled a bit. "I just bet they did," she stated cryptically. "Another difference between you and them is that their blood is unclean. Yours ain't. They can't touch or pass over anything holy."

Viktor gave a rude snort, letting her know what he thought of all things "holy."

"I know you ain't a man of faith, Viktor Brandewyne." She clucked at him impatiently. "Now be still and listen, boy. This is important."

He obediently gave her his full attention. She was, after all, Mother Celie, and she was helping him. Well he knew that information was often more valuable than doubloons for survival. "Please, continue," he motioned.

"An undead vampire can't go inside a church. They can't touch crosses, bibles, holy water, communion wafers or wine, or anything that has been blessed by a priest. You need to remember that. It'll help you discover their true nature, should you ever meet one." She fixed him with a hard stare. "You don't want to mingle your blood with theirs or theirs with yours, Viktor. To be honest, I don't know what it would do exactly. Normally, when a vampire bites someone, they get power over their victim, provided they don't outright kill them. It might or might not work that way with you, if you was to get bit by one of 'em. Or they might turn you into one of them. That, you do not want. It would give you the same weaknesses. So, you don't want to go biting one of them, either. Might give you power over them, but more'n likely it'll turn you or maybe just make you real sick. You can't make blood clean once it's been made unclean. It just don't work that way."

The old woman's words made no sense to him. A fog of confusion seemed to envelope his mind. He shook his head, trying to clear it, to no avail. His vision blurred, and he felt both weak and as if he were starving. "What's wrong with me?"

Celie saw the dull glow of his eyes and was careful not to look at him directly. "You need to feed, Viktor. I bet you haven't fed since that poor girl."

"No, I ate several meals a day during the voyage here."

Celie cackled. "And I reckon not one of them made your Hunger go away."

He had to cede her point. "No, they did not. How did you know?"

"Old Mother knows things, boy. Thought you'd learned that long time ago. Your dinner is out by the fire. You go out and eat, then, we'll talk some more."

"You've cooked something for me?" Childhood memories of Mother Celie's cooking made his mouth water.

"You brought your meal with you, Viktor."

He looked hard at her, realization dawning on him about what she just implied. "Rigger is my friend, or as close to one as I'm ever likely to come, Mother. He's a good mate, too. I'll not feed on him," he stated stubbornly.

"Time for being a fussy eater is too far past, boy!" she barked at him. "You need blood, and you need it now. You need blood, Viktor. You're dying. If you don't go out there and feed now, I won't be able to help you. Now git!" She emphasized the command with a sharp rap of her stick against the table leg.

Viktor got up and gazed at his reflection in a shallow wooden basin of water on a shelf set into the wall of the tabby hut. His color was sickly, rather than his usual robust sailor's tan.

He glanced at the old woman glaring imperiously at him. Something in him felt queasy at the thought of feeding on her blood. Too thin and sour, he thought.

He had no choice. He would have to drink his first mate. He was too weak to return to town and catch some stranger.

Rigger looked up, blinking, at the sound of the door opening. He stood as he saw Viktor coming out. His captain approached him; the man's eyes seeming to glow a bright green. It must've been some trick of the firelight, but they looked as if the eerie light came from within them rather than reflected its glow.

Jim Rigger's only thought at the moment was of how much he admired this man. Viktor Brandewyne was the best, most successful pirate captain he'd ever sailed under. He was worthy of respect, and Rigger would gladly die for him.

Viktor looked at his first mate standing next to the fire, and all he saw was food. For the moment, only his Hunger mattered. He locked eyes with Rigger, instinct taking over. He felt a connection with his first mate's mind. Rigger's will was his to control; it was a deliciously powerful sensation. "Rigger, come here."

Jim obeyed immediately. Viktor wasted no time in feeding. He held Rigger's will with his mind, preventing the other man from presenting even an involuntary struggle. He was in no mood to play with his food. His only concern was to take the blood he needed as quickly as possible. He had to sate the monstrous Hunger that threatened to usurp his own will.

Viktor stormed back into the hut. "Dammit, Mother, that man was my friend!"

"I know that, boy," she stated simply. "Tell me how you feel."

He stopped and thought about it before answering. "I feel... alive, powerful, almost rejuvenated."

"I knew you would, boy. Blood's a mighty powerful thing. This curse might just suit you, Viktor. I know you, boy. Watched you grow up. I don't think this will be the hardship old Juma thought it would be. Oh, there is a bad side to it. You're gonna have to feed often. If you don't, you'll grow weak, sick. You go without blood for too long, and you will die."

Viktor scowled, "So far, I see nothing about this curse to appeal to me. Already, it has cost me. Jim Rigger was a good pirate and an excellent seaman — and he was one of the very few men I could trust."

"He still is, boy," Celie smiled. "You go fetch him in here and put him on the table." When he hesitated, she snapped, "Do as I say, boy! You want old Mother to help you or not?"

He went out and scooped up the body of his first mate. The ease with which he lifted the deadweight briefly amazed him. As he carried the body into the hut and laid it out on the table, he said, "I suppose you will claim you can bring him back to life, old woman," skepticism painfully evident in his voice and expression.

Mother Celie turned around from the wall shelf, where she'd mixed up some strange concoction in a small stone bowl. "No, boy, I can't bring him back — as a man." She cackled and sprinkled the powdery substance over the dead man. "But as a cat, I might can do something for him."

Viktor blinked. Where the body of Jim Rigger had lain, he now saw a large, dead, black cat. It sported extra thumb-like toes on its forepaws and was the largest tomcat he'd ever seen.

Celie went to the window and whistled. A raven soon perched on the windowsill. She flicked a few flecks of the same powder on the bird and took it in her hand. With her other hand, she stroked the cat. It started to breathe but made no other movement. "I'm gonna send him back with you, but it'd look mighty strange for you to keep calling him Jim Rigger. He gonna need a new name." She continued petting the cat. "Hmm, now what would be a good name? The good Lord brought that boy, Lazarus, back from the dead. I think Lazarus be a fine name for a cat."

She locked eyes with Viktor and held the raven toward him. "Old Lazarus here gave all his blood to you, so he gonna have to have blood, too. Quick as you can, take your knife and cut this bird's head off. Now!"

Puzzled, but curious, he did as she told him. Grasping the raven by the head, while Celie held its body, he quickly beheaded it. The old woman upended the bird, so that its blood would drip into the cat's mouth.

"Lazarus, come forth," she summoned the creature that had once been Jim Rigger.

The cat sat up with a chortling meow and snatched the dead bird from her hand. He then proceeded to eat it, feathers and all. Once he had finished, he sauntered over to Viktor, purring and butting his head against the pirate's hand to be petted.

Viktor normally didn't care for animals, but it felt perfectly natural and oddly comforting to pet the cat. It even pleased him greatly when the creature leapt to his shoulder and draped itself there, as if that was where it belonged.

"This is all well and good, mother, but I've still lost his services as an able-bodied seaman and navigator."

"Aye, I know." She nodded with a mischievous twinkle in her eye. "But you've gained an extra set of eyes. Lazarus, get ready to go look."

The cat sneezed, as the old woman blew another pinch of the powder concoction onto him. In the midst of the sneeze, his body grew amorphous. It soon solidified as a raven.

"In this shape, ol' Lazarus here can go where you can't. You can see what he sees, if you want to, with no one the wiser. Who's going to take heed of a bird, after all?"

Viktor smiled, quickly grasping the possibilities. "Will he go where I tell him to?"

"Oh, aye. He's more your creature now than he ever was as a man."

"How so?"

"You bit him, boy." She looked at him as if he should have known that already. "Weren't you listening, when I told you about vampires? When you bite someone, you get power over him. They have to obey."

"So, if I were to bite all of my crew, they would obey me unquestioningly."

Celie gave him a knowing smirk. "Knew this curse would appeal to you, boy. But," she held up a gnarled finger, "you might not want to be doin' that."

"Why not, old woman?" He gazed at her cautiously.

"Well, I ain't sure if it'll work the same way, what with you bein' alive instead of undead, but for regular vampires, if someone they bit died, they'd become a vampire, too. Don't reckon you want a ship full of 'em competing for blood. Plus, they wouldn't be able to sail except at night. Oh, they'd still be yours to command, but they'd be useless to you during the day."

He thought about it for a moment. "Do you know of another way to get the same obedience?"

She nodded, "You can hold 'em, like you did Jimbo, your will over theirs, although that works best one-on-one instead of a whole crew at one time. But there may be one more way. Instead of drinking their blood, make them drink yours. It shouldn't take much."

Viktor raised an eyebrow at her. "And just how do you propose I accomplish that?"

"Never seen a pirate yet that'll turn down free rum." She was rewarded by a rather toothsome grin, as he caught on to her plan.

"Are you sure that will work?"

"No, but it can't hurt to try. I'd say try it on a stranger, before any of your crew."

"So as not to look the fool, if it does not work." He agreed.

"Exactly. You might want to keep in mind there's a way to prevent those you feed on from becoming like you. If you take their heart or their head, they'll stay dead, instead of becoming undead; if your bite works the same way a regular vampire's does."

"I will keep that in mind," he assured her, then, seemed to think of something. "Mother, you say I have to have blood, or I will die.

Would it be possible for me to bleed someone without biting him? I realize that I may not always have the luxury of being selective about my meals, but there are many of whom the thought of putting my mouth on is rather repulsive."

"Don't see why not," Celie shrugged. "Probably want to drink it faster, though, before it gets cold and clots on you. You never cared much for clotted milk. I don't think clotted blood would appeal to you, either. But you wouldn't have to worry about turning any of them."

Chapter 4

A light breeze, ripe with the scent of marsh mud, blew through the window. The old woman lifted her face, snuffling and listening. Her eyes grew unfocused for a moment before they cleared again.

"You might want to send Lazarus to check on your crew, Viktor," she warned him. "Smells like a change in the weather is coming, if you know what I mean."

His face darkened. He knew well that his crew was untrustworthy. Except for a small core band, the entire lot had been on the brink of mutiny against their former captain. Now, their pockets would be full, and they'd be drinking and wenching with abandon. Savannah had always been a safe port for him; if the wrong drunken tale got back to the wrong ears, that situation could quickly change.

"How do I send him?"

She gave him a look that told him she thought he was being dense. "You tell him to go, boy. His shape may be different, but, that saucy whelp you called Jim Rigger is still in there. He can understand you."

When he glared at her, she remained unfazed. So, he went over to the window and set the raven on the sill. "Lazarus, go find our crew. Watch them well."

The bird gave a caw that sounded very like and "aye" and flew off into the darkness.

Mother Celie got up and started rummaging about in a small cabinet. Her voice came back to Viktor, as he gazed out into the dark. He clutched the windowsill hard enough to crumble the edges of the oyster shell tabby, a wave of vertigo gripping him. He saw trees and marsh zip along below him, as he flew towards the docks and taverns along River Street. He also saw Mother's fire, blazing away, unattended. It felt very disorienting.

Glancing over her shoulder, Celie quickly grasped the problem. "Ease up on your grip, boy, afore ye rip out my entire window," she spoke gently. "It helps to close your own eyes, when you want to look through his. You'll learn to control it."

He did as she suggested and found that it did indeed help. The dizziness and slight nausea vanished immediately.

Lazarus found the tavern where the pirates had gathered to spend their shares. He settled into the shadows among the rafters and kept his eye on them, as he'd been bid.

Several minutes later, Viktor opened his eyes to find Mother Celie seated and watching him. She wore a knowing smile. He narrowed his eyes at her. "There is nothing out of the ordinary with my crew's behavior. But then, you already knew that didn't you, Mother?"

Celie's smile turned into a grin. "Aye; the exercise served two purposes. It let you get a feel for just how useful Lazarus will be."

"And?"

"It kept you distracted long enough for me to collect a few things from my cabinet," she replied smugly. "There's things in there ain't no one but me needs to see or know about."

The pirate remembered well the switching he'd gotten as a child. Mother had caught him trying to pick the lock on that cabinet. He was still curious about its contents and amused by her diversionary ploy.

She saw the slight smirk on his face and shook her stick at him. "Don't think I don't remember how to tan the hide of a young buck like yourself, boy," she warned, earning a chuckle from him. "Oh, hush up and sit down."

He did as she told him. Waiting patiently, he knew she would tell him about or show him what she'd retrieved from the mystery cabinet in her own time and her own way.

"You're going to have to start relying on your instincts more than ever, boy. Of course, I think you got better instincts than normal folks, anyway."

He smiled. "I agree, but tell me why you think so, Mother," he encouraged her, knowing that was what she wanted him to do.

She nodded to herself. "Yup, I knew it. Viktor, you always called me Mother, but you know we ain't real kin. And you never asked about your family. I always admired that about you, boy. You're so independent; always lookin' forward and never dwellin' on the past." She looked dead at him. "But it's time I told you about your parents."

"Your pa was a real bad man. He weren't no pirate, like you. If he had been, he might have been remembered. But he did some mighty bad things. You got your hardness from him, and that's helped you keep alive this far. But your ma, she was something special. She was a full-blood Indian, but she weren't no Creek or Yamacraw, like we got around here. No, she was a Cherokee that yer pa stole away from up north in the mountains. She was also a daughter of a medicine man."

"What is a medicine man? Do you mean a healer?" Viktor interrupted.

She waved her hand. "Sometimes: it's an Indian word for wizard, witch, or healer — or their kind of a preacher."

"I see."

"Anyways, I always wondered if you got any of your ma's talents. Now, with this curse, I guess we'll find out."

"Talents?' he raised an eyebrow.

"Magic, boy, magic; if you have, you're going to need every bit of it to do what you have to do, now."

Viktor leaned back on the stool. "And why should I have to do anything?" he asked, his rebelliousness surfacing.

"Because," Celie stated patiently, "if you don't, this curse will kill you. Oh, it won't do it right away. No, it'll kill you slow and painful."

His gaze darkened. This was not news he wanted to hear. He leaned forward, elbows on the table and fingers tented in front of him. "You've told me how this curse will benefit me and what it entails to maintain these new abilities. Now, you say that it will kill me? Make up your mind, old woman."

"Now that I have your attention," she said with a smirk, "I don't know how long it will take, but if I don't take certain actions, your need for blood will take you over. You won't be able to think about anything else but blood, and you'll need to feed more and more often. But you'll never be satisfied. It'll get to the point that you'll start wasting away and grow weak, no matter how often you feed."

"So, you are saying that this curse will eventually make me starve to death, but you don't know how long I have before that starts happening. That is not good. What actions do you need to take, and why are you waiting?"

She sighed. "When I was younger, I might have been able to help you on my own, but I can't do it by myself now. You are going to have to help me help you, Viktor."

"What would you have me do, Mother?"

"There are some women, my Sisters in a way, scattered here and there. I need you to find them."

"You want me to bring them here?"

"No! No." She gave him a fearful and alarmed look. "No boy, don't you dare bring them here. For all of us to be together in one place at one time would be very, very bad."

Viktor snorted impatiently, "If you and your sisters dislike each other so much, what makes you think they'll help us?"

"Didn't say I didn't like 'em, boy," she clucked at him. "I said it would be bad for us to be together. They're not my sisters by blood; they're my Sisters by power. That much magic in one place at one time could very well start the end of the world." She gave him a very intense gaze. "However, my Sisters can send back a small part of their magic. Together, we can make it so you can conquer this curse."

"You mean you can lift it; make things like they were before, and I'll be free to go my way?" he asked, sitting up.

"If that's what you want," she said, like she didn't think that was what he really wanted. "Or we can alter it to make you immortal and let you keep all the power you have gained and will gain."

Immortality: he liked the sound of that. "Very well, Mother, how many of these women do I have to visit, and where do I find them?"

"There are six that you need to find and a seventh you already met. As for where the six are, I don't know. Like I said, we were never meant to be together."

"A seventh…," he trailed off. His face darkened, and his eyes blazed green, as he realized whom Mother Celie meant.

She nodded solemnly at him. "Aye, Viktor, Juma is one of my Sisters," she confirmed. "You don't want to be goin' after her first, though. She will not help willingly."

"Obviously," he stated dryly.

Celie rapped the table leg with her stick. "Don't interrupt, boy. If you go after Juma now, she'll kill you outright. You have to go to my six other Sisters first. They ain't going to be easy to find, and they're going to set you difficult tasks to prove yourself before they'll give you what you need from them. You're gonna have to earn their help, boy."

She reached into her apron pocket and pulled out a small silver vial and a blue drawstring pouch. The vial, suspended from a fine silver chain, had a pin-lock on its hinged cap. Sliding these items across the table to him, she instructed, "You'll need these, Viktor. The silver bottle is for keeping what each of my Sisters will give you in. It will keep their magic contained and keep it from going stale. Stale magic is no good to anyone; too weak."

He reached over and took the vial, hanging it around his neck and tucking it into his shirt. "What is the bag for?"

"Once you've visited my Sisters and earned their gifts, you will have to return to *Mamaan* Juma. By then, you will have grown into your powers, and will be strong enough to stand against her powers and win. When you meet her again, you must kill her, burn her, and bring her ashes and the vial back here to me. Then, I'll be able to help you. The blue bag will contain her black magic and keep her from harming anyone from beyond the grave."

"Burn her, you say." He gave a rather toothsome and sharp grin. "That task appeals to me greatly. If you don't know where the other Sisters are, how do I find them?"

Celie help up one more item she'd kept palmed up to that point. She knew the pirate well enough to know it would have distracted him while she was instructing him about the bottle and the bag. A milky crystal set in silver wire and hung on a somewhat heavier chain than was used for the bottle sparkled as it slowly twirled.

"This is a key," she told him. "You need to go see old Uncle Zeke. He can tell you how to find the Sisters. You'll find him on Hell's Breath Island."

"Mother, I've sailed these waters for years. I know every island from here to Cartagena. There is no island called Hell's Breath," he protested.

"Been there myself, boy. It's a real place."

He started to think she was more than a little mad. He knew there was no such place, but he decided to humor her. "Very well, Mother, if you say so. But how do I find it? I've never heard of it, nor seen it marked on any chart."

"You don't find Hell's Breath, boy," she cackled. "It finds you! You sail on out to sea. The first full moon, you dip that there key in the water. You do that, and Hell's Breath will find you. Then you go ashore — alone — and talk to Zeke. He'll help ya, boy. You just tell him Mother Celie sent you."

Viktor took the crystal, eyeing it skeptically. "I would say you are mad, old woman, but I've already seen enough to know that if you are mad, then I must be mad, as well." He slipped the chain over his head and nestled the amulet next to the silver bottle.

"Always knew you was smart." Celie cackled. "I've done all I can for you for now, boy. You scat on back into town and collect your crew and a ship. You'll have to pirate a new one, I imagine. I'm sure the Navy will be looking for the one you came here in by now."

Viktor stood, bowed to Mother, and went out into the humid and black Georgia night. Celie continued to chuckle to herself.

"Yup, he's the One, all right. Finally, we'll be able to fulfill our task."

Chapter 5

The man, if man he could be called, stood looking out the window at nothing in particular. Absolute rage consumed him. *That bitch! That meddling bitch! he thought. How dare she interfere! She just won't give up, even after all these millennia.*

He turned and strode out of the room. At the end of the corridor, he came to a large room with an enormous fireplace. He moved to stand before it, staring into the roaring blaze.

A slight rustle of fabric and a soft footstep sounded behind him. She was not late, smart girl.

"You sent for me," the woman stated.

"I did," he replied, never turning around. "There is something you must do."

"Anything you ask."

"Ask?" he chuckled, but there was no humor in it. "I ask nothing; I command."

"Forgive me, I didn't mean to…."

"Spare me your feigned apology," he said, as he turned to face her. "I must send you away."

"Away?" she asked; the uncertainty showing plainly on her face.

"Relax, you are not being punished. I need you to conduct some business for me. It is nothing more than that."

Her eyes sparkled with mischief. "Oh?"

"That's better," he purred. "How would my little cat like to catch a mouse?"

"It is what I live for," she replied, her curiosity running wild.

"How true." Their eyes met. "Listen to me very carefully. You are to leave this very evening. My carriage will transport you to the harbor. A ship awaits you there. All that you will need has been provided. The captain has been given detailed instructions. He knows where you are to be taken, and he will help you find this mouse. You must find this pirate — this pretender, Viktor Brandewyne, and you must do it quickly."

"This pretender you speak of; this pirate — once I have found him, is he to be brought back here?"

He smiled, and she stepped back quickly. "Just bring me his heart." The temperature cooled noticeably.

"Consider it done," she said.

His eyes held her; his voice deepened. "I cannot begin to stress the importance of the task you have at hand. I would not send you, if I did not trust you to complete it. Captain Wormsloe will be able to answer any other questions you may have. The carriage is waiting. It is time for you to leave. But hear me and hear me well. Do not fail me."

"Have I ever?" She replied in a voice as cold as ice.

"Do. Not. Fail. Me," he repeated, turning back to the fire, a tacit dismissal.

Chapter 6

Viktor quickly found the tavern his crew was utilizing to part themselves from their ill-gotten gains. He'd seen the sign above the door using Lazarus' eyes, thus he didn't have to waste time looking in every similar establishment in Savannah.

Spotting Jon-Jon purchasing a fresh bottle of gin at the bar, he made his way over. Viktor snagged the bottle before Jon-Jon could. "A word with you, Mr. Jon," he said, and walked off toward a back table with his mate's precious alcohol. There was no need to see if the man would follow.

A small group of pirates held a table near the bar. Givens, one of the newer crew members, remarked, "Did you see that? He just took Jon-Jon's bottle and walked off with it."

Murph, who'd sailed with Viktor longer, gave a rough bark of laughter. "That's because he knew Jon-Jon would follow it. He's a smart bastard."

Viktor stopped at a small, unoccupied table near the back of the tavern. Jon-Jon joined him only seconds later, reaching for his gin. He held it out of the man's reach, broke the seal and took a pull. He promptly spat it out against the wall, grimacing. Finally handing the bottle over to his mate, he said, "I don't see how you can drink that bilge, man. I hope you didn't pay much for it."

Jon-Jon took a long swig from the bottle, swallowed, coughed once and thumped his chest to force it down. "Mother's milk, Cap'n." He winked.

"Then your mother was a drunken whore."

"Aye, she was." He laughed and waggled the bottle. "All this does is wake me up. Take something a lot stronger than this to make me full drunk."

"And you are a far better sailor drunk than many men are sober. I want a new ship, Jon-Jon. Tell me a big fish story," Viktor got around to the purpose for this little conference.

The larger man grinned and said, "Spotted us a fat one, Cap'n. She's a package ship bound for Bristol. Sailed down from Virginia half-laden with tobacco, to take on passengers and finish out her cargo with indigo and rice."

"How well armed is she?"

"There's the rub, Cap'n. She's well gunned. I think maybe her master has had dealings with pirates before. I counted five swivels, two starboard, two port, and one aft, as well as twelve heavy cannon on the gun deck. She's heavily crewed, as well, for a merchantman. We can take her, but it won't be quiet."

Viktor smiled slyly. "You're a gambling man, Mr. Jon. What would you wager that your dear captain can walk on board that prize and take her single-handedly?"

Jon-Jon nearly choked on his gin. "Have you been drinking tonight, Cap'n?"

Viktor gave a low chuckle. "Aye, powerful stuff."

"Maybe you should go on drinking whatever it is, if it makes you think you can take a fully armed and crewed ship by yourself, Cap'n."

"Will you wager me or no, Jon-Jon?" he goaded. "Time to put yer dick on the table; or won't it reach?"

"Oh, it'll reach," he rose to the challenge. "What do ye fancy for wager, should you pull this off?"

Viktor mulled it over for a minute, then replied, "I'll take two casks of fine Jamaican rum delivered to my cabin, as well as a bundle of those good cigars and a couple bottles of brandy."

"Is that all? Would ye like a tumble with my daughter, as well?"

"Is she in port?"

"Bastard."

Viktor chuckled. "And what will you take in wager, should I fail?"

"Well, Cap'n, I believe I'd fancy those casks of rum, and the cigars, and one of your coats," Jon-Jon answered readily.

"Which one?"

"The black velvet one with the silver embroidery."

Viktor eyed him. "Seems a might fancy for the likes of you, Jon-Jon. What would you want with such a fine garment?"

He puffed up, stung. "I might decide to go a-courting."

"Why Mr. Jon, is there something I should know about?"

"Not sure, Cap'n. It's a bit early to tell yet," he hedged.

"Well, I tell you, Jon-Jon. When you're sure, just let me know, and we'll have him aboard," the captain continued to tweak him.

Jon-Jon's face grew redder than normal. "If you wasn't the captain...."

"You still wouldn't have the balls to take me on, Jon-Jon. Make sure the lads cut it short tonight. I don't want any hangovers in the morning. Tell them to have anything they want to keep off our current vessel by dawn, and don't post a watch. I've a buyer in port who'll pay well for her," he ordered.

"Aye, Cap'n." He hesitated before asking, "Don't you usually have Jim see to that, Cap'n?"

Viktor's face grew deadly grim. "Mr. Rigger will not be joining us."

"Understood, Cap'n." He let it drop.

Viktor stood. "I'll need the names of our new ship and her current captain."

"Her captain is a Swede named Lars Stoddard. The ship's the *Frigga's Folly.*"

He grimaced, "We'll take the ship, but not her name."

"Bad luck to rename a ship."

"Only for the fool who misnamed her to begin with. Have the rum, cigars and brandy ready for delivery by dusk tomorrow, Jon-Jon."

"Aye," the pirate laughed. "Y'sure you don't want me to send a couple of the lads along with ye, Cap'n?"

"They'd just get in my way and bugger things up." He went to the bar, purchased a bottle of brandy, and strode out the door. Jon-Jon could have sworn he saw something dark and vaguely bird-shaped fly out behind Viktor.

Captain Stoddard was not pleased to see a stranger enter his cabin the hour before dawn. An early riser, he'd been expecting the cabin boy with his breakfast tray. "Who do you think you are, barging in here like this?" he barked at the intruder.

Viktor suppressed his natural inclination to kill the man. Instead, he bowed and smiled, doing a passable imitation of a well-bred country squire. "My apologies, Captain. I know it is early, but I need to book passage aboard this fine vessel."

"Why are you bothering me about that?" Stoddard grumbled. "My quartermaster handles all that sort of business."

"Ah, but you see, my situation is rather, shall we say, delicate. I've important documents to deliver to England, and there are some in this port that would try to deter me, if they knew of my departure," Viktor countered.

"I see," Stoddard replied, suddenly more civil. "You are a Loyalist, then."

"Aye," he lied. "So, we can come to a mutually beneficial arrangement?"

Stoddard nodded, "We can, sir."

Viktor smiled and produced the brandy and a small bag of coin. When the Swede's eyes gravitated to the bag, he knew he'd hooked his fish. "I trust you've no objection to payment in advance," he said, as he handed over the coin.

"None at all, sir," Stoddard hefted the bag, pleased with its weight.

"Count it, if you like, Captain. If you've a couple of glasses, please, share this fine brandy with me."

"Should be some in there." Stoddard waved his hand at a nearby cupboard, as he emptied the bag on the table and began counting the gold guineas which poured from it.

Viktor retrieved the glasses and poured the brandy. While the captain was preoccupied with the money, the pirate surreptitiously nicked his finger and allowed a few drops of blood to drip into one of the glasses. The dark color of the liquor hid the blood's presence.

Handing the tainted glass to Stoddard, he toasted, "To a safe and swift voyage."

He watched the man closely, as they drank. Stoddard shook his head and looked a bit confused.

"Strong stuff, isn't it?"

He looked at the half-empty glass unsteadily. "It is rather potent," he agreed.

"Nothing stronger," Viktor laughed. "Have another drink."

The Swede obediently downed the rest of his cup. His face immediately went slack, eyes blank. Viktor felt the man's will submit and bond to his. The sensation filled him with a powerful, nearly orgasmic rush. He enjoyed it very much.

"I'll have my coin back," he ordered. Stoddard immediately complied, placing the gold back into the pouch and handing it to him with a smile.

Viktor looked around the cabin, taking in every detail. "This cabin suits me. I'll take it," he stated arrogantly, "and the ship, as well."

"Of course, sir."

"So, tell me, Lars, is it?" The man nodded. He continued, "How many souls aboard this fine vessel?"

"Counting myself, forty."

"That seems a bit much for a mere merchant."

"We are bait. We have hidden gun ports, as well as the guns which are visible, and we make sure to carry tempting cargoes," Stoddard informed him.

"So, you are a pirate hunter," Bloody Vik Brandee said with a grin. "Well, damn, you caught one!" Stoddard just smiled idiotically. "How many senior officers do you have, Lars?"

"Six."

"Your cabin boy is just out the door. Send him to fetch them back here. Tell them I am your new partner, with Letters of Marque from the King himself, or whatever you wish. It won't make any difference."

Stoddard dispatched the cabin boy to summon his mates to his cabin to meet his new partner in their venture. While they waited, Viktor slit his thumb and squeezed a good amount of blood directly into the bottle. He swirled the contents to mix them. When he moved to wipe the wound, he was pleasantly surprised to find the cut had completely vanished without so much as a scar.

He set the bottle down, took a chair and put his feet up on the table. "Fetch glasses for your mates," he ordered the captain, as if the man were a common servant. Stoddard obeyed without question or complaint. Rather, his expression was of one eager to please.

"This is a learning experience for me, Lars. If I were to tell you to strip naked and dance a jig on the fo'c'sle, would you?" Viktor asked.

"Yes, sir."

"Interesting." He chuckled. "That might actually be worth seeing, but not today. Pour the brandy."

Soon after, there was a knock at the door and the sound of confused-to-irate voices. Viktor stood and moved to the shadows, then said, "Open it and invite them in."

As Stoddard moved to obey, Viktor flexed his new powers to test them. Without speaking, he thought a command for the man to do a quick little skip of a dance as he opened the door. His puppet performed perfectly.

"I know it's early, gentlemen," Stoddard soothed his mates, "but I've some important news. Please sit down and have some brandy, and my new partner in our mission will explain everything." He motioned to the table and glasses. The six men found their seats, murmuring in confusion about this new partner.

Viktor stepped forward, smiling and holding his own glass, his hand hiding the fact that it was empty. The murmuring stopped, as all eyes fell on him. One of them, a grizzled, older man who seemed the sharpest of the lot, eyed him particularly closely.

"You are this new partner Captain Stoddard is talking about?" he asked. "You seem familiar. Your name, sir?"

"Names aren't really important right now." Viktor dodged the question. "Have a drink." He raised his own glass, mentally nudging the man to drink. As he did so, the others following suit, Viktor announced, "Things are going to be different aboard from now on. There has been a change of plans. You will tell your crew to stand down. We won't be needing them."

The grizzled mate downed his drink, smiling appreciatively. "Damn! This is some mighty fine brandy; never tasted anything quite like it. Name's Joseph Burns. I'd like another glass of that, if you don't mind. Curious to hear why we don't need a crew."

As Stoddard poured another shot for his mate, Viktor made a mental note to himself that it might take a stronger dose of blood to capture strong-willed individuals.

Burns quickly downed the fresh glass. Viktor gave a mock bow, smiling wide enough to show off his new fangs. "Allow me to introduce myself, Mr. Burns. Viktor Brandewyne, your new captain."

Burns grinned back, laughing. "The devil, you say! I knew you looked familiar. Pleasure to have you aboard, sir. So, we're to be pirates now, rather than pirate hunters."

Viktor chuckled, "Oh, no, sir. I wouldn't dream of sullying the reputations of such fine gentlemen as yourselves, by forcing you into piracy. No, I've other uses for the seven of you."

At a silent order from the vampire, Stoddard moved to his side, took a small knife and bled himself at the wrist into the empty glass. Once it was full, he tied a handkerchief around the wound tightly. Viktor lifted the glass, took a whiff then, drained it.

"Self-righteousness flavored with greed, interesting blend. I'll be bringing my lads aboard at dusk. I want your crew off the ship by then. The seven of you will be sharing the smallest of your passenger cabins. Make sure all cargo and passengers are aboard, as well. We sail before midnight. Now be about your business."

The men exited the cabin except for Stoddard. He began gathering his effects. Viktor quickly put a stop to that. "Why are you still in my cabin?"

"I was just getting my things, sir."

"You have the clothes you are wearing. That's all you need. Now get out, and do not enter my cabin again without my permission."

"Aye, Captain." He stopped what he was doing, set down the items he had gathered, and left.

"Lazarus, come forth."

The cat instantly materialized. He began nosing around, inspecting the cabin.

"Stay here and keep an eye on things — and don't spray anything, or I'll cut your balls off," Viktor told the cat. "I have to go see a man about a boat."

Jon-Jon had the crew dispersed around the docks near the *Frigga's Folly*. They'd been instructed to blend in as much as possible. Viktor had found him around noon and told him to have the men ready to board and to bring his wager. A local porter stood by with the casks of rum on his handcart. The cigars and brandy, Jon-Jon had hidden in his sea bag.

"Very good, Mr. Jon. I see you brought my winnings," Viktor's voice came from behind him, making him jump.

"Didn't hear ye walk up, Cap'n."

He just smiled smugly. "I did not intend for you to. Now, shall we board our new vessel?"

They sailed down river, passing Skidaway, Cockspur, and Tybee Islands on their way to open sea. Viktor's intimate knowledge of the local waters eliminated the need for a harbor pilot. They made the night passage as easily as if it had been full daylight.

Once they were in open waters, he had Jon-Jon assemble the crew on deck and bring up the two casks of Jamaican rum he'd won from his mate. Viktor "doctored" the liquor before they'd left port, while the crew was still boarding.

"Listen up, lads," Vik bellowed for their attention. "It seems we've netted ourselves a damned pirate hunter's ship." The crew roared and hooted in response to this announcement. "Be that as it may, she's a pirate now. And, as such, she needs a new name. Some idiot gave her the sorry name of *Frigga's Folly*. Mr. Murph!"

"Aye, Cap'n!" Murph called back.

"Take a few lads at first light and chisel that damn name off my ship."

"Aye, Cap'n. What name do you want to replace it?"

"The *Barracuda*. She looks to be rigged for speed, and, with the hidden guns, she'll pack a hell of a bite."

The crew roared their approval of the new name.

"Mr. Jon, break open this rum for the lads. Let's have a drink to our new voyage."

"Aye-aye, Cap'n!" Jon-Jon grinned, looking forward to getting a taste of the rum he'd lost. The captain's generosity made the crew very happy, as well. All agreed it was some of the finest and strongest rum that they had tasted. A few joked with Jon-Jon about it surpassing the usual swill he'd select.

"I'd bet on it with the Cap'n," he explained. "I might be a drunk, but I ain't suicidal. Couldn't risk anything but the best with him; he'd take the difference outta my hide."

Viktor let them revel for a while before calling for their attention. "All right, lads. I know some of you are new to sailing with me. I do things a bit differently from other pirates. There'll be no votes on where to make port or what prizes to take. My word is law. Serve well, and you'll be rewarded well. Disagree with me, and you can get off my ship."

"Oh," he added," and there's only one way off my ship. Dead."

The men didn't utter a single sound of protest. It made things easier, but he had been looking forward to making an example of someone to get his point across. There had always been at least one idiot to mouth off, when he'd given that speech to past crews.

"Jon-Jon," he waved his mate over. He came obediently. "Have the men assemble at noon. I want the former captain and his mates, as well as all passengers brought to the fo'c'sle at that time. For now, though, get the passenger list from Burns and bring it to my cabin. Bring Burns, too; I need to have a word with him."

Jon-Jon left immediately to carry out his orders.

Viktor turned his attention back to his crew. "Those of you not on duty turn in and lights out. The rest of you be about your business."

There weren't as many passengers as he'd feared there would be. Savannah was too valuable a port to him to hold hostages from there for ransom. It would cause too much animosity among the family's powerful enough to make trouble for him. The passengers would have to be disposed of. He had an agent in the Caicos, who would pay well for any women or youngsters, but white men were hard to get rid of that way.

Still, he could get some use out of the three male passengers. One was young enough to press into service. The other two could be both food and object lessons.

Viktor ordered the five passengers lined up on the fo'c'sle, where the entire crew could see them. Stoddard and his mates trailed along behind him like a mock military inspection. The passengers consisted of a lone, middle-aged man and a family of four. The son would make a passable cabin boy or powder monkey. The father was too old to be worth his keep to Viktor, although the mother was still young enough to fetch a good price. The daughter — ah, now she was a prize.

He trailed around her, inspecting the texture of her hair, admiring the curves of her body. She proved a bit jumpy, but not too. His newly heightened sense of smell told him her nervousness came more from excitement than fright. It also told him she was untried.

Decisions, decisions, he thought. Should I keep her intact and get a higher price, or do I want to break her in, before I sell her?

Apparently, the inspection went on too long for the father's nerves. "Captain Stoddard! What is the meaning of this treatment?!" he demanded in outrage.

Viktor didn't even look at the man. "Mister — Stoddard, explain the situation."

Ever obedient, his puppet turned to the man and told him, "I have turned this ship and all aboard it over to Captain Brandewyne."

The lone traveler responded to this news. "Vik Brandee? My God, man! You've handed us over to pirates!"

Viktor was in front of him faster than the eye could follow, causing him to clutch his chest in fright. The vampire grinned, as the mother grabbed both her children and clung to them. Laughing, he told them all, "If you did not want to encounter pirates, you should not have booked passage aboard a pirate hunter's vessel."

The crew roared with laughter at the statement.

"Jon-Jon."

"Aye, Cap'n."

"Have Stoddard and his companions returned to their cabin and see that they are well-fed. Put the lad to work. If he gives you trouble, beat him. If he continues to give trouble, use him for fish bait. The crew can have the woman but see that they don't overuse her. She won't bring a good price if she's damaged, and she's worth nothing to me dead."

"What about the girl and these two, Cap'n?"

"Business before pleasure, Mr. Jon," he answered. "I want a word with these gentlemen. When I'm through with them, bring the girl to my cabin — untouched."

"Understood, Cap'n." Jon-Jon walked over and pulled the girl away from her mother amid much screaming and weeping. He had to backhand the woman to get her quiet. He set a man to herding the former captain and his mates and told him to take the boy as well. Other crewmembers wasted no time in getting acquainted with the mother. The father and other passenger were seized and dragged to the captain's cabin.

About an hour later, Viktor dragged out the two headless bodies and tossed them over the side. He set Jon-Jon to remove the heads from his cabin and tidy the place up before sending him the girl.

There was very little blood to clean up. Jon-Jon also noticed a couple of liquor bottles on the table held rather thick, reddish contents. Strangely, he felt no desire to sample the unknown liquid, even if it hadn't been the captain's.

He finished straightening things and fetched the girl.

Viktor soon returned to his cabin. "Well done, Jon-Jon. Tell Piggot he has the watch. I am not to be disturbed for any reason tonight. If you want, you can have the widow for the rest of the evening."

Jon-Jon exited the cabin, closing the door behind him.

No one aboard dared comment about the screams then moans that emanated from the captain's cabin that night. Although there were a few knowing chuckles among the crew.

Chapter 7

Two nights after Viktor sold off his hostages and cargo, the first full moon rose since he'd left Savannah and Mother Celie. The white crystal pendant she had given him grew heavier, and the chain felt warm, bordering on hot, as if it had lain next to a fire for too long.

"Dammit, Mother," he grumbled under his breath. "I'm not going to forget to do what I have to do." Louder, he shouted to the riggers, "Furl and secure all sails!" Once the task was accomplished, the ship began to slow noticeably.

"Douse all lights," he ordered, reducing the ship to a shadowy form on the moon-silvered waters. Only a few stars glimmered close to the horizon. The full moon's glow washed out the rest of the night sky to a dull pewter color.

He removed the pendant and tied a lifeline securely to its chain. The milky crystal seemed to almost glow in the moonlight. Carefully, he lowered it over the side and into the sea. The moment the crystal touched the water, it flashed. A slow, glowing wave spread out from it. Then, with a loud creaking, the ship slammed to an abrupt stop.

"Cap'n, we've run aground!" the lookout called.

Pulling the pendant back up and replacing it about his neck, Viktor ordered, "Lower a boat. I'm going ashore. Top watch, light one lantern only."

A dense fog descended on everything shortly after he entered the lowered boat and began rowing toward the dark bulk of the island. The fog rendered the lantern on the topmast almost invisible and reduced the moon to a pale watery spot in the sky. The strong, reddish glow of a fire flared ahead of him and gave him a heading. As he steered in that direction, the fog cleared a tunnel for him.

A short time later, he beached his boat and followed a path through the rocks, toward the fire's glow. Climbing over the rise that separated the cove from the rest of the island, he was surprised to find the fire was much smaller than its glow had led him to believe. Only a small driftwood fire with an ancient black man seated next to it greeted him.

"Uncle Zeke?" Viktor asked, stepping into the rocky, barren hollow.

"Pull up a rock, boy," the old man said by way of greeting. "Been expecting you. You don't happen to have any tobacco on you, do ya, boy?"

Seating himself opposite the old man, he reached into his vest. He pulled out a cigar and offered it. "Just cigars. I sold a load of baled tobacco two days ago."

Zeke made a face but took it anyway. "Thankye. Bit sharper than what I like, but it'll do," he said. "Hard to come by tobacco on Hell's Breath." He proceeded to crumble up the cigar and stuff the loose bits into a pipe that he seemed to have pulled from thin air.

Viktor made a mental note not to underestimate the old man. The magicks at work in this place were very subtle, but he found he could almost smell the power resonating around the figure before him. "I'll remember to bring pipe tobacco next time."

"Much obliged."

"Mother said you could help me find her sisters," he came right to the point.

"Mayhaps I can, mayhaps I can't," Zeke mumbled around the stem of his pipe.

The vampire scowled in irritation. "Can you help me, or can you not, old man?"

"You keep that tone, boy, and I won't help you," Zeke snapped back. "I'm too old to waste time on some snippety, sass-mouthed whelp."

Viktor seethed but held his tongue. He needed the old man's help; a fact that truly galled his prideful nature.

Zeke sat, silently regarding the vampire for a while. As he puffed on the pipe, his black eyes shone bright as coals with reflected firelight. He stared at Viktor for what seemed like an eternity. Finally, he seemed satisfied with what he saw and nodded to himself.

"So, you be the One. Mighta known it would turn out to be a scourge of a pirate like you. But then, the One needs to be a ruthless sort — strong — resourceful — and mean." He nodded again.

This puzzled Viktor. "What do you mean by saying I'm the 'One?' Mother Celie mumbled some nonsense about that, as well, but never explained."

"Well, if ol' Celie didn't see fit to explain, I reckon you don't really need to know just yet," Zeke replied. "You look to be a smart 'un. Imagine you'll figure it out for yourself, when the time's right."

He puffed the pipe again. "So, Celie's set you to find the Sisters."

"Aye," Viktor nodded. "She said I need their help to stop this curse from killing me — that she couldn't counteract it with just her magic."

"Mm-hmn!" The old man nodded. "Well, boy, seein' how you's the One, an' we can't have you dyin' on us, guess I better help you find the Sisters."

"It would be appreciated," he stated dryly. "Where do I find them?"

Zeke started chuckling, and continued to do so, until Viktor began to think him mad. The old man finally wound down. "Hee! Oh, this is goin' be a mighty entertaining undertaking," he laughed.

"What do you find so amusing?" Vik glowered at him.

"Why you, boy. Hee!" Zeke wiped a mirthful tear from his eye. "You think the Sisters be that easy to find? That I can just tell you where they be, an' you'll walk right up to them and get what you want?"

The vampire growled, "Of course I don't expect it to be easy to get what I need from them. Mother already told me that much."

"Just so's you understand." The old man sobered. He took a puff on the pipe, blew out the smoke, and watched it mingle with the smoke of his small fire. "The Sisters ain't easy to find. No one can tell you exactly where each is, but those that have the feel for such things can get you to the right place to hunt."

"So, you can at least navigate me in the right directions."

The old man shook his head. "I can't go with ya, boy. I don't leave Hell's Breath anymore."

Viktor nodded. He hadn't really wanted the old man underfoot on board, anyway. "Then, I'll just have to sail back here for new coordinates after each Sister is found."

"It don't work that way, boy," Zeke chuckled. "Ain't no guarantee Hell's Breath will be here, if you try to come back." He held up his hand to forestall Viktor's response. "Oh, we'll be seeing each other again. Don't doubt that Viktor Brandewyne. But it may not be in this part of the sea. When it's meant to be, Hell's Breath will find you."

"Mother said something like that." He frowned. "I'll accept it, but I'm not sure I like the arrangement."

Zeke puffed for a while more, staring into his fire. After a few moments, he spoke again. "This old island has a mind of its own. I know it'll find you, but I don't know when or where. It ain't called Hell's Breath for nothin'. There's some as say it's just a breath away from Hell, then there's others as say it travels on Hell's breath."

He sighed, then, brightened. "Myself, I don't care why that's its name. I suspect you don't really care, either."

"What I care about is finding the Sisters."

"Right. The Sisters. Well, boy, since I can't go with you, and I don't know when we'll meet again, I reckon I better send someone with you who can keep you on your course."

It's about time, Viktor thought. Aloud, he said, "I see no one else here. Where do I find the man?"

The old man grinned. Yes, Brandewyne was definitely going to be a source of entertainment. "She," he emphasized the word, "will come to you."

"A woman," Viktor scowled. "That can cause problems among a pirate crew."

"Oh, I think this one can protect herself," Zeke said with a chuckle. "She's not a typical female. Figure you need to set a witch to find a witch."

"So, I'm to take some old hag," the vampire sneered.

"Hee! Boy, you is funny as Hell. Not all witches are old or ugly." The old man had to wipe a tear from his eye. "What you need to do now is get back in your little rowboat and take it around the island three times. Then, your guide will come to you."

When Viktor didn't move right away, Zeke shooed him. "Go on now, boy. The faster you get on it, the sooner you'll find what you're looking for."

Belladonna watched the lone man rowing around Hell's Breath Island. She'd been watching ever since the damned island appeared and grounded the pirate ship. The crystal's reawakening had called to her, just as it had summoned up Hell's Breath.

Finally! Some excitement, she thought.

She followed the boat, swimming silently. The fog shifted to obscure the island by the end of the first pass. Before the second pass had been completed, the island vanished, leaving only the fog bank.

Belladonna swam closer. To her amusement, she heard the man grumbling under his breath about witches and the old man and their bloody stupid rules.

From her closer perspective, she could tell that he seemed well formed, rather than too bony or too flabby, like so many sailors she had encountered. It was hard to tell in the darkness, even with her excellent night vision, if his hair was black or dark brown. He wore it long, tied back then draped over one shoulder. His eyes were a vibrant emerald green. The fact that they literally glowed with his irritation made the color easy to discern. She also noticed that he seemed rather well groomed for a sea faring man. His mustache and goatee were neatly trimmed, rather than bushy or scraggly, as was more common. The neatness accentuated the shape of his cheekbones and jaw line, something she found quite appealing.

He looks good enough to eat, she thought, *and what a fine feast he'd make, too. It's almost a shame I'm not permitted to do that with this one. Oh well, time to make my introductions.*

Viktor had just completed his third circuit of the island, when a loud splash startled him.

"Hi. You look lost," a nude young woman spoke to him. She was in the water with her arms resting on the side of his boat, smiling coquettishly at him.

To his credit, he only flinched a little at her appearance. He was a little relieved to see her. He'd begun to think the old man had been full of bilge.

He found the woman to be quite attractive. The dark made it hard for him to determine what color her wet hair was. Her eyes were some light shade. For the moment, they were moon silvered. She was full-breasted, with the firmness of youth. Her waist tapered in pleasingly before curving back out for the swell of her hips. What was below was hidden from sight by the dark seawater.

Belladonna raised an eyebrow at his scrutiny of her. "You are being quite rude, Viktor Brandewyne," she pointed out. "Are you going to invite me into your little boat, or shall I rip it in half and dump you in the water?"

The thought of this slip of a woman ripping anything, let alone his boat, in half amused Viktor. "Come aboard, then, lass. I wouldn't mind getting a full view of you." He chuckled lewdly. "You are the witch that Uncle Zeke is sending with me?"

She deftly flipped herself over the side and into the boat, showering Viktor in the process. "Yes, I'm Belladonna."

"Dammit wench!" he cursed over the soaking. Then, he sat back in astonishment. "What are you?"

Where her legs should have been, she had a black shark's tail with a silvery underside. Her eyes glowed amber. As he stared, her tail split, shrank and reformed into shapely legs.

"I'm a siren," she stated, as if she thought him simple-minded. "Don't you read?"

"Sirens are just bilge wash spouted by men who couldn't navigate their way out of a gunny sack." He dismissed her claim.

Belladonna sat back, lounging against the side of the boat in a pose that he found both arrogant and provocative. "This coming from a vampire hunting for witches." She smirked.

"Point taken, lass," he ceded. "I am curious as to how you know both who and what I am."

"Oh, I know lots of things." She smiled. "But I don't know why you've been rowing around out here for over an hour, muttering and cursing, instead of going back to your ship."

It was his turn to look at her as if she were the slow wit. "The old man told me I had to row around the island three times in order to summon you."

"What island?"

Viktor was about to point out the obvious answer, when he finally noticed that the obscuring fog had vanished — and so had Hell's Breath Island. The moonlight was strong enough that he could have spotted his ship, even without the aid of the lantern on the topmast.

"I think Zeke was having a joke at your expense," Belladonna giggled. "He has a strange sense of humor."

"I do not find it amusing." The vampire's voice was warm and low with a deadly anger. "I do not suffer ridicule or wasting of my time lightly."

Belladonna sensed that the man before her was a formidable predator, possibly her equal, or maybe even strong enough to master her. The siren had never encountered a human male that she'd felt could not only escape her wiles but might even be capable of entrapping her. She found the thought disturbingly compelling. She also found that his contained anger made him very attractive to her.

"I promise you, Captain, I will never waste your time." She gave him a sultry smile.

Viktor eyed her up and down, a slow, arrogant smile spreading across his face, as lust began to replace his anger. "No, I can see that you would definitely not be a waste of time."

The siren was pleased and appreciative of the view when he stripped his shirt off. It puzzled her, however, when he handed it to her. She took it and held it up to look at, her face showing her confusion plainly.

"Thank you, but — what am I supposed to do with this?"

"Put it on."

"Why?" she questioned, even as she complied. The scent of male on the garment awakened her appetite.

Viktor leaned forward over her, a hand on each side, effectively pinning her in place. "Because I would find myself obliged to kill about half of my crew before I could get you back to my cabin, if I were to bring you aboard naked," he purred, his wicked grin wide enough to reveal his fangs.

Belladonna's eyes fixed on them immediately. She reached up a hand, fingers delicately brushing their razor-sharp tips. "Nice," she smiled mischievously, "but only two?"

"Oh, I find them sufficient," he confided.

"I guess they are, if you're only after blood," she shrugged. "But, if you're eating meat, I find a whole mouthful much more suitable."

Her lips peeled back in a grin that was much wider than any human mouth could ever stretch, revealing neatly interlocking rows of needle-like teeth.

He quickly sat back and away from her. "Damn! I would never have thought a mermaid would have teeth like a barracuda!" he exclaimed, seriously reconsidering his ideas about seducing her.

Belladonna frowned at him. "I am not a mermaid! I'm a Siren," she corrected him irritably.

"A moment ago, you were half fish," he argued. "What is the difference?"

It was her turn to lean in over him, getting so close they were almost nose-to-nose. He watched as her eyes went from golden amber to an almost human gray. Her teeth reverted to human, as well. She whispered in a purring voice, "Mermaids don't eat Sirens."

She kissed him, only their lips touching, then sat back and smiled coyly at him. "Shall we go back to your ship and start looking for the Sisters?"

Chapter 8

A solitary figure exited a dimly lit shop onto a dark back street in Havana. The heavy rain led him to tug his hat down more firmly and pull the collar of his topcoat up to his ears. Turning his feet toward the waterfront, he headed back to the tavern where his mates awaited him.

Three disreputable looking men watched from a nearby alley.

"That him?"

"Aye, that be the buggerer."

"You're certain?" The third man sounded doubtful. "There'll be no reward, save a flogging, if ye be false with us."

"'Tis him, I tell you," the second insisted. "Bla'guard beat me feet bloody over nicking a pair o' boots. I'll not be forgetting him anytime soon."

The man in question drew even with the mouth of the alley. Heavy rain and darkness prevented him from seeing his attackers, until it was too late. He was tackled, a gunnysack thrown over his head, and a cudgel applied to the base of his skull.

Consciousness returned to the kidnapping victim gradually. A dull ache in his head, as well as a tender spot close to his left ear made their presence known. His vision remained dark despite his open eyes. The close, stale air led him to realize some sort of bag covered his head. A gentle rocking motion and faint creaking told him he was on board a ship.

"Talmidge, you better be right about this one," a raspy voice said. "If you've lied, it'll be you swinging in the breezes of Port Royal."

"I've told ye afore, 'tis the man himself," another voice whined.

A rough hand snatched the sack off the man's head, stirring up dust and causing a violent coughing fit.

Once he'd managed to catch his breath, he looked up to see who had finally managed to capture him. The man wore finer clothing than the last time they'd met, but he still wasn't very impressive. Lank, dirty blond hair and a height just shy of six feet were the only markings of his Nordic sire. Muddy brown eyes spoke of his Carib mother. Rather than blending the natural beauty of both races, his form seemed to sully them. His appearance was plain, bordering on ugly.

"Been a long time, Hezekiah," the blond man spoke.

"Not long enough," Hezekiah Grimm answered. "Still a coward sending others to do your dirty work, are you, Jorgen?" The taunt earned him a kick in the ribs.

Jorgen turned to a scurrilous, greasy looking man. "You spoke true, Talmidge. You have delivered the Grimm Reaper, as promised. Marle, give him his pay and get him off my ship."

Talmidge snarled, baring yellowed, rotten teeth. "Cap'n Jorgen, you promised me passage to Tortuga. Ye can't put me ashore here! Grimm's mates will kill me!"

"Not my problem; and I promised no such thing," Jorgen refuted. "Mr. Marle, why is this creature still aboard? If he utters another word, toss him over the side without his pay."

The burly sailor shoved a small leather pouch into the informant's hand, then grabbed him by the scruff of the neck and began forcing him toward the gangplank. The little weasel made a protesting squawk, when he felt how light the pouch was. Marle followed his captain's orders to the letter. Snatching the pay back, he cold-cocked the traitorous pirate, hefted him over one shoulder, carried him to the opposite side of the ship and dumped him into the bilge-polluted water without further ceremony.

Jorgen turned back to his captive, a cold smile on his face. "You're going to fetch a pretty reward from the Governor of Jamaica, Hezekiah, but my crew has to eat, as well. Where is your ship and cargo?"

"Go bugger yourself, Martin," Grimm spat. "You're naught but a sneak thief and, it seems, a lapdog for the powers that be."

The privateer, never a patient man, backhanded him. "Damn you, Grimm! You always tried to lord it over me, when we sailed together; always acted like you were better than me. Where is that ship?!"

Grimm just looked at him. Jorgen slapped him again with enough force to cut the inside of his cheek against his teeth. He spat blood onto the deck and gave Jorgen a bored stare.

Jorgen turned to his mate again, "Mr. Marle, put him in irons and keep him on deck. He is not to have any food or water, and flog him three times a day, until he gives us his ship, or we reach Port Royal."

"Aye sir."

Later that night, after the privateer set out to sea and headed due east toward the Florida Straits, the helmsman dozed at his post. The crew was below decks, drinking and gambling pay they had yet to receive. Grimm sprawled half-conscious on the deck, iron manacles at wrists and ankles. His back was raw, cut by the whippings and blistered by the unforgiving tropical sun.

Slowly, a shadowy form lowered toward him from the rigging. It resembled nothing so much as a fat spider.

"Cap'n?" The shadow spoke low, so as not to rouse the helmsman. "Can ye hear me?"

Grimm managed to turn his head. "Who?" He croaked through chapped, cracked lips.

The stumpy shadow chuckled softly. "Just ol' Sniff, Cap'n. Didn't expect you to know me without me legs. Brought you some water and saved ye a bit o' fruit from me dinner." He held a small flask to Grimm's mouth. Once the wounded man had his fill, Sniff slipped a chunk of papaya into his mouth, with instructions to chew slowly. He used the remainder of the water to wash the salt from Grimm's face.

"If we get close enough to land, I'll steal a small boat at night and get ourselves away from this right bastard. Bla'guard's turned against his own kind."

Just as silently as he'd descended, he disappeared back up into the rigging.

Viktor had less trouble bringing the siren on board than he'd thought he would have. As dark as it had been, even with the moon at the full, the few crewmen who'd seen her come aboard had assumed she was a marooned young sailor. They were only puzzled as to why the captain would rescue the lad.

When it became known Belladonna was female, Viktor gave the order she was not to be touched. His appreciation of his hold over the crew grew considerably, as a result. Not one, not even Jon-Jon, protested or made any attempt to defy the order.

Belladonna, on the other hand, seemed determined to test his patience as much as possible. She insisted on dressing in men's clothing, if she absolutely had to wear something. He ceded to that only because pants were more practical than skirts on slippery, heaving decks.

What he found truly irritating was her almost constant flirting with his men. Bound by his will, they either wouldn't or couldn't give in, but he could tell most of them really wanted to. His own sense of self-preservation kept him from fulfilling his desire to bed her, temptress that she was. Some inexplicable instinct told him that could lead to disaster. But it didn't stop his jealousy from flaring.

Then, the mysterious rash sprang up.

Almost half his crew sported painful red welts on face, arms and chest. Fears of plague raged on board, testing the strength of his hold on his men. Some of the victims became delirious, as the welts began to blister and fester.

Almost a week passed before Viktor discovered the source of the infection. None of the men could tell how they'd gotten it. That day, he witnessed it rise on the flesh of one of his sailors. Belladonna had taken her flirting to a more physical level, nearly draping herself on her target. The man remained unresponsive. The siren made an irritated growl then got a cold, almost cruel smile on her face. She backed away from her victim with a parting caress to his face. Viktor saw the welts spring up where her fingers had brushed the man's skin.

Lightning fast, he grabbed her by the wrists, careful to keep her hands away from him, as she tried to sashay past him. "What have you been doing to my crew?" he demanded, his voice cold as steel.

She looked up at him, not the least bit perturbed at being restrained. "I've been trying to seduce them, but your magic is blocking me," she stated. "I don't take rejection very well."

Viktor would have slapped her, if he hadn't been using both hands to hold her wrists. He leaned down and snarled in her face, "So you give them some strange disease? Some are too sick to work! Did it never occur to you that they are needed to sail this ship? You were brought aboard to aid me in my quest, not to cripple my crew!"

Belladonna tried to move her body as close as she could to her captor. "You are magnificent when you are angry," she purred. "I'll tell you how to cure your men, if you'll give me a kiss."

He just stared at her for a moment. He was tempted, but he was not about to let this troublesome female have the upper hand. "First, you will tell me the cure."

"Salt water," she stated simply.

He transferred one of her wrists, so that he held both with one hand, tightly. With his now free hand, he stroked her face. He found her eager response to the caress gratifying.

Without warning, he started for the hatch at a brisk stride, jerking the siren off balance.

"What about my kiss?" she demanded.

"I don't trust you, lass." He didn't even look at her, as he dragged her along. "I want to see the cure work."

Keeping a firm grip on her, he ordered the worst stricken of the pirates lowered over the side by ropes. The crewmen assigned the task dunked the man briefly, then, raised him back up to the ship. Though the welts no longer festered and oozed, they still showed angry red against the man's sickly pale skin.

"That is not good enough," Viktor growled and flung the siren halfway across the deck.

She caught herself by elongating one hand into a talon and digging it into the deck. She stood, her fingers shifting back to human, and stalked seductively toward the vampire. He eyed her suspiciously, readying himself to fight.

"You'll not get that kiss, wench," he told her. "The man is not cured."

"Of course, he's not, Captain. That one is too far along for just the salt water to work. I'll have to use magic — and sacrifice to work a complete cure."

"What kind of sacrifice?"

"Give me the least important member of your crew and have all those I have stung get in the water at the same time," she instructed. When she saw he was still distrustful of her, she dropped her playfulness and gave him a serious face, putting just enough magic behind it to assure him that she meant what she was saying. "I give you my oath, Captain Brandewyne, that I will not harm your men in this manner again. The only man who will die, will be the one you give me for a sacrifice."

"You will cure my men," he warned her. "If I see so much as one more of those welts on any of my crew, I'll slit your throat and throw you to the sharks."

She chuckled, as if amused by his threat. "Don't worry, Captain, my magic will undo what I have done. I do require you to release my victim completely from your power, however. My magic cannot be hindered by yours, if this is to work."

"Very well," Viktor agreed to her terms.

Within the hour, everyone who'd suffered from Belladonna's poisoned touch went over the side. Some jumped, others, either too sick or unable to swim, had been lowered by their healthy shipmates.

The chosen victim, still under Viktor's control, stood by patiently, face blank, mind blank.

"How long do the men have to stay in the water?"

The siren smiled, not a comforting sight, since her true teeth were in view. "When the time is right, they'll come out of the water on their own; probably much faster than they went in."

She sashayed up to him and grasped his goatee, pulling him down into a kiss. That she was able to do so before he could react spoke of her power and speed. He realized she might be a match for him.

"I wanted to take my payment now," she purred. "I've a feeling you won't be inclined to grant my kiss after what you are about to see. Now, if you'll release young Saunders to me, please."

The sailor shook his head and appeared to be disoriented, as Viktor cut his hold on the man. "Captain? You wanted me for something?"

"I'm giving you to Belladonna." Viktor scowled at the siren as she busied herself disrobing.

Saunders followed his captain's gaze and broke into an eager grin. "Yes sir!"

Belladonna glanced up and noticed the vampire's glower. She shrugged, "Garments would just be in my way for this." Then she smiled, careful to hide her teeth, "Come join me for a swim, Saunders." She turned and strode to the rail, fully aware that two sets of eyes were following her every move. She looked back over her shoulder, smiled, crooked a beckoning finger then jumped over the side.

Saunders rushed at breakneck speed to join her in the water. Viktor had to exercise his full will to keep from diving in, himself. The siren was truly tempting. He did go to the side to see how she was going to work her cure.

The siren surfaced. Her eyes shone amber. Her fingers had turned into razor sharp talons, and he could clearly see her shark tail. She raised her arms to her victim. The man swam to her embrace eagerly, oblivious to the changes in her physical form. She pulled him into an open-mouthed kiss. The man's pleasure soon turned to horror, when she bit off his tongue and ate it.

Blood curdling screams drew the attention of the other men in the water. As soon as they realized what was happening to their crewmate, they started scrambling up the ropes, frantic to get out of the water.

Not one bore even a scar from Belladonna's caresses.

The siren drew back, still clutching her prey to her. She opened her mouth impossibly wide, her jaw appearing to unhinge, and revealed multiple rows of needle teeth. Viktor glimpsed pure terror on Saunders' face for just a moment. Then the siren struck, her mouth entirely enveloping the man's face. There was a sickening crunch as her teeth crushed his skull. With the man's head still in her jaws, Belladonna rolled her yellow eyes up to lock gazes with the vampire.

It was the gaze of a true predator, and Viktor knew his expression matched hers at that point.

The siren dove deep, taking her prey with her.

The first beating of the day came shortly after sun-up. Marle hooked a line to the chain on Grimm's wrist manacles and hoisted it until he'd forced his victim to stand on his toes. Marle then commenced to reopen the scabbed over gashes from Grimm's whippings of the previous day.

Thirty lashes. After each lash, Jorgen demanded the location of Grimm's ship. The captured pirate stubbornly held his silence.

A repeat performance took place at midday, with the same results.

During the afternoon, Grimm became aware of a shadow blocking the worst of the glare from his tortured body. He knew it was probably Sniff, up in the rigging, but wisely never looked up. He did not want to draw Jorgen's attention to his secret ally.

The afternoon beating proved the most vicious. Already, Jorgen's patience wore thin. If it took too long to find out where the ship was, Grimm's erstwhile crew would have the stolen cargo offloaded. Collecting the bounties for the pirates and whatever price the prize brought at auction would be the best he could hope for then. That might prove a dicey proposition, at best. The prize would most likely be severely damaged, when they moved to take her.

His frustration with Grimm's uncooperativeness played out as five lashes added to the thirty. Grimm merely grunted.

After the beating, Grimm managed a raspy chuckle. "These scratches will fester and kill me of fever before you'll get any ship from me, Martin."

The blond tormentor growled and kicked him savagely in the knee.

Marle made a cruel suggestion. "Wash him with rum, Captain. That should kill any fever."

Jorgen greeted the idea with a malicious grin. "Make it so, Mr. Marle."

A small cask of liquor was brought up from the ship's stores. Before he would allow the "treatment," he had Marle pour them each a cup. "After all, we wouldn't want to give our guest anything but the best rum," he said with a harsh laugh.

Marle then began pouring the liquid over their victim's back. The alcohol felt like liquid fire as it poured over and into the gashes cut by the whip. Finally, Grimm screamed. The scalding pain was just too much. He blacked out.

Viktor ignored the knock on his door, sure in the knowledge that none of his crew would dare enter his cabin without permission. Lars Stoddard slumped, unconscious, at the table. He was the last of the *Barracuda's* former officers. Frankly, it amazed Viktor that the erstwhile pirate hunter had lived this long, given how much blood he'd taken from him. None of his shipmates had.

Now, it looked as if he had exhausted the last of his larder. The man's heart slowed noticeably with each passing minute. He would have to go hunting soon or be forced to feed on his crew.

He snarled in anger, when the door to his cabin opened, and a figure entered his cabin unbidden. Belladonna shut the door behind her. "What?" she stated irritably. "I did knock."

"I did not give you permission to enter."

She shrugged and hopped up to sit on the table. "We need to talk."

"I am busy at the moment." He waved a hand at the dying man.

She glanced over, then, returned her gaze to Viktor. "You've gotten all the blood you can out of that one. If you're done with him, I'll take care of the rest."

The vampire realized she wasn't going to leave until she said what she came to say. After witnessing what she was capable of, he didn't think it wise to antagonize her. "You're welcome to him, lass. What exactly did you want to talk about?"

"Two things, really, and you can call me Belladonna or Belle," she instructed him. "The first thing is that I had a vision while feeding. I saw you talking to one of the Sisters. Her features were unclear, probably due to her spells of protection, but I sensed her power. She's somewhere near the Isle of Youth, but she may move. Visions like that often go both ways."

"Then we best set course, before she can escape," he stated dryly. "I was starting to wonder if you really were going to help me find the Sisters, or if sending you with me was another of that old man's jokes."

Belladonna gave a throaty chuckled that provoked a response from his body against his will. "Knowing Zeke, both."

He moved around the table to stand behind her. Placing his hands on the table, he leaned until his lips were just inches from her throat. The recent feeding had his predatory side close to the surface. "You say you had your vision while feeding," he whispered. "Is that the only time you get visions? I can't very well keep feeding my crew to you, little fish."

She leaned back on her elbows between his arms to look up at him. "That's the other thing I wanted to talk to you about." She smiled. "You might want to replenish your stores. That meat you gave me was severely undernourished."

He enjoyed the view she offered him in their current positions, but he remained strong-willed enough to keep it from distracting him from business. "I have already planned to do some hunting, my deadly Belladonna." He smiled smugly at her.

"I was hoping you'd take that course." She returned his smile with a grin. "You haven't really been living up to your reputation, since I came on board."

He stood straight and crossed his arms. "And what reputation would that be?"

She rolled over onto her belly to face him directly. "Oh, you're famous among the sea folk, Viktor Brandewyne. Your bloody acts of piracy have kept us very well fed indeed."

"Hmm," he grunted.

Glancing over, he spotted Lazarus gnawing on the dead man's hand. Belladonna saw it, too. She darted off the table and snatched the body off the chair. The demon cat dangled from the hand, jaw locked and growling.

"Get off!" The siren hissed, trying to shake the cat loose.

Lazarus growled louder and swatted a clawed paw at her, missing.

Chuckling, Viktor grabbed a sword and severed the hand, dropping Lazarus unceremoniously to the floor. The cat darted under the bed with his prize.

The siren started after him, but Viktor stopped her. "Let him have it, little fish. You've got the rest of the body," he ordered.

Turning at the door before going out, he added, "I don't want either one of you eating that in my cabin. Take it outside."

Chapter 9

A few days later, top watch noticed something moving toward the ship very fast. The sea mounded up ominously in front of the unknown object's submerged approach. Little waves spread from its wake. The lookout thought maybe it was a dolphin or small whale, no serious threat. A few yards short of the ship, the wake stopped abruptly, as the creature dove deep.

A sudden, geyser-like eruption on the opposite side of the ship startled everyone on the deck.

Belladonna dropped from the geyser, catching hold of the rigging to break her fall. By the time she lowered herself to the deck, her siren form had melted away to reveal her human form. She strode naked and unmolested to her cabin. The crewmen, the vivid memory of her feeding habits still fresh in their minds, gave her a wide berth.

Once in her cabin, she slipped on trousers and a loose shirt. Viktor's insistence that she wear clothes both puzzled and amused her. At least he didn't insist on all the foofaraw that human females ensconced themselves with. She didn't see how they could have any mobility with all those binding garments and layers on. No, men's clothing suited her tastes much better; loose, comfortable, and easily removed.

Satisfied that she was properly clad to avoid annoying the vampire, she padded the short distance to his cabin.

Viktor had already heard the report of the siren's return. When he heard the knock at his door, he said, "Enter."

Belladonna closed the door behind her. She thought she caught a hint of a smile on his face, before his expression returned to its usual impassiveness. "I've found us some food," she announced.

The pirate raised an eyebrow but remained silent.

Grinning impishly, the siren elaborated. "If you stay on this course, you'll encounter a small fishing fleet that seems to have gotten lost."

"Lost," Viktor echoed.

"Mm-hmm," Belle feigned innocence. It had the desired effect of provoking a chuckle from him.

"I suppose you had something to do with their getting lost." He laughed. "What did you do, my naughty little fish, lure them off with your song?"

"So, you do read!" she chirped. "Don't believe everything you read, Viktor. I don't sing — well, I should say, I do sing, but there's nothing magical about it. But I can scream really, really loudly. So loud, in fact, that it will drive any mortal who hears it quite mad. It makes them very susceptible to suggestion."

He stood and strode over to her. Leaning down, he caressed her face. "Naughty little fish," his voice was warm and low with amusement and admiration.

She fairly purred under his touch. She blinked in surprise, when he suddenly just wasn't there. She turned to find him holding the door.

"Shall we go hunting?" he invited.

The three fishing boats were easy prey. Viktor found out the siren's magic scream had all but destroyed the minds of the helpless fishermen. They could perform simple tasks but seemed unable to reason or act for themselves. The very mindlessness of the men reminded him of the zombies *Mamaan* Juma had sent to fetch him. He found the similarity disturbing.

The salted fish as well as the fresh provisions the fishermen had brought along made the crew happy. The watered-down rum barely held any potency, but none of the pirates complained.

Viktor picked out the five healthiest of the fishermen to keep alive. The remaining seven he hung up and bled into a couple of barrels. He mixed some of his private stock of rum and brandy with the blood to prevent clotting, a barrel of each.

Belladonna made short work of two of the bodies. Sharks schooled nearby but did not approach to feed until the siren left the water to return to the ship.

None of the fishing boats proved of value to Viktor, so he let his gunners use them for target practice.

Favorable winds helped them make good time. Already, they were preparing to round the western end of Cuba. If the weather stayed with them, they'd make the turn south then east and arrive at the Isle of Youth within the week.

Supplies held out well, but the pirate kept an eye out for potential prizes. Not only was piracy profitable; Viktor Brandewyne truly enjoyed the occupation.

The aft lookout called out, "Sails to the southeast! Wind's with her. Gaining fast."

"What colors she runnin'?" Jon-Jon called from the helm.

"She just struck the Spanish and ran up the French, same as we're flying."

"Sounds like Brethren, Cap'n," Jon-Jon said. "Should we outrun them or turn and fight?"

"I want a better look," Viktor told him. He took the glass his mate held out for him and peered through it. Unsatisfied with the limited range, he summoned, "Lazarus, come forth."

The cat appeared, seemingly from out of nowhere, and jumped up on the railing. "Mmmrrow."

"Go see what ship that is."

Lazarus leapt from the rail, dissolving into a smoky mass, and reformed as a raven. He flew up high, then dove and arrowed in on the pursuing ship. Viktor closed his eyes, watching through his familiar's eyes, as Lazarus did his fly by. A wry smile curved his lips when he recognized both the ship and her captain. "Lazarus return."

The cat materialized as if he had never left.

"Mr. Jon, hold your course and maintain our current speed. If he can catch up with us, we're about to give Wally Cornell a rude shock."

The pursuing ship overtook the *Barracuda* about two hours later. As soon as she pulled even, she fired a shot across Viktor's bow.

"Heave to and prepare to be boarded!" a shout came from the pirate.

Calmly, a peaceful smile on his face, Viktor ordered, "Return fire. Chain shot to her foremast." Within minutes, they crippled the attacking ship.

"I think it is you who should heave to, Cornell," Viktor called across.

Cornell stood at the railing of his ship, his blood running cold, as recognition hit. "Vik Brandee?! I heard you were dead."

"I got better."

"If I'd known it was you, I'd have steered clear and given you a wide berth," Cornell called.

"As well you should have," Viktor smiled grimly.

Cornell had a stubborn set to his face. "I know you'll not let us pass. However, we outgun you."

At a silent signal from the vampire, the gunners removed the false sections of hull to reveal all the *Barracuda*'s guns. "Oh, do you now?" He chuckled. "Your ship is already crippled, Wally. You can't outshoot me. This was a pirate hunter before I took command."

"A parley, then, to negotiate safe passage, Vik," Cornell requested.

"Come aboard, man. We'll have a meal and talk. You have my word none of my crew shall harm you or your ship while I draw breath."

Wallace Cornell entered Brandewyne's cabin with a great sense of apprehension. He knew the chances of leaving this ship alive were almost nonexistent. Things had gone too far. Shots had been exchanged. Still, he knew Brandee to be a man of his word. He held some hope he could bargain his way out of this, albeit a slim hope.

It stunned him a bit when the enormous black tomcat occupying one of the chairs growled and hissed at him. He'd never heard of Brandee being one to keep pets.

"That is Lazarus' chair," Brandee warned. "I would advise against trying to move or pet him. He's fond of finger food."

Cornell eyed the cat warily as he took a chair further away from the ill-tempered creature. Turning to the table and the captain of the vessel, he was impressed with the hearty meal laid out. Though the fish proved no surprise, the fresh bread, fruit and vegetables were.

"Came across a fishing fleet a few days back and re-provisioned; they had no further use for the food. Help yourself."

The pirate wasted no time in accepting the invitation. Brandee threw a piece of fish to Lazarus to shut him up, then, joined Cornell in the meal.

"What news in these waters?"

"North shore's been busy, not so much the western tip or the southwest shore. But then, with this ship, I don't reckon you worry too much about pirate hunters."

"Not particularly."

Something about the man, something Cornell couldn't quite put his finger on, seemed more menacing than he'd remembered Brandee being. He felt much like a rabbit finding itself in the fox's den.

"No," he proceeded warily, "I'd warrant they'd best watch out for you instead. There is one been spotted around Havana, though, you might want to keep an eye out for. Don't know the hunter's name, but word in port is that someone's caught the Grimm Reaper."

Brandee's eyes flashed at the name. "Hezekiah Grimm has been taken? I find that difficult to believe."

"It's true," Cornell insisted. "Talked to some of his mates just a few days ago. They haven't seen him since he went to negotiate with his agent for their cargo. The first mate had to renegotiate the whole deal, at what was probably a loss, just so they could offload and get clear, before the hunters came after them."

Brandee sat silently, sipping his drink and considering what effect, if any, this news had on his course of action. He'd known Grimm for a long time. They'd sailed together, when he'd first put out to sea.

Finally, he spoke, "A pirate's life has no guarantees save for a chance of an early death. You're a good man, Wallace. You deserve a sporting chance for the information you've given. I can't just let you go, since you fired on me. It would look weak to my crew."

"Aye," Cornell agreed. "Just as my crew would think I'd lowered myself by begging for my life. They'd mutiny and maroon me before the week was out."

"There is a way we can both save face with our crews. A duel: winner take all."

"First blood?"

Brandee shook his head. "You know me better than that, Wally. I do not accept defeat graciously. One of us will have to die."

Cornell nodded grimly. "You're right. So be it."

They finished their meal in silence. Wallace Cornell resigned himself to the fact that it was his last.

As the two pirate captains came on deck, Viktor called Jon-Jon to him. "Mr. Jon, clear the decks. Captain Cornell and I are going to have a little duel. I want no interference from the crew." Then, in a voice too low for his opponent to hear, he added, "When he cuts me down, kill him and have the lads ready to take his ship."

Belladonna sat perched in the rigging, watching. Her inhuman hearing permitted her to eavesdrop, catching every word being said. She found the vampire's instructions to be puzzling.

Viktor and Cornell drew their cutlasses and circled each other warily. Each man tried to spot the other's weakest point. Finally, the clash of steel on steel rang out.

His opponent's skill both pleased and impressed Viktor. It meant he didn't have to hold back as much to keep from killing the man early in the fight. He always enjoyed a good challenge.

After about ten minutes, they broke off. Cornell was sweaty and winded. Viktor was not, but he feigned fatigue to keep from raising Cornell's suspicions. "You've gotten better since the last time I saw you fight," he complimented.

"A man does what he has to, to survive," Cornell panted.

"True, he does." Viktor raised his weapon and rushed at the still resting man.

Cornell saw his opening. He wondered only a moment that the infamous pirate would be so careless as to attack without keeping up his guard. The moment passed. He stabbed upward, skewering Viktor through the ribs, before he could bring his weapon down.

Viktor collapsed, Cornell's sword still in his chest. More than anything, he looked surprised by the rapidly growing red stain on his shirt.

Wallace Cornell stood stunned. He hadn't expected to leave this ship alive. He most certainly never dreamed he could've won a duel with Viktor Brandewyne. The man's dueling prowess was legendary among those who sailed under the black flag.

He never saw Jon-Jon climb up from the cargo hatch. Still marveling at his victory, he flopped forward over Viktor, as the pistol ball tore the top of his skull off.

A roar of outrage went up from his crew. Unlike Viktor's crew, they had stayed on deck to see what the outcome of the duel would be.

At a signal from Jon-Jon, the crew of the *Barracuda* boiled out of the hatches, armed to the teeth. They let out a battle cry of their own.

Silence fell over both ships, however, when Viktor Brandewyne shoved the body off his torso, got to his feet, and removed the blade from his chest.

"That damn well hurt!" he commented, dropping the cutlass next to the fallen pirate. "Ruined my shirt, too." He stripped the bloody garment off and tossed it aside. The wound no longer bled. In a matter of seconds, the smear of blood on his chest remained the only indication he'd been skewered.

Belladonna dropped to the deck close to him. "Ooooh, you look tasty," she teased.

"Don't be looking at me like that, lass. There's a whole ship there for us to feast on," he warned her. Loudly, he called to his crew, "Have at lads! Take them now but save twenty alive."

The men needed no further goading.

The battle was remarkably short. Viktor's men were ferocious, but the speed and sheer bloodiness exhibited by the vampire and the siren took most of the will to fight out of Cornell's crew. A few made the mistake of jumping overboard to escape. Belladonna swiftly dove in after them. The waters around the two ships soon turned as crimson as the blood soaking the decks.

In the aftermath, more than the requested twenty had been captured alive. Viktor ordered the prisoners chained below decks, until he could sort through them and decide their fates.

He ordered the body of Cornell wrapped in sailcloth, weighted, and dumped overboard. He forbade Belladonna to consume the remains of the fallen pirate captain.

He set Jon-Jon to organize some of the crew to strip and scuttle the captured ship.

Once back in the privacy of his cabin, Belladonna questioned him on his choice of action. "If you were going to kill him anyway, why did you even bother with that silly farce of a duel?"

"I wouldn't expect a woman to understand."

"Try explaining; you might be surprised by how much I can understand." She bristled at his condescension.

Viktor gave her a measuring gaze before giving his reason for what he had done. "Wallace Cornell was a good pirate. He'd given valuable information. Under different circumstances, I might have invited him to sail with us. But, since shots had been exchanged, the duel was the only way for both of us to avoid appearing weak to our men."

"I know that, Viktor. What I want to know is why you let yourself be run through, and had Jon-Jon kill him, instead of just doing it yourself."

"I held him no more ill will than I do any other man. He deserved to die happy, thinking he had accomplished the great feat of defeating me. Besides," he smiled slyly, "I'd given my word that neither I nor my crew would harm him or his ship while I drew breath. My 'death' allowed me to keep that vow."

"Sneaky," the siren smiled appreciatively. "So, what did he tell you?"

"Don't get too curious, little fish."

Belladonna pouted, but it had no effect on him. Rather than satisfying her curiosity, he left to check on what progress his crew was making with their prize.

Chapter 10

Apparently, Cornell hadn't been long out of port. Other than a few personal stashes from his crew, they found very little treasure aboard. However, provisions, timbers, lines and lanyards, and sailcloth, as well as powder and ammunition for the guns proved plentiful.

Jon-Jon had some of the men toss the poorer weapons from the *Barracuda* and replace them with Cornell's newer guns. To his particular pleasure, he found Wally Cornell's private stock of liquor. The man had had a fondness for gin. Hopefully, the captain would let him have a few bottles when the prize was divided into shares among the crew.

By the next morning, they had everything aboard the *Barracuda* that was of any value. Cornell's ship was scuttled, and the crew of the *Barracuda* put as much distance between them and the wreckage as possible. Before long, the charges left on board went off, speeding the sinking ship to the bottom.

"Mr. Jon, turn her about," Viktor ordered. "Set course for Havana."

"Aye, Cap'n."

Belladonna looked alarmed. Keeping her voice low, so as not to be overheard, she insisted, "A word with you in private, Captain."

"Later."

"This is too important to wait until later," she hissed, her tone adamant. When he ignored her, she added, "Remember those fishermen. We talk now, or I will scream!"

Viktor's eyes flashed emerald fire as he whirled on her. Grabbing her upper arm with one hand, he dealt a vicious backhand with the other. Before she could recover, he dragged her to his cabin door and flung her through. Many among the crew wore knowing grins, as he stalked in and slammed the door.

Knowing no one would interrupt, he closed the distance to her with inhuman speed. Grasping her arms, he hefted the siren until they were eye to eye. "Never threaten me again," he growled. "I am Captain!"

Belladonna's voice was low and deadly, "And I was sent to help you on your mission. I may play with you, but when I say something is important, it would be in your best interest to heed what I say. I have no desire to undermine your authority as captain. A ship is nothing more to me than a plaything and floating larder."

He set her down, pushing her away from him. He found her fearlessness of him aroused him a little too much for his comfort, and the proximity of her body to his made it difficult to concentrate. "What was so bloody important that it could not wait?" his voice remained gruff.

His reaction to her was not lost on the siren, but she let it pass for the time being. Now was not the time for play. She started to answer him.

But she never got the chance.

The ship's forward motion halted with a lurch that flung her against him hard enough to tumble them both to the deck. She landed on top of him. She was immediately aware that his body, at least, did not mind her being there. The inconvenience of the timing irritated her immensely. She knew what had stopped the ship.

"Dammit, Zeke, I was going to straighten this out," she muttered.

Viktor, who had started to enjoy the distraction of her warm weight on him, pushed her off at the mention of the old man. "What the hell does he want?"

The two of them emerged from the cabin to find Hell's Breath within wading distance. Organized chaos reigned on the deck of the ship, as crewmen recovered their footing and checked for broken bones. Murph was already sending a few of the carpenter's mates over the side to check for damage. Just to port, a jetty of rocks protruded from what had been open water moments earlier.

"He wants to see both of us," Belladonna stated.

"What makes you say that?"

"The rocks; Zeke knows I change if I get into sea water."

Viktor just grunted. He let Jon-Jon know he wanted a full damage report when he got back, then headed ashore.

They found the old man sitting at his fire with his back to them. Never even turning around, Zeke spoke, "You're getting off course, boy. Here you are, almost to the first of the Sisters, and you turn around to go the other way? Don't make sense."

"I haven't abandoned my search, old man. I have my reasons for this side trip."

"And what could possibly be more important than finding a solution for your curse before it kills you?" Zeke sounded skeptical.

"A life debt."

At that, the old man did look up at him. His gaze was searching. Viktor never flinched. "So, you are determined to go after the Grimm Reaper, even though it may mean you'll never be able to find all of the Sisters in time?"

"I am."

"Boy, he was taken well over a week ago. How do you know he's even still alive?"

"Then I will slaughter those who took him." He remained resolute. "Pirate I may be, but I have my honor. I swore a life debt to Hezekiah years ago. I will fulfill that vow."

90

Zeke frowned and shook his head. "Thought you was the One. Maybe I was wrong. Can't seem to stay focused."

Viktor's voice was pure ice, "Oh, I am very focused, old man. I have not forgotten, nor will I forget the importance of finding the Sisters. I will find them. I will also retrieve or avenge Hezekiah Grimm, before I sail another league on that mission."

Zeke spat into the fire. "Then you can go fetch him without my help. You don't need Belladonna's help, either."

"So be it."

The siren sputtered, "Wait just one minute! What, are you sending me away? You aren't my master, Zeke."

"You was sent to help him find the Sisters, not to go flitting about after every whim or fancy."

"Fine!" she grumped. Turning, she stomped off in a huff.

Zeke shook his head after her departure. "Females. Well, boy, I suggest you get off my island and back to your ship. Move too slow, and you might find yourself in the water with a very upset sea-witch."

Vik wasted no time getting back to the *Barracuda*. Already, Hell's Breath was growing hazy and indistinct. Knowing the old wizard was unhappy with him, he wouldn't have been surprised if he made the island vanish from under his feet.

Hell's Breath vanished completely mere seconds after Viktor boarded. The ship groaned, as the sand and rocks disappeared, letting her float free again.

"What's the damage, Mr. Jon?"

"Just bruises and a sprain or two among the men. Best we can tell, the ship's in good shape for now. She'll probably need to be careened in another month, though. A bit more barnacles than I'm happy with."

Viktor raised an eyebrow. "As best you can tell? Does Mr. Murph need to be replaced as ship's carpenter?"

"Don't blame Murph, Cap'n. The lads came back up over the sides the minute that sea demon came back without ye."

"Where is Belladonna, by the way?"

Jon-Jon shrugged. "Can't rightly say, Cap'n. She never came aboard. She was raising a ruckus in some tongue I've never heard before. Then she just up and dove into the sea and disappeared."

"Very well; keep on heading toward Havana." He returned to his cabin; confident his orders would be followed.

That evening, there was a knock at his door. "Who is it?"

"Jon-Jon, Cap'n," came the voice through the door. "Littlefoot wants a word with you."

"Send him in."

A nervous looking sailor entered the cabin. He was wringing a shapeless, moderately filthy stocking hat in his hands. His eyes darted a quick glance at his captain, then fixed on the floor. "Thank ye for seeing me, Cap'n. Y'know my brother and I have sailed w'ye for a while now...."

"Out with it, man. I've no time for tales."

"Right, Cap'n. Hrmm," Littlefoot cleared his throat. "Well, it's about me brother, Charlie."

"What about him?"

The sailor shuffled his feet a bit before answering, "Poor Charlie, he's kind of simple. I've always looked after him. Been noticing lately that he's been acting kind of different. Made me suspicious, so I watched him close. Sure enough, I caught him sneaking and getting into the ale."

"My — ale?"

"Aye, Cap'n. I boxed his ears for it. Told him he knew what'd happen if anyone else had caught him. He won't do it again." He glanced up, hopeful.

Viktor's face might as well have been made of stone, for all the emotion it showed. "No. He won't. You know the rules, Littlefoot, as does Charlie."

He started to realize the terrible mistake he'd made. "Please, Cap'n. Charlie's just a simpleton. He meant no harm. He won't do it again, I promise."

"You want me to be lenient?"

"Please, Cap'n."

"I am not a stingy man. Ask, and you shall receive. But steal from one, and you steal from us all. Charlie may be simple-minded, but not so much that he couldn't understand our rules. He knew that, when he took the ale rather than just asking for it." Viktor remained cold and stern.

"Mercy, Cap'n! I'm beggin' ye!"

"The rule stands, as does the punishment. But, since you want mercy for him, you can be the one to kill him."

"He's my baby brother! I couldn't!"

"You should have thought of that before you snitched him out, Littlefoot!" Anger warmed his voice. "You will kill him for the crime of theft, or you will die with him. Mr. Jon, see that my orders are carried out."

"Aye, Cap'n." Jon-Jon seized the still protesting man and dragged him from the cabin. Before he could shut the door, Belladonna pushed past him, then, shut it herself.

"How sweet," she purred. "You missed me so much, you arranged a little feast to lure me back. You didn't have to, you know."

The vampire blinked at her unexpected appearance. "Don't flatter yourself," he finally replied. "What are you doing here?"

"Well! You're awfully grumpy," she pouted.

"That is not an answer."

"I'm here to help you, remember?"

He leaned back, smirking, and folded his arms across his chest. "Odd. I distinctly remember old Uncle Zeke saying I didn't need your help."

The siren rolled her eyes. "He obviously doesn't know you like I do."

"So, you're saying that I do need your help."

"In all honesty, you really don't need it," she admitted, "but I'm offering it, anyway."

"Why?" That one word was loaded with suspicion.

"Several reasons," she shrugged. "I like you, Viktor Brandewyne. Sailing with you has been the most fun I've had in ages. And you intrigue me. Just when I think I've got you figured out, you go and do something that puzzles the hell out of me. I'm curious to see what happens next."

Viktor laughed. "Then, welcome aboard, my little fish."

Chapter 11

Viktor and his crew found themselves fighting the wind. The more determined he was to sail east, the stronger the wind seemed to blow northwest.

"Damn this wind," he muttered. "At this rate, it'll take us a week to reach Havana."

"Problem?" Belladonna asked, striding over to him.

"We can't seem to make any headway. The winds are against us."

"Oh, is that all?" she smiled. "That's solved easily enough."

He just looked at her as if he thought her daft. She gave him a condescending smile, patted him on the cheek, and sashayed to the bow of the ship. Nimbly padding out on the bowsprit, she perched on the end and started singing.

Gradually, the wind changed direction. Once they were pushing the ship in the correct direction, they increased to near gale force. The bosons called out orders through the rigging to adjust the sails to take the most advantage of the now favorable winds.

Satisfied with her spell, the sea-witch sauntered back to rejoin Viktor at the helm.

"I thought you said there was nothing magical about your singing."

"I lied."

They made Havana by the next night. Belladonna agreed to keep her powers secret, an order that only made sense to her. She balked, however, at having to wear women's garments.

"Why do you even have a dress in your possession?" she demanded irritably.

"It is a trophy. Now, put it on," he ordered, holding the offending garment out to her.

She just looked at it with a mixture of disgust and horror on her face. "Why? They're such binding things. I don't see how human females can move about in them."

He wasn't sure whether to be amused or irritated. His impatience made the irritation win out. "Only the undergarments are binding. You don't have to wear those; just the dress," he growled.

Reluctantly, she took it from him. "But why do you want me to wear it? Shirt and trousers cover me just as well as this would."

He glared at her. "Even with your breasts bound, you couldn't pass for a boy. A woman dressed as a man draws a certain kind of attention in a port like Havana."

"I'm perfectly capable of defending myself," she returned his glare.

He smiled at that, his ire lessening a bit. "Oh, I have no doubt of that, little fish. But, as entertaining as that would be to see, it is a distraction I can ill afford right now. I need to get information about Hezekiah and who took him as swiftly as possible. You will draw much less attention dressed as a woman."

"Well, if I'm going to be such a distraction and a burden to you, I could just stay on the ship," the siren grumped.

"Oh no, pet. I want you where I can keep an eye on you. I owe my crew that much. Now, are you going to put that on, or am I going to have to dress you?"

She narrowed her eyes at him. "You'd enjoy that, wouldn't you?"

He loomed over her. "Much more than you would, I can promise you. Put. The damn. Dress. On. NOW."

"Fine! I'll wear the silly thing. Give me some privacy to change."

He gave a harsh bark of laughter. "I know you're not modest, Belle."

"No, I'm angry and not feeling very generous. You don't deserve to enjoy the sight of me."

At that, he truly laughed. "Very well, you shall have your privacy, although this is my cabin," he said as he moved toward the door. "You have much too high an opinion of yourself."

Once the door was closed behind him, she replied softly, "The same could be said of you, Viktor Brandewyne."

It surprised Belladonna to find Viktor had been right about the dress. Although she noticed several appreciative glances, no one approached her.

Making their way through the narrow streets, they soon came to a tavern. The placard proclaimed it to be the Crescent Moon Inn. She could tell it enjoyed a high level of business just from the noise. The noise didn't exactly stop when she and Viktor entered, but it did lessen considerably. Murmurs rippled through the crowd. Several eyes followed them, as he led her to a vacant table. No sooner were they seated, than one of the serving wenches came over.

"Well, if it isn't Captain Vik Brandee," she cooed, leaning over the table to reveal much of her generous bosom and completely ignoring Belladonna. "It's been a long time. What'll your pleasure be?"

"Pleasure will have to wait, Valerie." He gave her a wistful smile. "For now, bring us a bottle of your best rum."

She gave a pout but was quick about filling his order. Belle's eyes followed her with a murderous glare, as she made her way back to the bar. The look wasn't lost on the pirate, who kicked her under the table. She shifted her glare to him. He just smiled smugly.

"Here you go, Captain." Valerie set the bottle down on the table along with one glass.

Viktor took her hand and placed several more coins in it than he knew the liquor was worth. She looked hopeful when he didn't release her right away. "There's more where that came from, pet," he purred seductively. "Spread the word that I want information on the fate and whereabouts of the Grimm Reaper."

The girl paled at that. Viktor's grip tightened imperceptibly. "I will fetch Manuel. He can help you."

"Good girl," he gave a predatory smile. "And bring back two more glasses, one for Manuel and one for my companion."

Valerie finally acknowledged Belladonna's presence. As Viktor released her hand, the two women exchanged glares. The vampire chuckled and swatted the wench on the rump.

"Off with ye, lass."

As she scurried off, Belladonna growled. "She's plump enough. I wonder if she'd taste as good as mermaid flesh."

He laughed salaciously, "Oh, she's a tasty one, all right."

The siren growled at him, making him laugh harder.

A few moments later, a short burly man joined them, setting down two glasses. He gave the still irritated siren an appreciative leer. "*Hola*, Captain Brandee. Now I see why Val was being such a shrew. She was your favorite, but here you bring a replacement she has no hope of competing with."

Viktor glanced over at Belladonna, then, gave Manuel a wicked smile. "You should know, Manuel, a woman is so much more passionate if she thinks there is a threat to her favor."

The tavern keeper laughed. "*Si*, Captain. They are very territorial creatures."

"That they are. But pleasure is not my business tonight. Sweet Valerie said you could tell me about what has become of the Grimm Reaper."

Manuel's face darkened. "*Muy* bad business, that." He spat on the floor. "To be taken or killed in a fair fight is one thing, but what they did to Captain Grimm? They were not true men!"

Viktor slid a hefty pouch of coins across the table. "Tell me everything you know."

Manuel glanced at it, then, pushed it back. "No, Captain. I will not charge for this knowledge. Men like those who took the Reaper are bad for business. They scare away customers. That will make my *chicas* get fat and lazy. I know your reputation, Captain Brandee. You find these bastards; you kill them all."

"That is my intention."

"A few nights ago, I threw a bilge rat out of here. He was drunk and whining about how he'd been cheated by some pirate hunter. He said he gave him the Grimm Reaper but got thrown overboard instead of paid. I told him he'd get no pity here, just a slit throat. Then I kicked him out." The tavern keeper seemed very indignant over the whole thing.

Vik leaned forward, a faint glow to his eyes. "Did this bilge rat have a name, or give the name of the man he claimed cheated him?"

Manuel's face grew a bit blank as he made the mistake of making eye contact with the vampire. "He never named the hunter that he sold Captain Grimm to, but the bastard is a little sneak thief called Talmidge."

"Where can I find him?"

"Probably in some back alley. By now, no one in this port would allow him to enter their businesses. Captain Grimm did much trade here in Havana."

Viktor released the man from his sway. He stood and helped Belladonna to her feet. Once again, he shoved the gold toward the tavern keeper.

"I told you, Captain, I will not take your money," Manuel insisted.

"Give it to Valerie, then. Tell her it is a gift, since I did not have time to spend with her this night. But I want her ready for the next time I make port."

"You have my word, Captain; even if I have to take her away from the Governor, when you return."

"She services the Governor?" He seemed surprised.

"*Si*, he comes here every month, when his wife has her — well, you know," Manuel winked.

Vik chuckled, "Useful knowledge, that. The man has good taste."

"I wish you'd let me kill that rude female. She kept acting like I wasn't even there."

"You are not to touch her, my naughty little fish," he chuckled. "She is far too useful to me. Be satisfied that she fears you may replace her as the object of my attentions."

The siren sidled up to him, sliding her hands up the front of his shirt. "Shall I prove her fears right?" she purred.

He grasped her wrists gently, but firmly, removing her hands from his shoulders. Giving her a wicked smile, he said, "I do not trust you that much, little fish. I've a feeling you like to play with your food just as much as I do." He placed a kiss on her palm before releasing her.

Belladonna gave a throaty chuckle. "In that, you would be correct. So, how do you propose we find this Talmidge person?"

"Lazarus, come forth."

The demon cat which had once been Jim Rigger had little trouble in locating their prey. Talmidge lay piss-drunk in a gutter. The gutter ran down an alley behind one of the less reputable whore houses; the kind that would take anyone with coin or anything to trade, regardless of the customer's health, reputation, or cleanliness. The pimp had just thrown Talmidge out.

Within minutes, Viktor and Belladonna arrived, following the cat's visuals, just in time to see Lazarus swat at the drunken traitor as he tried to pet him.

"Lazarus, return."

The cat hissed, turned around and sprayed Talmidge full in the face, before he bounded over and leapt up to the vampire's shoulder.

"Bloody damn cat!" the man cursed, wrinkling his nose at the pungent odor.

Belle sniffed the air. "You know, I think he actually smells better now." She grinned maliciously.

"Indeed."

Talmidge focused bleary eyes on the pair. "C'mere, luv, and I'll show you just how good I can smell."

Viktor lifted the man by the neck, feet dangling, in a split second. "Actually, you are coming with us. Word has it you know who took the Grimm Reaper."

The drunken man scrabbled at Viktor's hand, trying to get loose. He tightened his grip in response. Before long, Talmidge's eyes started to bug, his face turning purple. The only sound he emitted was a weak gurgle.

"He might be able to answer questions, if you'd allow him to breathe," Belladonna suggested.

"Hmm," he grunted, dropping the man back to the ground. "You have a point, pet."

Talmidge lay there, gasping.

"Speak up, you worthless barnacle! Where can I find Hezekiah Grimm?"

He coughed and glared up at Viktor. "Bastard, why should I tell you anything?"

Vik smiled evilly. "Belladonna, pet, why don't you give our friend a few of your special caresses to convince him to cooperate?"

The siren giggled, as she knelt beside the man. She gave him an angelic smile in answer to his expectant leer. She gently brushed the matted, filthy hair from his face, then, trailed her fingertips down his cheeks to his throat and shoulders. Within seconds, he was screaming in agony; angry red welts rising on his skin where her fingers had passed.

"Where is the Grimm Reaper?"

"Bugger off!" Talmidge hissed in pain.

"Belladonna, go for his jewels."

She grinned, her barracuda-like true teeth showing. "With pleasure."

She extended her talons, slicing through his shirt like paper. Slowly and deliberately, she raked her fingers down his chest and belly. His screams increased in pitch, as she reached the band of his pantaloons.

"No! nonononononono! Please stop!" His eyes were wild with pain and terror. "I'll tell you anything! Just make her stop!"

"Belle."

The siren removed her hands from his skin.

"What manner of hell spawn are you?" he asked, shying away from her as much as he could.

"I'm a siren. Don't you read?"

Viktor squatted next to him, grasping his chin to draw his gaze to him. "For the last time, where can I find the Grimm Reaper?"

"He's aboard the *Montcrief*, if he's still alive. Oh, God, this hurts," he moaned.

"Tell me who her captain is and where she's headed, and I'll make the pain go away."

Talmidge grasped Viktor's shirt desperately. "Oh please, God, make it stop burning!"

"Captain and heading."

"Martin Jorgen, may he rot in Hell. I heard they were making for Tortuga then Port Royal. Now please, I'm begging you, whoever you are, make it stop!" the man writhed in agony.

"Where are my manners? Allow me to introduce myself. Viktor Brandewyne at your service," he said with a smile, using his dagger to gut the informant.

"Can we go back to the ship now? I want to get out of this filthy dress," she waved a hand at the now muck stained skirts.

Wiping his dagger off on his victim's shirt, Viktor stood and gave her a wry look. "You mean you don't want to have yourself a quick snack?" He nodded at the dying man.

"The rats have to eat, too."

"Mr. Jon, have the men prepare to cast off."

"Aye, Cap'n. What's our heading?"

"Make best possible speed to Port Royal."

Belladonna caught the last of that exchange, when she joined them at the helm. She was in shirt and trousers once again. She'd been more than happy to throw the ruined dress over the side.

"What is your plan of attack, Captain?"

"I intend to intercept the *Montcrief*. They've had ample time to have made Tortuga."

"Then why not go there?"

He gave her an indulgent smile. "If I did that, we would most likely miss them then be hard pressed to overtake them before they could reach Jamaica. But, by going toward their final destination first, then turning north, we should meet them head on."

"I see, however," she argued, "they've also had time to reach Port Royal, already."

He shook his head. "If it was any other captain, then yes, perhaps; but, although I've never sailed with the man, I know Jorgen's reputation quite well. He was always a greedy bastard, when he was still a pirate. Now that he's gone privateer, he'll want to capture as many prizes as he can. That would explain why he'd head to Tortuga first; plenty of pirates to hunt."

She looked puzzled. "That's something I don't understand. Why would a pirate want to hunt his own kind? Don't privateers have to share their prizes with whoever commissioned them? Pirates only share among their crew."

"Aye, that is how it's done. He may have turned a deal to save his own hide."

Jon-Jon picked that moment to pipe up. "I sailed with Jorgen once. He may have been trying to save himself, but more likely, he did it to get command of a ship. God knows no pirate crew worth their salt would pick that bastard for a captain."

Viktor considered what his first mate had to say. "Mr. Jon, what are the chances that Jorgen is unpopular with his crew?"

"Depends, Cap'n. If their take has been good, and he hasn't cheated them on their shares, then they'll stand with him. But, if he's the same man he was when we sailed together, then it wouldn't take much to get them to mutiny."

Viktor smiled tightly. "Thank you for that useful information, Jon-Jon. When you go below, help yourself to one of the better bottles of rum."

"Aye, Cap'n!" He grinned.

With Belladonna helping with the weather, the *Barracuda* made good time to Port Royal. Since he'd not permitted anyone to leave the ship in Havana, he dispatched Jon-Jon to take a few trusted men ashore for provisions. They were given strict orders not to reveal they were pirates. It had been more than a century since this had been a pirate-friendly port.

The siren left the ship a few hours before they made port, to hunt. She planned to return after dark, when it wouldn't draw attention.

Satisfied that his crew was safe and soon to be well fed, Viktor went ashore on errands of his own.

Jorgen and Marle had given up trying to get Grimm's ship and crew from him days ago. Both were well away, sailing under a new captain now. It irritated Jorgen to no end that Grimm continued proving himself the better man by refusing to sell out others to save his own neck from the noose. It was what he had done, even offering to hunt down his fellow Brethren. Granted, it hadn't been as profitable as he would have preferred. He had to turn his prizes and prisoners over to the Governor, who took more than a captain's share before distributing the profits among the privateer crew.

Of course, even if Grimm had cooperated, Jorgen would still have done everything possible to make sure he was hanged anyway. He truly hated the man.

Now, further aggravated by a fruitless hunting stop in Tortuga, determination to find the traitor in his own crew fueled him. Grimm's health seemed much better than the meager provisions he'd finally permitted him could account for. Someone on the crew sneaking food to the prisoner seemed the logical explanation.

Jorgen held no delusions about his lack of popularity with his crew. The poor take on this trip out meant it wouldn't take much to incite mutiny. He must find the man who dared disobey his orders, before the bastard's actions encouraged others to follow suit.

Viktor, gambling that he wouldn't encounter anyone in Port Royal that knew the man, used Stoddard's name as an alias. He learned from the harbormaster that the *Montcrief* had been out for a little over two months. The man wasn't sure when she'd be back but mentioned that her captain usually didn't stay out for more than three months at a time, and usually had to replace most of his crew each time he returned to port. He opined that it would probably be impossible for Jorgen to find willing seamen to man his ship before another year passed.

Having gotten the information he needed from the harbormaster, Viktor wiped away any memory of having met or talked with him from the man's mind. As far as he knew, the captain of the *Barracuda* had never come ashore.

Viktor left the docks in search of a tavern. His appetite had roared to life during his questioning of the harbormaster. By the time he found a place, he was ravenous. He ate a hearty meal, large enough to draw a few curious looks. Yet the Hunger remained.

He soon realized that food and drink would not satisfy this craving. He was going to have to hunt.

Catching the eye of one of the serving wenches, Viktor smiled and silently summoned her to him. When she reached his table, he rose and started leading her toward the upper rooms. He tossed a handful of gold coins on the bar as they passed it. The coins quickly vanished into the tavern keeper's apron.

Although he meant to pleasure himself with the girl first, his blood Hunger would not be denied. All he could think about was the vital fluid flowing through her veins. Once in a room, he shut the door and pulled her to him.

"Such a hurry, love," she giggled.

"Hush, pet," he shushed her, answering her smile with a dazzling one of his own.

She gasped and tried in vain to pull away at the sight of his fangs. In a flash, he latched onto her throat, before she could scream. He fed greedily. The girl died within minutes.

Keeping in mind the warnings Mother Celie had given, he made quick work of beheading the corpse. He didn't want to draw attention to himself while in port, so he stripped the body and arranged it in the bed. A strategic placement of the covers hid the fact that her head no longer connected to her body.

Slipping back downstairs, he exited through to a back alley. Only a kitchen scullery saw him. A quick glance and suggestion from him erased the memory of it.

Belladonna sat waiting for him in his cabin, when he returned to the ship that night. She was amusing herself by teasing Lazarus with some large, iridescent fish scales dangling from some twine. The second Viktor entered the cabin the demon cat leapt up to a shelf and made a show of ignoring the siren.

"Hmph," the vampire grunted. "What is that?"

"Leftovers."

Viktor went to the cupboard and poured himself a glass of brandy-blood mixture. "Going by his current habits, the harbormaster expects Jorgen to return in the next few weeks."

"Try two days from now, given his current course and the weather conditions," she smiled smugly.

"You've spotted the *Montcrief?*"

She nodded, as he downed his glass. "If you set sail before dawn, you should intercept him by dusk tomorrow."

"Good."

Belladonna eyed him warily, when he grabbed the bottle he had just poured from. He turned it up and drank straight from it, draining it quickly. Lazarus gave a low growl from his perch. Viktor set the empty bottle on the table and turned glowing emerald eyes on the siren.

"Viktor?"

In half a heartbeat, he was across the cabin. He'd moved faster than she'd anticipated. Before she could dodge, he'd grabbed her and had her pinned beneath him, fangs exposed and mouth wide for the strike.

Chapter 12

Sniff's frustration ate at him. Jorgen had kept the ship locked down so tightly when they'd been in Tortuga he'd been unable to free Grimm. Jorgen had allowed no one, except Marle, to go ashore. He'd been afraid, and rightfully so, that some of the crew might try to jump ship in the pirate port.

Of course, the fact he'd forbidden shore leave raised suspicions among the locals. It hadn't taken long for word to get around that a privateer was snooping about. They soon made it clear to Jorgen he and his ship were not welcome in Tortuga.

Now, he had cut off Grimm's rations again. Worse, he'd posted a guard. Sniff found it almost impossible to smuggle him so much as a crust. Grimm's time was running out.

Sniff wondered if he should spread rumors about something he'd seen on watch that day. He was sure it was just a sun-dream, but if he worked it right, he'd soon have half the crew convinced the ship was cursed, and the only way to lift it was to free Grimm. Even if the ploy didn't work, the unrest it would cause would bedevil the hell out of Jorgen. Sniff had come to truly despise the man.

Martin Jorgen was convinced he was surrounded by enemies. Grimm's secret compatriot continued to evade him. Now, superstitious rumors ran rampant among the crew, including wild talk of bad omens and curses.

"Mr. Marle!" he bellowed.

"Aye, Cap'n."

"Inform the crew that they will be placed on half rations and lose three quarter of their pay, if these insidious rumors are not stopped. But there will be generous reward for whoever turns over both the man who started the rumors and whoever has been aiding our prisoner against orders."

"Aye."

Scorching blind Hunger. He had to feed. The trollop earlier only whetted his appetite. The drunken sailor near the dockside warehouses also failed to sate him. The brandy diluted with blood he kept handy wasn't satisfying, either.

He had to feed!

Searing pain in his throat pushed the Hunger back somewhat. It was still there, but Viktor was back in control of himself.

Slowly, he realized the siren pinned under his weight had her poisoned talons buried in the flesh of his throat. She had the strength to hold him off, but not the leverage to dislodge him.

"Get. Off. Me," Belladonna demanded, once she saw sanity return to his eyes.

"Release my throat first, pet."

She shook her head, her eyes never leaving him. "Not until we're both standing."

Slowly, Viktor knelt and helped her to sit up. She kept her arm extended stiffly. Once they'd both gotten to their feet, she withdrew her talons, her hand returning to human. Viktor caught a brief glimpse of the extended stinger cells in her fingertips, before skin covered them again.

With a speed to rival his, the siren suddenly stood by the door, ready to bolt if he tried for her again. Lazarus remained on his shelf perch, ears flat, tail bristling and twitching, and a low growl emanating from his throat.

"Don't ever do that again," she warned him. The punctures from her talons on his throat had already closed over, but the welts from her stingers were still in full blaze. "I was afraid something like this might happen," she stated, eyeing the wounds from a safe distance. "You are going to have to feed to heal those."

He gave her an evil smile. "That was precisely what I was about to do, when you gave them to me." He rubbed the tender skin.

"You don't want to feed on me, Captain Brandewyne. That would be a very bad thing."

"For you, perhaps." He stalked around the table, slowly.

"No. For you," she corrected. "Be you the One or not, you try that again, and I will kill you."

"You will try."

"If you don't feed soon, I won't have to. Viktor, your time is running short. Apparently, the further you stray from your quest, the more your Hunger grows. I can smell that you've already killed today."

"I will not turn back from Hezekiah, now that I am so close," he said stubbornly.

Belladonna gave him a resigned sigh. "I thought you might say that. I may have a solution for how you can keep your Hunger at bay long enough for you to retrieve your friend. Then we can get back to business."

Viktor gave her a dangerous glare.

"Don't give me that look. I'm trying to help you. You'll need to drain at least five more humans. That many bloodless, and hopefully headless, corpses would draw too much attention in port. Plus, you'll need to set sail tonight if you hope to intercept the *Montcrief*, before she's close enough to signal for help."

"True enough," he inched closer, her heartbeat singing its own siren song to him. "So, what, pray tell, do you suggest; I kill some of my crew? I have already mentioned, I believe, that I require my entire crew to sail this ship."

"If I may continue?" She glared at his continued progression toward her. He waved her on. "Pick men from your crew who are good fighters, but easily controlled. Bring them over instead of just draining them. Then, use them to help take your prey."

He stopped advancing and considered the idea carefully. "It would mean attacking at night. Most of the crew would be useless in a nighttime sea battle."

"True but considering that you would have at your disposal five or six warriors with your greater speed and strength, all of whom would be completely loyal and obedient to only you, there'd be no need to risk the majority of your crew in battle."

Viktor smiled tightly. "Lower casualties. I like the idea. It would leave more men available to strip a prize. And," his smile widened to a grin, "attacking at night will scare the living hell out of anyone unlucky enough to cross my path."

"You will, of course, have to pirate more often than you've been doing since I came aboard. Wouldn't want your fledgling vampires to start feeding on and turning the whole crew," she added as an afterthought.

"No, that wouldn't do at all, but I've no objection to doing more of what I do best. Now, let's go select my cadre. I'm starving."

It took Marle until late afternoon to catch the rigging rat he hunted. He'd been against taking the legless barnacle on as a part of the crew, but the captain had overruled him. It didn't matter now. He'd finally caught Sniff trying to sneak food to Grimm. He'd also learned that Sniff started the 'cursed ship' rumors. He dragged the unconscious man over to the mainmast and chained him alongside Grimm.

"You're a right bastard, Marle," Grimm accused, "beating on a cripple."

"Cripple my ass." Marle spat at him. "Bugger damn near took a chunk out of my leg before I beaned him. I'd like nothing better than to use the worthless barnacle as shark bait."

He stomped off to inform Jorgen of his success.

Belladonna stood at the ship's railing, watching the sun get lower in the sky. Viktor moved up to stand beside her.

"It is almost dusk. If you are right, we should be spotting the *Montcrief* soon."

She nodded. "Provided it stayed on course."

He stroked his beard, anticipating the coming fight. He felt more alive than he had in days. Below deck, he could sense the six new vampires lying dormant, soon to rise for the first night of their new existence.

Still, he wanted to be sure they did not miss their prey.

"Lazarus, come forth," he summoned. He sent the demon cat in raven form to scout out their quarry.

A face full of rancid mop water brought Sniff fully awake. He sputtered and snorted, trying to clear the foul water from his open nasal cavity. He'd lost his false nose sometime during the fight with Marle. A vicious kick in the side knocked the wind out of him.

"Leave off, Marle," Jorgen ordered. Standing over the chained man, he demanded, "Why did you disobey my order that the prisoner not be given food or water?"

Sniff glared up at him. "Because it ain't right. A pirate ain't supposed to hand over his Brethren to the hangman."

"I. Am. Not. A. Pirate," Jorgen bit off the words.

"That's a fact," Sniff spat. "Ye're naught but a goat-fucking son-of-a-whore, and ye've brought down a curse on this ship and all that sail with you."

"Enough! I'll not have you trying to incite mutiny with your lies!"

"'Tis no lie, Cap'n. Yesterday morning I saw two of the most beautiful mermaids following the ship. One had hair yellow as gold, and the other had hair as red as blood. They was playin' tag, it looked like. The redhead was chasin' the blonde. They both dove under just as they neared the side. They never came back up, but the water turned all bloody. It's a bad omen, I tell ya."

"Mermaids," Jorgen sneered. "Mr. Marle, beat this man until he is bloody. Then, throw him over the side. I'll not tolerate such stuff and nonsense on my ship."

"Aye, Cap'n."

Marle proceeded to hang Sniff by his wrists. He then hoisted Grimm up, as well. Jorgen raised a questioning eyebrow.

"He sassed me for kicking this cur. Why wear myself out beating one at a time, when I can beat 'em both together?"

"Very good, Mr. Marle. You may proceed."

Fifteen minutes into the beating, Grimm hung unconscious. Even with the smuggled food, the constant abuse proved too much for his starved and battered body to withstand.

Sniff, however, shouted obscenities at Marle with every stroke of the whip. He got quite inventive.

"Sails off the port bow," the lookout bellowed from the crow's nest. Everyone on deck strained their eyes in that direction, Marle and Jorgen included. Looking through the spyglass, the privateer could make out the topsails of a ship. A few minutes later, more sails appeared below those, just above the horizon.

"She's flying French colors," he announced. "A bonus for you if we catch this prize, Barlings. Strike our colors and run up the French flag! Shroud gun ports one, three, five and seven on the port side! Helmsman, steer to starboard and put us on a gradual intercept course. Not too sharp, man. We don't want to scare our prize."

"Aye, sir."

"Cursed ship, indeed!" Jorgen crowed. "Lads, this prize will make our voyage a success. Our letter of Marque from the Honorable Lord Governor of Jamaica instructs we take all French and Spanish ships, as well as pirates. Riggers aloft! Be ready to put us full sail, if we have to give chase. All other hands, remember we're just a Frenchie lot. Hide your toys until it's time to play."

The ship rapidly turned into a floating anthill of activity. For two hours, the winds proved a frustration. It seemed the closer they got, the more the wind died. Finally, at dusk, the winds picked up again, puffing the sails out, like a fat politician's belly. They swiftly came within hailing distance.

Oddly, no one aboard the *Montcrief* seemed to notice that, although the wind filled their sails, those of their prey hung nearly limp.

Another thing which went unnoticed save by the now ignored prisoners, was a large black cat. Grimm and Sniff watched the cat gnawing and pulling at the knots on the ropes holding them suspended. It seemed as if the beast knew exactly what it was doing.

Their prey finally hailed them. *"Bonjour! Quelle nouvelle?"*

Jorgen ordered his gunners to fire a warning shot across the ship's bow. "Heave to and prepare to be boarded!" At his signal, they struck the French flag and replaced it with the British.

Their prey responded with raucous laughter. A tall, black clad man called back with a clear commanding voice, "It is you, sir, who is about to be boarded. Have at, lads!"

"Bloody pirates," Jorgen growled. "Give 'em hell, boys! There's a shipload of bounties to be collected, dead or alive!"

The privateer started lowering its pirogues to row over to their enemy. Some of the boats made it to the water, but few sailors made it to the boats. The pirate ship fired her guns, not all, but enough. Four harpoons speared the *Montcrief*'s side, too low to be reached by those on deck, too high for those on the gun deck. Ropes were drawn taut to the swivel guns mounted fore and aft on the pirate.

Pirates began swarming across. Jorgen's sharpshooters, stationed in the rigging, fired on them but with little effect. They hit and dislodged only one pirate, but he caught the rope before he could fall into the water and continued across as if the shot hurt no more than a bee sting. The pirate ship fired its largest bore cannons, and two smallish figures launched into the privateer's rigging.

Jorgen's first thought was that the pirate was firing dead bodies at him. Then, one of his sharpshooters crashed to the deck at his feet, the man's throat torn out.

The rope-swarming pirates divided ranks. Most of them swung down into the gun ports. Three, however, leapt up to the railing, a seemingly impossible jump. They possessed an inhuman agility and grace. They also appeared to be smoldering ever so slightly in the last rays of the setting sun.

Jorgen's men hesitated only a moment, before rushing the trio. Screams, shots and clash of steel on steel rang out from all parts of the ship.

The cat finally succeeded in loosening the knots. Sniff and Grimm dropped to the deck, ignored by the combatants around them. As soon as circulation returned to his hands, Sniff dug around in his trousers, until he found his set of lock picks. Within minutes, he had the manacles off both of them. Grimm's wrists and ankles were chafed raw from his sweat and the heavy irons.

"You had those all this time?" he raised an eyebrow at the picks.

"Aye," Sniff confirmed. "This is the first chance I've had to use them with any hope of us getting away. That bastard, Marle, keeps everything locked down and watched."

"True. You'd think he and Jorgen don't trust their crew."

Sniff's face split into a near-toothless grin, "Aye, you would. Can't imagine why."

They sat leaning against the mast, taking in the situation around them. The cat joined them, sitting just out of reach. Pirates boiled up through the hatches, confirming that the gun decks had been taken. A slime of blood covered the deck, dismembered bodies strewn all about.

A blood-soaked pirate spotted them and rushed forward. He resembled a feral beast more than a man. Grimm noted it looked as if he'd filed his canines down to sharp points. Even as he considered the merits of such a scare tactic, he was looking around for something to use as a weapon against the attacker.

"Brave kitty," Sniff chuckled. Grimm looked to see the cat puffed up, ears flat, standing between them and the sharp-toothed pirate. It let out a low warning growl.

Grimm and Sniff were amazed to see the man stop in his tracks and cower like a whipped dog. The cat gave a staccato, "Meh," and the pirate turned in search of other prey.

"I'd been about to suggest we steal a boat and escape in the confusion," Grimm said. "But perhaps we should stay put. Jorgen appears to be losing, and there's something unnatural about this cat."

"Aye. It's almost like he was sent to help us," Sniff agreed.

Jorgen and Marle survived the battle, along with fifteen of their men. Most of the survivors had surrendered. The captain and his mate had not.

The pirates rounded them up into a tight group. They huddled together, one or two of them crossing themselves in horror, as six of the pirates drank from the torn throats of some of their fallen shipmates, in full view.

Grimm and Sniff were so engrossed in watching the disturbingly bizarre behavior, that they didn't notice the black-clad figure approaching them.

"Good job, Lazarus. Go feed," the man said. The cat bounded off. "It's been a while, Hezekiah. Glad to find you still alive."

Looking up, Grimm instantly recognized the man. "Bloody Vik Brandee! I'd heard you were dead," he grinned. "Surprised and grateful to see that is not the case."

Viktor reached down and gave him a hand up. He raised an eyebrow at Sniff.

"Sniff, here, saved my life. I owe him a life debt."

"Sniff?" he questioned the name.

The bald little man gave him a gaping grin. "Had me nose bit off in a tavern brawl over a fine whore."

"I hope she was worth it," he laughed, flashing fangs.

"Oh, she was," Sniff chuckled.

Grimm stared hard at his old friend. "I see you've changed your tactics somewhat, attacking at nightfall."

"More than that has changed, Mr. Grimm. We'll talk on it later, once we're back aboard my ship. Now, however, we've some prisoners to deal with." He spotted the raw and bleeding lash marks on his friend's back from the daily beatings. His voice held icy steel. "If the bastard that did that is among them, point him out. He'll soon learn the true meaning of pain."

Grimm had a smile to match his name, as he approached the prisoners. He spotted the pirate hunter and his mate immediately. Marle glared at him. Jorgen was more concerned with the black-clad pirate captain standing next to him.

Pointing out the large first mate, Grimm accused, "That's Marle. He's a vicious bastard. Prides himself on inflicting as much pain as possible. That weaselly sack of entrails next to him is Martin Jorgen."

"Anvil, bring me the two men Mr. Grimm pointed out."

The hulking giant of a smithy, who'd been set to guard duty, waded in and seized the two men by the scruffs of their necks, as if they were kittens. Both struggled and complained loudly of the treatment, to no avail. As large of a man as Marle was, the smith dwarfed him considerably.

Viktor eyed the captain with a condescending smirk. "So, you fancy yourself a pirate hunter? Well damn! You've caught one," he laughed. His crew obliged with a chorus of guffaws.

Jorgen pulled himself up to his full, unimpressive height as best he could. The weight of the indigo-dark meaty hand on the back of his neck made it very difficult.

"Just who the hell are you?"

"May I do the honors, Captain?" Grimm asked. Viktor nodded, so he continued, "Martin, I don't believe you've ever met Bloody Vik Brandee." He took great pleasure in watching the color drain from Jorgen's face.

"You're supposed to be dead."

"How ironic. By my reckoning, so are you," Vik told him. "We shall have to remedy that. Let him go, Anvil. Mr. Jon, give him your sword." The pirate complied.

"Defend yourself." He gave warning before lighting into the pirate hunter. Jorgen's lack of swordsmanship soon left him thoroughly disgusted. He wondered how the bastard had survived this long, even as he brought his sword down with all his supernatural strength.

Jorgen's body dropped to the deck, innards spilling out where he'd been cleaved neatly in half. Viktor wiped the blade off and examined it for nicks. Finding none, he proclaimed, "This is a really fine blade. Good quality steel. The Spaniard I took it from didn't deserve such a fine weapon."

"Oh?" Grimm asked, unfazed by the carnage at his feet.

"Aye. He was a worse swordsman than this bastard," he nodded. "Barely knew hilt from blade."

They turned their attention to Marle. Viktor stared at him long and hard. Neither he nor Grimm spoke.

Eventually, the man broke. "Why don't you just kill me and get it over with, you bastard?" he snarled.

"Belle, pet."

The siren smiled hopefully. "Yes, Captain?"

Viktor turned to face her, his expression never changing. "Take your new swimming partner. Just make sure he suffers well before you eat him. Give him a taste of what it's like to be on the receiving end of pointless torture."

She turned to eye her prospective meal. "Oh, I'm going to really enjoy this. Nothing seasons the meat like pain and terror." She stalked around him. "Hmm. I think I might peel him before I'm through. Would that be satisfactory, Captain?"

"Quite; Mr. Jon, cull out the three healthiest of this sorry lot and hold them for my future attention. The cadre can have the rest."

"Aye, Cap'n."

This brought loud protests from the prisoners. "We surrendered so you wouldn't kill us!" "We never liked that bastard, Jorgen!"

"Let us join your crew!" "Let us go, if you're not going to enlist us!"

Viktor gave them a chilling stare that quelled their cries instantly. "You have seen what we are, so I cannot let you go. I have no need for any new hands. Besides, my cadre and I require — sustenance." The last he said with an evil grin that left his fangs in full view; a grin echoed by the grins of the cadre of new vampires.

"Mr. Jon, you have your orders."

Chapter 13

In Viktor's cabin, Hezekiah took full advantage of the pirate captain's hospitality. After weeks of near starvation, he gorged himself on the meal he had been offered. He barely noticed how Viktor drank more than ate.

Not until nearly sated did he realize his friend drank from a different bottle than his. The liquid in Viktor's bottle looked reddish and muddy, rather than the clear dark amber of the rum in Hezekiah's.

"Never seen liquor like that," he commented. "Almost looks like blood. What is it?"

"Blood," Viktor replied, matter-of-factly.

Knowing the man had an odd sense of humor, Hezekiah laughed, "Of course it is. Seriously, Vik, what is it? It can't be real blood, or it would be clotted and as thick as buttermilk."

He chuckled, "Not if you dilute it with something like rum or brandy. Granted, it's not as good as fresh, but the liquor does give it an interesting flavor."

Grimm tried not to let his growing unease show. Something about his old friend was not right, but he hadn't survived as long as he had by showing his fears.

"I've heard some of the old legends about men who were turned into blood-sucking demons, and I've seen the filed teeth that you and some of your crew sport. It's a wonderful scare tactic, and intimidating as hell, but we've known each other a long time, Vik. Don't you think you're carrying the ruse a bit far?" He waved a hand at the dark liquid in Viktor's glass.

Viktor set the glass down on the table. His face grew solemn, and his gaze locked on the far bulkhead. "You're one of the very few I can trust with this, Hezekiah. What you've seen this night is only all too real. It's not just some ruse to frighten a bunch of superstitious sailors into surrendering. I told you, much has changed since last we met."

He shifted his gaze to his friend, and Grimm saw that his eyes seemed to be glowing. A split second later, Grimm felt his head forced back, baring his throat. Viktor had one hand in his hair, the other on his shoulder, holding him in his seat with an unimaginable grip. He'd never seen the man move. It sent a jolt of terror through him.

Close to his ear, Viktor whispered, "You need to remember, old friend, that there is always a small grain of truth in every legend." Then just as suddenly, the vampire was back in his seat across from Hezekiah, as if he'd never moved.

Grimm's eyes were just a tad too wide. "You mean you really are a…?"

"A vampire?" he grinned, showing off his fangs. "In a manner of speaking, yes; I do have fangs, and I'm cursed with a Hunger for blood. But I'm also hundreds of times faster and stronger now."

"What about sunlight? The stories I remember say that vampires are creatures of the night," Grimm stated curiously.

"True vampires are, but then, they're undead. I never died. I was cursed by an irate old witch-woman. The sun is no bane to me," he explained. "I've also noticed that I don't need sleep anymore."

"Other than the blood drinking, it sounds like more of a blessing than a curse."

"You would think," he smiled wryly. "But the Hunger can grow strong enough to almost rob me of reason. Mother Celie believes that it may eventually kill me." He poured himself another glass and stared into it for a while.

Grimm sipped from his own glass, his eyes never leaving the man sitting across from him. He knew nothing he could say would dissuade his friend of his fate as pronounced by the old witch who raised Viktor. He, personally, had never been comfortable the few times he had encountered the woman. She'd proven right about too many things she should never have even known of.

Finally, Viktor spoke again. "I have a proposition for you, Hezekiah. I want you as my first mate."

The sudden change of subject caught him off guard. "I thought Rigger was your first mate."

Lazarus sauntered over, leapt to the table and draped himself over Viktor's shoulders. The vampire reached up to scratch the cat's ears, resulting in a rumbling purr.

"Let's just say that I'm not the only one who has changed in recent months," he smiled cryptically. "Jim is no longer able to fill that role, although he does serve other purposes now. Jon-Jon has been my acting first mate, but he's a bit too fond of the bottle. He's also more of a follower than a leader. I've business to attend to concerning my curse and its possible cure. I need a first mate that can keep the crew under control, when I'm busy elsewhere."

It was Hezekiah's turn to sip and contemplate his response.

"Three shares and first choice of the wenches and geegaws, after you, of course," he named his terms.

"Two and a half shares, first choice of geegaws after me, and you can have first choice of the wenches before me," Brandee countered.

Grimm tossed back his drink, slammed his glass down, and offered his hand with a grin. "Done."

Brandee shook it with an answering grin. "Welcome aboard, Mr. Grimm. Shall we go see what progress Belladonna has made with Marle?"

"Hmm, sounds like he's either dead or unconscious. I don't recall hearing any screams for at least ten minutes."

The raw, bloody, man-shaped hulk dangling by its wrists made for a disturbing sight. Marle's skin lay in a slimy, bloody heap on the deck. Only his hands, feet and genitals had not been peeled. His face and scalp hung from a hook. What was left of him still breathed, but it was impossible to tell from his lidless eyes if the man was conscious or not.

Belladonna stood nearby, cleaning several cutting instruments. Her clothing lay neatly folded a few feet away. Her victim's blood smeared and spattered her nude body from head to toe. Grimm found it hard to tear his eyes away from the barbaric spectacle. The combination of her unabashed nudity and the grisly remains of her recent activities made her both alluring and disturbing to him.

Curiously, none of the crew would look in her direction. It was unusual behavior for any kind of sailors, let alone pirates, when presented with a willingly naked female. Glancing once more at what had been his tormentor, Grimm decided that fear, rather than respect, was the cause of their aversion. Even Viktor was not looking at her. He seemed to be more interested in her handiwork.

"Why did you leave some of his skin, pet?"

"Seasoning," she replied.

Grimm, already convinced that Viktor's vampirism was no act, had to ask, "Are you a cannibal, lass? Do you really eat people?"

She gave him a condescending smile. "No, I'm a siren, don't you read? And, yes, I eat people, when I can get them. The captain won't let me have any of his precious crew." Viktor ignored the taunt.

Grimm moved a little closer to her, inexplicably drawn, despite the blood and gore. His voice took on what passed for a seductive tone in his mind. "So, what do you eat when you can't get hapless sailors?"

The siren took a step closer to him, in turn. "Sharks make good snacks." She shrugged. "My favorite food, however, is mermaid. They're tricky and very hard to catch, but they're absolutely delicious!"

"So, I wasn't dreamin'!" a voice crowed from the rigging. "I did see a couple of mermaids!" Sniff swung down to dangle, leering at her.

Belladonna narrowed her eyes at him. "I am not a mermaid! I'm a siren, you disgusting little troll!"

Viktor and Grimm both laughed at the retort. "You still have such a winning way with the ladies, Sniff," Grimm chuckled.

"Aye, I have to beat 'em off me all the time."

"Was that you he saw, lass?"

She stepped in even closer, so that she was forced to look up to see his face. Fully aware that Viktor watched her closely; she gave Grimm a sultry smile. "Yes," she purred. "Tell me, do you swim?"

Before he could answer, Viktor was just there, directly between them. "Mr. Grimm is not food." His tone brooked no argument. "He is the reason I gave Marle to you for torture. Now, if you don't mind, I'd like you to make sure that Mr. Grimm is the last thing this bastard sees before he dies."

"Very well," she shrugged, giving up her game. She took Marle's skinless head in both hands and pointed his face in Grimm's direction. She held it that way for a few moments, then, dug her thumbs into his eye sockets. A shrill shriek emanated from his lipless mouth. Using her talons, Belle cut the orbs free from their optic nerves.

Lazarus bounded over to her, as she popped one of the eyes into her mouth. Stretching his forepaws up to her knee, he gave her an inquisitive, "Mrruh?"

Ignoring the cat, she proceeded to eat the other eye.

He growled and moved over to inspect the discarded pile of skin. Giving it a sniff, he turned and sprayed it quite thoroughly.

It was her turn to growl. "You wretched beast! I was saving that for later! Now you've ruined it!"

"Meh!" Lazarus stated rudely then bounded off.

"I thought you'd learned by now, pet, that pirates share their spoils," Viktor said with a chuckle. "You can finish this off now, if you like."

She glared at him before cutting down her victim. She dragged Marle over to the railing and jumped over the side with him.

"You don't want to get too close to that one, old friend," he warned Grimm, as they watched her dive under with her kill. "She has a tendency to bite."

The *Barracuda* skirted along the south side of Cuba, heading west-northwest and cutting between the large island and Jamaica. Once again, Viktor made course for the Isle of Youth, near Cuba's northwest tip, and the Sister waiting there.

The further west he went, he found his blood Hunger returning to normal, if such a hunger could be called normal. He no longer felt it threatened to take over his will.

He explained to Grimm most of what had happened to him in the last few months. His friend and first mate didn't understand most of it, but he seemed to accept it readily enough. He knew Grimm would have no qualms about leaving no survivors of any ships they took. It had long been the older pirate's practice to kill anyone he didn't conscript or sell. It was how he'd earned the nickname "Grimm Reaper."

The way he saw it, even those he'd personally found useless could now serve a purpose. "Better them than me," was what he'd told Viktor.

Belladonna proved to be a bit of an adjustment for Grimm. To keep himself from seeking a place in her bed, he kept telling himself she was the captain's woman. It was the surest deterrent. He wasn't stupid. He'd known Brandee long enough to tell when he was being possessive of any given female. He had no doubt his old friend would gut him on the spot, if he'd made a try for the siren.

Now, he believed he understood why Viktor had given him first choice of any wenches that might happen to be on the ships they would take. He was puzzled, however, at why the man tolerated the saucy lass flirting with him. He finally decided to risk just asking.

That afternoon, he went to the captain's cabin. As they sat over drinks, he commented, "That little firebrand of yours seems to be quite friendly my way, Vik. I've tried to discourage her. I know you don't share your wenches. But she seems to make a point of tempting me whenever you're in sight or earshot."

"I've noticed," he replied. "That's why I've been ignoring her behavior. She's trying to use one of my tricks on me."

Grimm's eyes lit up with curiosity. "I smell an interesting tale there. Care to share?"

Viktor poured them each some rum, foregoing the blood mixture for the moment, then sat back and smiled. "Aye. I had our lovely Belladonna accompany me in Havana, while I searched for news of who'd taken you."

"Didn't trust the crew with her, eh?"

"Actually, I didn't trust her not to eat the crew. Her presence drove a tavern wench to be more attentive and informative. The lass behaved quite rudely to Belle, however. I thought I was going to have to tie and gag her to keep her from killing the wench."

"So, it's retribution she's after," he understood. "Thinking she can use me to make you jealous. Who was the wench, by the way?"

"Sweet Valerie. She'll be quite a pleasure to have the next time we make Havana," he answered smugly.

Grimm gave a lascivious chuckle. He'd enjoyed the girl in question a few times himself. "Oh, aye; nothing like a good Crescent wench to tighten your nuts."

"And Val is one of the best," Viktor laughed with him. "Manuel told me she services the governor."

"Bah!" Grimm spat. "That's a waste of a fine wench on that old goat!"

"Aye, it is."

Chapter 14

Grimm found himself abruptly thrown to the deck. The ship lurched to a violent stop, accompanied by the unmistakable sound of eight-inch-thick timbers snapping like twigs. Viktor's superior reflexes were the only things that kept him off the deck, as well. Sad to say, he was starting to get used to stopping this way. Plus, the crystal Mother Celie had given him had grown warm, warning him of Hell's Breath's imminent reappearance, this time.

"Damn that old man," he growled, as he helped his first mate to his feet. "How the hell does he expect me to find the Sisters without a ship?!"

They made their way up to the quarterdeck. It surprised Grimm to see how few of the crewmen were hurt.

"Mr. Jon, report!"

"She's got a hole big enough to launch a boat from, Cap'n. She's taking on water, but we're too shallow to sink."

"Take a detail down to the ballast hold with enough sail cloth to wrap the cadre in and bring them up on deck."

"Aye, Cap'n."

"Where's Belladonna?"

"She jumped over the side about half an hour ago," Jon-Jon told him.

"Of course; Mr. Grimm, come with me. We're going ashore."

"You bring any 'bacco, boy?" Zeke said by way of greeting.

Viktor wasn't sure whether to laugh or yell. His response to the old wizard was not quite as furious as he'd originally intended. It ended up coming out more as just gruff and slightly incredulous. "You knock a gaping hole in my ship with your damn island, and all you can think about is if I brought you any smoke?"

"Priorities, boy, priorities; we'll deal with your little boat in due time. Now answer the question."

He realized he wasn't going to get anywhere with the old man until he'd filled his pipe. "Mr. Grimm, you've always got smoke on you. Give him some."

Grimm gave him a bemused look, which Viktor ignored, but did as he'd been ordered.

"Much obliged, Hezekiah Grimm. Thank you," Zeke told him, taking the pouch of tobacco and filling his pipe, before returning it.

"You know me?" Grimm asked in surprise.

Using a stick from his fire, he lit the pipe. He drew a few puffs, savoring the tobacco. "Known ye since you was a pup. Knew you'd bring some fine Virginny tobacco with you, when this rapscallion finally brought you to Hell's Breath."

Viktor's rage came back, full blown. "What game are you playing, old man? You practically forbade me to go after Grimm!"

Zeke puffed and grinned. "How else did you expect me to make sure you brought him back here, boy?"

"You expect me to believe that?" he argued. "Not two days before I finally caught up with his captors, the damn curse nearly got out of hand. If Belladonna hadn't suggested turning some of my crew, I'd have never made it to Grimm. Yet, oddly enough, the Hunger has come back under control since returning to my hunt for the Sisters. I can't help but think you had something to do with that."

"That girl never did listen too good." The old man shook his head. "It was a test, Viktor Brandewyne; one you passed quite well, I might add."

He tried to go for his sword, only to find himself paralyzed. This forcibly reminded of just how powerful the old man truly was.

"I'm well aware of what a selfish, self-serving bastard you can be, boy. It's what's kept you alive this long. But we had to be sure, without any doubt, that you are the One. Your persistence in rescuing your friend here, despite the discouragement sent your way and the very real risk to yourself has proved that you are. Now we know that you have what it will take to find and take on the Sisters. You actually have a chance of surviving whatever they may throw at you."

Viktor found he could once more move, but wisely kept his anger and irritation in check. His sarcasm remained in full evidence, however. "So, you put a hole in my ship that will sink her as soon as this island vanishes again," he smirked. "That'll make it so much easier to reach the Sisters in good time. Thank you so much."

The old man waved his hand in dismissal. "You don't need that leaky old tub anymore."

"Oh? Am I expected to swim from island to island? Or perhaps you'll tell me I can grow wings and just fly."

"Hee! That'd be a sight to see!" Zeke laughed.

"What this old fart is telling you, Captain, is that you now have a far better ship at your disposal."

Viktor and Grimm turned to see Belladonna approaching. To their relief, she was fully clothed. It meant she'd gone to the ship before coming ashore.

"Watch that sass mouth, girl," Zeke muttered. She blew him a kiss in response. Ignoring her, he turned his attention back to the two pirates. "Fog's going to be setting in pretty soon. You'll be wanting to transfer all your gear and tack over to the new boat."

Viktor was still irritated at him. Every time he encountered Uncle Zeke, he felt as if he had no control over his own life. That control was something he'd worked long and hard to achieve. It did not sit well with him that even someone as powerful as the old wizard could usurp that control so easily. If the Sisters were anything near as powerful as this old man, it did not bode well.

"The ship I have was adequate for my purposes, until you put a hole in her. How do I know this ship I have yet to see will suit me as well?"

Zeke just chuckled. "Go and have a look at her, boy." He turned back to his fire, dismissing them.

☠

"We're going to need a bigger crew," Grimm stated, when they topped the rise above the bay where the promised ship lay at anchor.

It was easily twice the size of the *Barracuda*. It was also fitted with a copper clad hull. Viktor could count thirty guns just on the port side, distributed between two separate gun decks. He suspected there was at least that many more, masked by false sides. It was lust at first sight.

"That — will do nicely."

Lazarus appeared, unsummoned, and perched himself on Viktor's shoulder. "Mrrow."

He reached up and caressed the cat's chin. "Lazarus, go inspect our new vessel."

The cat morphed into his raven form and flew over to perch on the railing. Returning to feline shape, he set off padding about the ship, slipping into every nook and cranny. The images Viktor received from his familiar confirmed his suspicions about the hidden guns. Better yet, the powder looked to be perfectly dry.

A couple of things Lazarus showed him puzzled him, however. Turning to Belladonna, he asked, "How much do you know about this ship?"

"Considering I'm the one who stole it and hid it here, quite a bit; was there something specific you had in mind?"

"Explain the pulley system attached to the fore and aft swivel guns."

She chuckled, "Oh, you'll love this. It's a little twist on one of the tricks I've seen you use; the harpoon lines you shoot into other ships. The pulleys allow you to attach the lines to counterweights. Push the weights out the lower gun ports and pull your prey to you."

"What's to keep the two ships from crippling each other when they collide?" Grimm asked.

Viktor answered, having "seen" the solution lying on the deck. "Corkwood buffers, like you use to protect small boats' sides, when you dock. But these are the biggest ones I've ever seen."

Grimm whistled, impressed. "This is definitely no merchantman."

"No," Vik agreed. "She's not a regular man-o-war, either. If you look closely, you'll see the masts are hinged. The lower sails are doubled as well. I'll wager the secondary sails are false ones, shot to bits. Couple that with supposedly broken masts and she'd look crippled enough to lure another ship close enough to take."

"Wasn't that one of old Billy Black's tricks?"

"Aye; one of them. He was a right clever bastard. Someone must've survived to tell whoever commissioned this ship."

"Fog's coming in," Belladonna reminded them.

Jon-Jon and Murph were set to organizing and carrying out the transfer to the new ship.

As night fell, no one noticed Hezekiah slip off in the fog. Those handling the transfer were using small boats. None of the crew had a desire to go ashore on Hell's Breath.

Before he even realized where he was going, the pirate found himself facing Uncle Zeke across the small fire. "Been waiting for you, Hezekiah Grimm," the old man smiled. "Pull up a rock and sit a spell."

"Why was I compelled to come see you, Uncle?" he asked, genuinely puzzled.

"Got some serious business to talk about. There's a job needs doin', and you're the one fated to do it. That's why you're here now."

"I already know Vik is going to need help finding these Sisters or witches or whatever they are." He was starting to understand why Viktor found the old man so frustrating to deal with.

Zeke chuckled, "You think you know what's going on, boy, but you don't know the half of it. Hell, even Viktor Brandewyne only knows what he needs to know for the present. There's a lot you both yet will learn about a great many things."

Hezekiah glared at him. "Then why don't you enlighten me, old man."

The chuckle grew to a cackle. Anyone else might well have been intimidated. Grimm's reputation as a ruthless pirate rivaled that of Vik Brandee. Together, they would be a force to be reckoned with. "Yup, you're the right one for this job. We need someone to go with him to keep him on course, besides that wild girl. She's always got her own reasons for doing what she does, and she's not always predictable. We can't trust her completely to act in Viktor's best interests."

Grimm smirked knowingly, "Can't argue with you there, old man. Belle does seem to be a bit mad. But Vik has never been one to let a wench control him or lead him about by his gonads."

"That don't mean she won't try. I'm sure you've seen how he lets her get away with behavior that would earn anyone else a slit throat by now," he pointed out.

"I'm not going to ask how you know that, but yes, he does seem to be more tolerant of her than is his wont."

"Mm-hmm, that's her magic at work." The old man nodded. Seeing the murderous look on Grimm's face, he smiled and added, "She can't help it, boy. Ol' Belladonna is a siren, not human. Drawing men to her will is just part of being what she is. If your captain were a weaker being, he'd already be completely in her thrall by now. But his magic is at least as strong as, if not stronger than, hers. An ordinary man would fall prey to her immediately, unless there was a stronger spell already on him."

"I think you overestimate her pull, Uncle," Grimm shook his head. "I find her attractive, but not that attractive. I'd gut the bitch and throw her over the side, before I'd become her puppet."

"Hee! That's what you think, Hezekiah Grimm. She just hasn't turned her attention to you, yet. Besides, that wouldn't kill her, anyway. It might make her mad, or she may think its foreplay. Hard to tell with that girl."

Zeke stirred his fire, while he let Grimm digest that bit of information. Hezekiah found himself staring into the flames. The dancing embers mesmerized him.

Once satisfied with the fire's effect, Zeke asked, "To what lengths will you go for Viktor Brandewyne?"

Grimm's voice came dreamlike, "He is my brother. I would do anything for that man; kill for him; die for him."

"That's good, but we don't want you to go so far as dying. A dead watchdog is no good to anyone. The time is coming, sooner than you might think, when he's going to need you to protect him."

"I fear no man or creature. Anyone or anything that tries to harm Vik will have to go through me."

"Yes, you will make a good watchdog against outside forces, but a true watchdog cannot be afraid of what it guards, either."

Grimm gave Zeke a hard stare, already fighting free of the old man's spell. "Vik is my brother. I am not afraid of him."

Zeke smiled to himself, pleased at the pirate's strength of will. "You need to understand; the Viktor Brandewyne you sail with now is not the man you remember. He's told you about his curse?"

He nodded.

"He's got abilities now that no ordinary man ever will. One of those is the ability to impose his will on others. Right now, he has total control over anyone he bites or who tastes his blood. He has partial control over someone he holds eye contact with. But his power is going to grow. Before all this is over, he'll be able to make people do what he wants simply by thinking about it. The worst part is that as his power grows, so will his blood Hunger. He'll come to care more about serving that unquenchable thirst than he will about finding the Sisters, so he can break the curse's hold over him. If that is allowed to happen, he will choose the Hunger over everything and everyone — even you, Hezekiah."

"That can't be true," he argued in disbelief. "Vik would never turn on me, unless I gave him good reason to."

"Jim Rigger has already fallen to the Hunger. He was Viktor's second blood meal."

Grimm realized the truth in the old man's words. "I remember Vik telling me that Rigger was no longer able to fulfill his duties, when he asked me to step up as his first mate."

"There's something I need you to do. You may not like it, but it'll keep you from suffering Rigger's fate. Hand me your knife."

Grimm wasn't sure why he obeyed. It wasn't like him to hand any of his weapons over to anyone else — ever. Yet, he found himself readily giving the old man one of his favorite blades.

Zeke took the offered knife and pricked the skin of his inner wrist. He handed the knife back and squeezed the wound until two drops of blood welled up, crimson against his dark skin. "That should be plenty. Now, come here and lick this blood off my wrist."

He had been right, Grimm didn't like the idea, and he didn't want to do it. "Vik's the one who likes drinking blood, old man, not me."

The old wizard gave the pirate a small taste of his true power. "We ain't got time for games, Hezekiah Grimm. Now, get over here and do what you're told."

He had no choice but to obey. His body moved of its own accord. His mind screamed against the pull, but he was powerless to resist. He put his mouth to Zeke's wrist and licked the blood off. Drawing back, he saw the wound vanish as if it had never been. He had a strong urge to spit, but Zeke wasn't having any of that.

"Swallow it, boy."

Grimm obeyed. Instantly, his thoughts cleared. He felt as if he just emerged from a fog he'd never realized he was in. All his senses grew sharper. Everything was in hyper-focus.

"I didn't want to have to force you, boy, but it's probably best that I had to. Now you know what it would be like to be defenseless against Viktor, once he reaches his full power."

Grimm gave him a hateful glare.

"Told ye you wouldn't like it, but you're safe now. Well, as safe as you can be. What you just swallowed was thousands of times more potent than that bloodied up rum he uses to control his crew.

He'll never be able to take your will, now you're carrying a little bit of my power in your veins. You're going to heal a lot faster and be harder to kill."

Grimm felt almost intoxicated with the sensory input he was getting. At the same time, everything Zeke had been telling him started to make sense. He stopped doubting and listened to what the old man had to say.

"For a while, Viktor won't realize what has taken place here. When he does, he's probably going to take it as a betrayal and try to kill you. You can't let him do that. He's really going to need you to keep him sane and on course. You're going to have to protect him from himself, before the end. But remember this; you are harder to kill now, but you ain't immortal. So, don't get cocky," he warned him. "Our business here is done for now, but don't be a stranger, Hezekiah Grimm."

Grimm woke up back in his cabin. He had the vague memory of a strange dream involving the old man he'd met earlier with the captain and the siren.

He also had a faint metallic taste in his mouth and the kind of headache he usually got from coming off a weeklong drunk.

It took the better part of two days to get everything they wanted or needed to take removed from the *Barracuda* and shifted over to the new ship.

As ships went, she was literally a new vessel, at only three years old. She'd been christened the *War God* and had been built to be the ultimate pirate hunter. She'd vanished at sea on her maiden voyage from the Bristol shipyards bound for the Caribbean.

Tales of the disappearance had spread like wildfire throughout the sea-going community. The story was she'd left the shipyard accompanying a convoy of merchantmen and at least two other men-of-war. Her mission: finally squelch the piracy and smuggling which interfered with English trade in the Colonies. Midway on the crossing, an unusually dense fog had enveloped the convoy. Several crewmen from the other ships later reported hearing piteous screams and tormented wailing. After about an hour, the fog dissipated. The *War God* was nowhere to be seen.

The official report was that she'd either hit an uncharted reef or run afoul of a pod of whales and been sunk.

The story the sailors who were there told was that Hell itself had opened up and swallowed the ship whole. They only heard the screams, not breaking timbers. They'd only seen the bloody water where the ship should have been, no bodies or wreckage — or whales.

Many had vowed never to set to sea again.

Viktor, Grimm, and Belladonna stood near the helm, watching the *Barracuda* slip beneath the waves. Hell's Breath had long since vanished. The *War God* lay at anchor near a natural shoal which had never been a part of the traveling island's topography.

Jon-Jon approached and reported. "I've set Murph and his lads to removing the name, as ordered, Cap'n."

"Good work, Mr. Jon. It was a good name for her, but given her history, it would draw too much of the wrong kind of attention."

Grimm leaned, forearms on the railing. "Any thoughts on what to rename her, Captain?"

In response, Viktor turned to the siren. "I believe I'll give you the honor of renaming this vessel, pet, since you procured it for me."

She gave him an enigmatic smile. "I've a name for it that should suit it quite well. How does *Incubus* sound?"

He thought about it for a few moments before replying. "It has a vaguely threatening sound to it. I approve. Mr. Jon, go instruct Mr. Murph to start work on the new placard."

"Aye, Cap'n."

"*Incubus*," Viktor tried the name out again, liking the sound of it even more. "Interesting word. What does it mean?"

The siren laughed, a throaty chuckle. "You may read, Captain Brandewyne, but you haven't been reading the right books."

He glared at her. "Don't test me, Belle. What does it mean?"

"Maybe I'll tell you some day, if you don't figure it out before then," she teased, perching herself on the railing. "Right now, I'm hungry." She slipped over the side and out of reach, just as the vampire made a grab for her. The two men watched as she changed from beautiful young woman to terrifying sea monster. Grimm looked a bit ashen at the transformation. Viktor had seen the show before. Both still couldn't decide if they were more disturbed by the transformation or by the fact that they still found her desirable, even in her true form.

"Irritating bitch," Vik muttered. Grimm silently agreed with him.

Chapter 15

Viktor stood on the bowsprit, one hand on the rigging for balance, enjoying the feel of the spray plowed up by his beauty of a ship. She was rigged for speed and was showing it. It was yet another feature that delighted him with its subterfuge. Ordinarily, a ship as large as the *Incubus* would be a relatively slow, cumbersome beast, difficult to steer in close battle. The copper-clad hull allowed her to cut through the water much more efficiently.

Grimm was right about needing a bigger crew, however. Viktor had no hope of utilizing her full firepower with the current compliment at his disposal. He simply didn't have enough men to man the guns, not even half of them, and sail the ship at the same time.

Since the ship was already set up for it, he decided to try old Billy Black's ship-in-distress ruse at the first sight of sails on the horizon.

He smiled. Billy Black. Now there was a name that brought back memories. A real pirate's pirate, the old barnacle had been well into his fifties when a fifteen-year-old Viktor had first encountered him.

Some lads played with marbles. Some played games, pretending to their fathers' professions. Most wanted to carry on their family businesses, but a few sought adventures and used their imaginations.

Viktor Brandewyne wanted to be a pirate.

He was already a bit of a river bandit. He'd learned early on that he could make a profit from raiding other lads' catches of crab, shrimp or fish. He also wasn't above a bit of sneak-thievery in some of the outlying communities along the Savannah River.

Of course, Mother Celie had repeatedly warned him to stay away from the docks, warehouses and taverns along River Street.

"There's bad sorts there, boy," she'd harped. "Thieves and cutthroats that'd slit you from navel to chin just for looking at them the wrong way and whatever coin you might have on ye. And then there are the press gangs. You're strong-built and tall for your age, just what they'd prize. They'll put things in your food or drink or just knock you over the head. Next thing you know, you're out to sea, forced to slave on some ship. Knowing you like I do; you'd end up getting' yourself killed. I know how much you hate being told what to do."

"Yes, you know me, and you know me well enough to know I know my way around the docks. I'm aware of all that goes on down there. I may not be a businessman, but I know the ways of the street — and the river. I can look after myself, old woman."

She gave him a slap for the sassing. "You'll keep a civil tongue in that head, boy! You will show respect for me or face the consequences."

Vik glared at her but held his tongue. He had a pretty good idea of what the old witch was capable of when riled. He may have been a headstrong teenager, but he wasn't stupid.

When he turned and left her tabby shack, Celie just shook her head. She knew, stubborn as he was, he'd have to learn the hard way.

Of course, Vik had made a point to go more often to the riverfront. Celie's warnings hadn't entirely been wasted on him, however. He always made sure to stay aware of everything going on around him and to eat well before going there. The last kept him from wanting much food or drink while in the city.

William Blackthorne was somewhat of a local legend. He'd made a name for himself as Billy Black, captain of the *Nightshade*, a wily and black-hearted buccaneer. He'd settled in Savannah and used his ill-gotten gains to establish himself as the proprietor of a tavern, inn, and brothel known as the Black Flag. The Flag was the haunt of Savannah's more disreputable and nefarious sea-going denizens.

Viktor could often be found lurking around the place, hoping to overhear tales or plots that could be useful to him. He was invariably run off as a pestering brat.

Realizing he would never receive the education in piracy he desired by lurking outside, he resolved to secure himself a place inside The Black Flag. Mustering his resolve, he pushed his way inside. Spotting the old pirate through the smoke, he strode over to him.

Bold as brass, he demanded, "I'm here for work, and if you'll not have me, then to hell with you!"

Billy gave the tall, skinny boy the once over with a smirk. "Y've got balls, lad. I like that." Then, he dealt Viktor a fist to the side of the head. The boy crumpled to the floor from the force of the blow, blood trickling from his ear.

"But I'll not be talked to thus by some pup! You will address me with respect, both as your elder and your employer. Now get up."

Viktor obeyed, wearing a smug look on his face. A boxed ear was a small price to pay for a chance at the knowledge he was after.

"Do y'know one end of a swab from the other?"

He nodded.

"Then grab one and get to work! There's piss, beer and puke stinking up the place."

He'd worked the boy to near-exhaustion that first day. Viktor had done every task set him with silent determination. Billy Black figured if he could make it through a week like that, he'd keep the boy on staff. Hell, he might even pay him.

The week passed. Not once had Viktor grumbled or sassed, regardless of how menial or disgusting the task given. Nor had he behaved like some bootlick. There was a pride and confidence in the lad.

"You've earned your keep, lad. What's your name?"

"Viktor Brandewyne."

"The Thunderbolt Witch's brat, hmm? Heard tell of you. Figured you'd find your way here eventually." Billy nodded to himself. "Of course, Viktor Brandewyne is too much of a mouthful for a place like this. Think I'll just call ye Vik Brandee. Easier to remember and it suits ye, boy. Now scat on home and let old Celie know where you've been and that you've got a job. I wouldn't want the old witch to get cross and hex me. You be back here tomorrow, sunup."

He did as he was told, smiling all the way back to Skidaway Island. Vik Brandee would make a fine pirate name.

They were maybe two days sailing from the Isle of Youth, when the call came from the masthead, "Sails on the horizon, sou' sou'west."

Viktor gave the order.

The crew lowered the hinged masts, counterweights in place to hoist them back into position, should there be need to give chase. They furled the good sails and hung false, ragged ones in their place, shot through and burnt as if from battle. Smudge pots smoked all about the deck. Finally, they masked most of the gun ports.

For all intents and purposes, the *Incubus* looked like a merchantman that had run afoul of pirates.

Belladonna questioned Viktor about the tactic. "How does virtually crippling your ship help you catch your prey? I would think they stand a better chance of escaping you now."

He smirked condescendingly, "Hardly, pet. They are going to come to us."

She raised a disbelieving eyebrow, causing him to chuckle. "I'll explain it the way it was explained to me. Have you ever seen a wounded duck? People see one and they are going to go to it. Some want to help it. Some want to eat it. But very few are going to pass it by."

"And we're pretendin' to be the poor defenseless wounded duck," Grimm concluded, joining them. "She's turning this way, Captain. Sniff reports she's flying British colors. Looks to be a courier ship."

Viktor peered through the glass, then with naked eye. He found his own eyesight clearer than using the distorting lenses. He gave a toothy smile, the tips of his fangs just showing.

"This should prove interesting. She's a courier, all right. Maybe ten, twelve guns. Rigged for speed," he observed. "Seems to be more dress uniforms moving around on deck than such a small command warrants. Must be carrying important papers or personages."

"Aye. Could be profitable. I've ordered most of the lads below. You'd best be getting out of sight, as well, lass."

Belladonna stared at the pirate, as if he'd sprouted a second head.

Viktor gave her a swat on the rump. "Do as you're told, pet. Pirates wouldn't leave a woman behind on any ship they'd taken, save perhaps a dead one."

"Not even that, if they're desperate enough," Grimm muttered. Vik chuckled at the face Belle made over that comment.

"Off with ye now," he ordered her. "If you're seen, our little trap will be sprung before the prize is caught." He gave her another swat.

She glared at him but went below without any argument.

Hezekiah smirked, "Bit of a temper on that one. Bet you'll have some fine sport of her later on."

Viktor's response froze his first mate's blood. "Attend to the business at hand, Mr. Grimm."

"Aye, Captain." Grimm instantly sobered. Apparently, the siren was a sore subject with his captain.

The smaller sloop pulled close to the larger, crippled ship. Viktor's opinion of her captain went down considerably. The fool didn't even have anyone manning the guns, what few there were. A seasoned captain would never approach a derelict ship so carefree. Apparently, the man didn't have a good sea-eye, or he would have noticed well before getting so close, that the hull bore no damage at all.

"Hulloooooo! *Incubus*? May we offer assistance?" came the hail. "Is there anyone alive aboard?"

"Ahoy, *Seafoam*," Jon-Jon replied, dressed in bloodstained clothes. "Most are dead or taken, but we've a few wounded aboard. Our surgeon took shot through the chest. Have you got someone as can help?"

Viktor stayed out of direct view, listening to the exchange. His superior hearing allowed him to pick up on a whispered conversation aboard the vessel. There seemed to be a disagreement between her captain and her main passenger about lending aide. The passenger was angry and suspicious of the delay in completing his mission. At least someone on the sloop had some intelligence. The captain sounded to be a complete fool.

Viktor decided it was time someone relieved him of his command.

"Stand by to receive a boarding party, *Incubus*. We've an excellent surgeon and several able-bodied seamen to help move the wounded."

"Much obliged, *Seafoam*. Our captain is among the wounded."

In the hold of the *Seafoam*, a shadow coalesced into a large black cat. Lazarus slipped in among the cargo, looking for anything out of the ordinary. Not finding anything unusual, he proceeded to snoop around the cabins.

In the quartermaster's cabin, he found what he was looking for.

The "wounded" were brought over from the *Incubus'* deck. They totaled nine, including Viktor, Jon-Jon and Sniff, as well as a select few with enough scars and old injuries to make it look convincing. There was enough scrap lumber and other flotsam on deck to hide the smudge pots. Jon-Jon told the would-be rescuers that he'd gotten all the wounded up before they'd arrived. The rest of the crew was said to be either dead or taken by the pirates they'd run afoul of.

The *Seafoam*'s captain insisted on having Viktor brought to his cabin. Both he and the surgeon agreed the man wouldn't last much longer. The surgeon said he could shove his intestines back in and sew up the gaping belly wound, but he'd never seen anyone live long after such an injury. They'd die of blood loss, if they were lucky, or swell up and endure an agonizing death by fever. Out of respect for a fellow officer, the well-intended men decided to try to make him as comfortable as possible in his final hours.

Viktor decided the *Seafoam*'s surgeon was as competent as the captain had claimed. Jon-Jon hadn't lied about their surgeon dying of a chest wound. It had happened months ago, when they'd still been sailing the *Redfish*. This one would make a good addition to his crew.

He waited until the man prepared to stitch him up before he made his move. Once his intestines had been shoved back in, the skin sealed over and healed instantly. Viktor used the shock this gave the surgeon as the opportunity to seize the man and sink fang. He was careful not to drink too deeply, although sustaining his "wound' had stirred his Hunger. He didn't want to kill the man, just ensure his control over him. Although, even undead, the surgeon would prove useful.

"Your name, man."

"Dr. Matthew Coffin, sir."

Viktor chuckled. "Can't say as I care for that name. I would think it would be bad for business."

"That it has been, sir."

He looked down at the needle and thread in the doctor's hands he'd been about to use to sew up the gut wound with. "I think I'll call you Stitches, instead. Fetch this vessel's captain. I'd like to thank him for his aide and use of such a fine surgeon."

"Of course, sir."

Dr. Coffin came through the hatch onto the deck. The *Seafoam*'s captain and Viktor followed close behind. The unfortunate captain looked to be torn between terror and apoplexy. Viktor's hand rested firmly planted on the man's shoulder.

The first to notice this little entourage was an officious, overdressed man. "Captain Brogan! What is the meaning of this?! My mission is of utmost importance. Why are we still tied up to this derelict ship?"

"I'm afraid my mission trumps yours, Lord Ferguson," Viktor informed him. He'd learned the courier's name from Dr. Coffin.

"And just who the devil do you think you are? The King himself issued my orders!" Ferguson puffed up.

"The devil indeed," Viktor grinned at him. "Hell has set my course. As for who I am, I'm sure you've heard my name before; Viktor Brandewyne, at your service. Mr. Jon, secure his lordship, if ye would, but try not to damage him too much."

"With pleasure, Cap'n," he replied. He delivered a light rap to the back of the man's skull, dropping Ferguson to the deck like a sack of grain. "Been itching to do that since we got on board. Pompous ass hasn't been quiet the entire time."

The sergeant in charge of the redcoats on board barked his men to arms. Viktor thought their response time admirable. If they could sail half as well as they soldiered, they'd be a welcome addition to his crew. If not, well, he and his cadre had to eat.

"You will pay for that pirate," the sergeant promised. "You are outnumbered. Release his lordship, the captain and our good doctor."

"No. I don't believe I will."

"Didn't you hear me, man? You are outnumbered. Surrender now!"

"That is where you are wrong, sir," he corrected him. "Mr. Grimm!"

"Aye, Captain," Grimm called back from the *Incubus*.

"These gentlemen seem to be under the impression that they outnumber us. Show 'em what we've got."

At that signal, the crew of the *Incubus* unmasked all sixty guns facing the *Seafoam* and raised the hinged masts.

Grinning, Viktor locked eyes with the sergeant. "It appears to be you, sir, who are at the disadvantage."

"Stand down, sergeant," Brogan ordered; his voice a bit too strident, his eyes about to pop from their sockets.

"You coward," the sergeant sneered.

"Aye, he is, isn't he," Viktor agreed. "Unworthy of his command. I think I'll relieve him of it." Before anyone could act to prevent it, the vampire shoved his hand in the captain's gut and up. The man just grunted in surprise, when he ripped his heart out. He sank fangs in the still beating muscle and sucked it white in minutes.

"He could have made a good sailor, someday, but his heart just wasn't in it. I'll be taking your surrender now." He smiled, licking a drop of blood from his mustache.

As one, the soldiers dropped their weapons. "What are you?" one of them whispered.

"We are the people your parents warned you about, and you'll soon be joining us. Mr. Grimm, send over a barrel of the good rum. We'll welcome our new crewmates with a toast. Then, we'll retrieve that little cask full of bribe money Lazarus is guarding in the quartermaster's cabin — and anything else of value on board."

Chapter 16

Of course, the specially spiked rum had the desired effect. The loyalty of the conscripted men to Viktor was now unquestionable. They stripped the *Seafoam* down to little else but hull, deck and masts. A few well-placed shots sent her swiftly to the bottom.

"What do you want to do with his lordship?" Grimm asked, once they were under way again.

"He may be worth some ransom, since he holds title," Vik shrugged. "Although I doubt it. Most of the fools who get selected for the kind of mission his papers detail are usually expendable."

Grimm chuckled, "Probably lifted the wrong skirt back at court."

"Like as not. If he doesn't quiet down by the time we reach the Isle of Youth, I'm going to cut his tongue out," the vampire growled. "Maybe Jon-Jon was too gentle with him."

They spotted their destination a couple of days later; a fact Sniff took as being as good a reason as any to celebrate. He perched in the crow's nest with a bottle of grog, singing, if it could be called that, at the top of his lungs.

"With a dick as big
As a full-growed pig
And a couple of cantaloupe nuts,

This here's the story,
In all of its glory,
Of the big-bellied pirate, Barney Butts!
Big-bellied Barney
Sailed Lake...."

Without even looking, Viktor fired a pistol over his shoulder, shattering Sniff's bottle. "Pick another song."

"Oh, Cap'n, come on," the rigging rat whined. "There's nothing like a good sea shanty."

"And that was nothing like a good sea shanty."

"Everyone's a critic," Sniff sniffed.

Viktor just shook his head. Spotting Jon-Jon, he waved him over. "What's the report, Mr. Jon?"

"We'll make harbor in about three hours, Cap'n."

"Good. Where's Belladonna?"

He shrugged. "Not sure, Cap'n. She's been sulking in her cabin since we took that sloop, but she wasn't there when you sent me to fetch her."

He growled in irritation. "Aggravating female. She's angry with me, I suppose, for not letting her join in our fun. If she went to feed, she better get back to the ship soon, or she'll have to wait until dark to join us in the harbor."

The siren chose that moment to make her appearance. Wearing a loose shirt and trousers, she strode up to him. She reached up, grabbed his goatee and pulled him down into a searing kiss. Then, with a dazzlingly wicked smile, she sashayed away.

Both Viktor and Jon-Jon admired the rear view she offered.

"I think she likes you again," Jon-Jon observed.

"I know — and that disturbs me."

Knowing he would need her help in dealing with the Sister, Viktor chose not to make an issue of wardrobe with Belladonna. He allowed her to wear the trousers she favored into port.

Feeling generous, since the gold take had been good, he had Grimm dole out shares to the crew and gave most of them permission to go ashore. A few of the more useless of the new crewmembers were bled for his own private stock, as well as to feed his cadre. He set one of the fledgling vampires to guard the noble prisoner.

Jon-Jon managed to finally silence Ferguson by threatening to find the most putrid, soiled rag of a garment among the crew and use it to gag him. He'd even produced said rag. The foul odor of the thing caused his lordship to wretch violently, when Jon-Jon brought it into the cabin. That area of the ship remained blissfully quiet ever since.

Once on shore, the crew scattered about, although a good number chose to follow where Brandee went. There was usually good sport to be had in his vicinity.

Almost invariably, some poor fool would have to be educated as to just who had come into port.

Viktor wasn't studying sport, however. He had a Sister to find. Grimm and Belladonna went with him, being the only members of his crew who knew what was really going on.

To his irritation, and the siren's as well, she had not been able to sense the Sister's location. In fact, she couldn't sense the Sister at all.

"She must be more powerful than expected," she grumbled.

"Why do you say that pet?"

"I can see how she could mask herself from me when we're a great distance apart. But we're on the same island, and it's not that big of an island. I might not be able to pinpoint her exact location, but I should be able to sense something." Frustration showed in her voice. "This is her territory. Her power should seep through everything and everyone here."

"You don't sense anything at all?"

Belladonna shook her head. "Nothing. Not even a faint tremor or echo."

It was Grimm who pointed out the obvious. "Maybe this witch isn't so powerful. Maybe she's just not here to sense."

The siren rounded on him. "My visions are never wrong, human. I clearly saw her on this island."

Viktor placed a warning hand on her shoulder. He didn't have time for this kind of bickering. "We'll ask around. Someone here should know something about her," he declared. "But Hezekiah has a point. It has been weeks since you had that vision. She may have sensed you then and hidden. The old man did say they wouldn't make themselves easy to find."

This mollified the siren until she saw the smug look on Grimm's face. She lunged at the pirate. If Viktor had not been gifted with superhuman speed, his first mate might very well have ended his voyaging right then and there, permanently.

The vampire dealt her a slap forceful enough it would have broken her neck, if she'd been human. Standing between them, he got right in her face, a vise-like grip on her jaw to make sure she paid attention.

"That man is my brother, bitch, and a most valuable member of my crew. Anyone — anyone who lays a hand on him, other than myself, will answer to me." His eyes flashed emerald fire. "I protect what is mine. Is that understood?"

Belladonna gave Grimm a glare of pure jealousy. "Perfectly — Captain."

He released her and turned to his mate. "Now stop antagonizing her, Hezekiah. We've a witch to find and a short time to do so."

Viktor's group found themselves in one of the more respectable inns in the port. He and Grimm took a table, drawing a few curious glances from the other patrons. The tag-alongs from his crew drew more attention, however, mostly in the form of distasteful sneers or frowns. The innkeeper, wisely, did not object to their presence. The gold the pirates flashed around proved sufficient to hold his interest and to make him overlook the general lack of social graces. He knew from past experience there was good profit to be made if he kept these roguish guests happy. Just as he knew he could suffer great losses if they were angered or made to feel unwelcome.

He sent his best serving wench over to Viktor's table, but he kept a close eye on her. She was his daughter, and if the guests got too familiar, he would find some excuse to substitute another server.

For her part, the girl gave them her full attention. The painfully obvious fact the two pirates were dangerous men proved very appealing to the girl, especially given her early stage of womanhood. The fact they were both roguishly handsome only added to the attraction.

Viktor and Grimm made no attempt to hide that they both enjoyed, and to some measure, expected the attention. Belladonna, who'd opted not to join them at the table, noticed this as well. Still stung by Viktor's earlier favoritism, the easy, laughing manner he used with the girl only fired her jealousy and ire more. She turned sulkily to the bar.

Noticing the siren's absence when the lovely Paella left to fill their order, Viktor scanned the dining room for her. He spotted her by the bar, ignoring some local drunk who all but slobbered on her. His temper flared immediately. In a heartbeat, he stood beside the man, one hand heavy on his shoulder.

"I don't take kindly to people accosting one of my crewmembers," he whispered in a low, deadly voice. "Tell me, sir, are your intentions honorable? A life depends on your answer."

Outraged, the drunk sputtered, "Sunbish! Wha'si'matter t'you?"

"Wrong answer."

Somehow, Viktor's dagger found itself buried in the man's ear. He removed it and let the body slump to the floor. It happened so quickly, no one saw the kill take place.

"I could have taken care of that myself," Belle stated, as she allowed him to grasp her arm and half-lead, half-drag her back to his table.

"I'm sure you could, pet. But I've already told you, I protect what is mine."

She jerked to a stop, forcing him to either stop with her or pull her off her feet. He stopped and stared hard at her.

"If you think for one minute that you own me, just give me five minutes with you in the water."

He leaned down until he was barely and inch from her face. "If you think for one minute that I don't own you," he purred, "I'll give you those five minutes."

He smirked knowingly, smelling the lust rolling off the siren in waves. But he had no intention of sating that desire, tempting though it was. There were more important things to tend to at the moment. He released her arm, turned and went back to his seat.

As he suspected she would, Belladonna followed him to the table. Grimm, wisely, refrained from commenting.

The three were discussing what would be the best way to track down the first Sister, when Paella returned with a tray of food. She began setting the dishes on the table, keeping her eyes downcast.

"I will return shortly with the rest of your order, *señors*," she spoke with a subdued voice.

Viktor and Grimm noticed the change in the girl's behavior and exchanged a look.

"Do you think she knows something about our business?" Grimm asked.

"Aye," Vik nodded.

Belladonna shifted impatiently. "Then just ask her when she comes back."

"What's troubling you, lass?" Grimm noticed the siren's irritability.

She glared at him, but answered, "The little slut practically reeks of fear, one of my favorite flavorings. Now I'm starving."

Vik chuckled, "That she did, pet. Here, take my roast. I'll be feeding some other hungers, while I find out what our little Paella knows."

Belle made a face at the offered food. "No thank you. I don't see how you can stomach this. It's practically ruined."

"Don't know what you're talking about, lass," Grimm countered around a mouthful of his own meal. "This is actually some of the best cooking I've had in a while."

"Ew! You actually like taking perfectly good flesh and scorching it before eating it?" she said incredulously.

"Well, I can't very well eat it raw."

She just shook her head as if she thought him daft. However, seeing that he genuinely seemed to be enjoying the food, she decided to pick at the meat on Viktor's plate.

"I guess it's not bad," she shrugged. "Not as good as fresh man flesh steeped in terror, but not bad."

Viktor chuckled at her observation. Paella soon returned with the rest of the meal.

"My compliments to your cook, lass," Grimm offered, still stuffing his face.

"*Gracias, señor.*" Paella blushed. Noticing Viktor had given his food to Belladonna, she asked, "Would you like me to bring another tray, *señor*? I did not realize *la señorita* would be joining you. Is there anything special you want *señorita*?"

The acknowledgement and courtesy raised Belle's opinion of the girl. "No. Thank you for asking, though."

Grimm raised an eyebrow at the siren's atypical behavior. Viktor ignored it.

"Another tray won't be necessary, pet." He reached around Paella's waist and pulled her abruptly into his lap. "I've got all I want right here."

She struggled, but without any true determination. She'd never been publicly handled like that, and it excited her. Her position on his lap let her know that the pirate was quite ready for her. It made her forget her earlier fear and brought a deeper blush to her cheeks.

The blush proved an interesting experience for the vampire. As a man, he'd always taken it as a sign of encouragement. Now, it also increased his appetite. All that blood — just under the surface of that oh-so-soft skin. He could even hear her pulse speed up from her arousal.

He found it intoxicating.

He nuzzled her ear and neck, the bristles of his always neatly trimmed beard and mustache scraping and tickling her sensitive skin. It raised gooseflesh and caused her to let out a giggling moan.

That caught not only his tablemates' attention, but the attention of the innkeeper, her father.

"Paella! You are needed in the kitchen," he called.

Obediently, the girl jumped and tried to heed her father. She found Viktor's arm around her waist to be immovable.

"She's going to be busy here for a while," Vik informed him without taking his eyes from his prey.

Grimm, Belladonna and several of their crewmates watched to see how this chain of events would play out. The sudden mass attention was not lost on the innkeeper. He was acutely aware of his predicament.

"Please, sir, let me send you another *señorita*," he pled. "My daughter, Paella, is young and inexperienced. She is virgin and knows nothing of a seafarer's appetites. Let me send you one of the more experienced girls."

Viktor grinned; making sure the man could see his fangs. The man blanched. The girl remained oblivious to the exchange between the vampire and her father. The noticeably hard lump in the lap she sat on completely distracted her.

"Then it is high time she learned," he stated. He stood and half-led, half-carried Paella toward the door. "Your daughter will be in high demand once word gets out that she was taught by Viktor Brandewyne."

The poor man grew even paler, looking as if he might pass out.

"Mr. Grimm, pay the man."

Once Paella realized the pirate was taking her toward the docks and his ship, rather than to a rented room, she began to panic and struggle. Horror stories of girls carried off by sailors never to be heard from again filled her head. Viktor responded by tightening his grip around her waist. The effect was two-fold: it reduced her leverage, and it kept her from getting enough breath to scream.

No one on the docks gave them a second glance.

On board the *Incubus*, he set her down, grasped her wrist and led her to his cabin. He then showed her to a chair, rather than the bed, and took a seat opposite her. Her confusion showed plainly.

"I believe you know something about my business here, pet." He smiled at her.

"No, *señor*."

"Oh, but you do," he insisted. "You overheard my mates and me talking about how best to find someone who is supposed to be here, a woman of magic and power."

Paella's eyes grew large, and she started shaking her head vigorously. "No! *Señor*, I know nothing!"

Viktor stood, the girl's eyes never leaving him. He walked over to the sideboard and removed a bottle of the thick, brandy-laced blood. The girl's growing fear fired his Hunger and threatened his self-control, a distraction he could not afford at the moment. He took a long pull on the bottle to quiet the urge to drain her on the spot.

"You aren't a very good liar, Paella," he told her as he replaced the bottle. "I marvel at your father thinking you are still virgin."

The sudden change of subject caught her off guard and made her blush again. "*Papi* still sees me as a child." She confirmed what his senses already told him.

"I don't see you as a child." He gave a lustful look to prove his point. It had the desired effect. Her own lust and excitement began overpowering her fear.

He walked over behind her, skilled fingers unlacing her garments. When she reached up to help speed up the process, he lightly slapped her hands away. "No, no, pet." He chuckled low. "Patience. Some things are better when savored."

He continued the tortuously slow process, causing her to squirm and make small, impatiently eager sounds. The deliberate slowness gave him time to get his vampire urges under firm control, as well as thoroughly seducing the girl. He could smell that she was ready to receive him.

"Now, tell me the truth, Paella," he whispered in her ear. "What do you know about the Sister of Power I seek here?"

"It is forbidden to speak of," she replied breathily.

"You can tell me, pet." He nuzzled her neck, as he slid her dress off her shoulders. She sat exposed to the waist. He reached around and fondled her breast. She moaned and arched her back, pressing herself into his hand. "I can make it well worth your while," he breathed against her skin.

Paella proved a wealth of information by the time he finished with her. She told him of how many believed their island to be under a curse. Blight and storms began destroying crops. Trade suffered, as well, and disease ran rampant. All this misfortune started only recently.

Some had gone out to seek *la Madre* Dorada, the Golden Mother. They were sure she could bring healing and good fortune back to the island's community. But she was nowhere to be found. Most of her followers were gone, as well.

Only three old women had been left behind to warn off any seekers. They told the islanders that a great evil was coming, and *Madre* Dorada had been forced to flee before it.

Paella woke in her room at her father's inn. Two days had passed since she'd been with Viktor. She had no memory of leaving the ship or how she'd gotten home. She felt tired and weak, as if she'd been ill. On her inner thigh, she found two neat puncture wounds, as if small nails had been driven into her flesh, then removed. She didn't know how they came to be there, but instinctively knew she should never let anyone know about them.

She cried inconsolably, when she later learned her pirate lover had sailed immediately after bringing her back to the inn, heartlessly leaving her behind.

Chapter 17

It miffed Belladonna a bit to learn Grimm had been right about the Sister having fled the island. She secretly took some pleasure from the pirate's misplaced guilt about the matter, even though she didn't understand the emotion.

"If I had been more cautious in Havana, you wouldn't still be trying to catch this witch," he apologized.

"Going by the dates Paella gave me, *Madre* Dorada left the Isle of Youth at least three days before I even learned you'd been taken, Hezekiah," Vik told him. "I still would have missed her, even if I hadn't gone to fetch you."

Something in Belle's mind told her that they would expect her to be remorseful, now, for having alerted the Sister. But, being a siren, she was incapable of that emotion. She was a predator, first and foremost. Her nature held no room for remorse.

Viktor turned to her. "Do you think you can find her again?"

"I can. You know the price. Who will you give to me?"

"Captain, we're still undermanned for a vessel of this class."

He nodded. "Aye. That we are." He thought hard for a while. Who could he sacrifice, when he could ill afford to lose any of his crew?

Then it came to him. A slow, evil smile spread across his face. "It seems Lord Ferguson will prove valuable after all. Does that meal meet with your approval, pet?"

"Mind if I play with him, first?" she asked impishly.

"If you like," he ceded, "but don't take too long. I need to know where to look for *Madre* Dorada, before she has time to get well hidden."

"Oh, all right," she sighed. "I'll keep it short. It won't be as much fun, though."

A knock sounded on Viktor's door.

"Enter."

Jon-Jon poked his head in, looking unsure. "Um, Cap'n?" he hesitated, then, decided to continue. "Belladonna just demanded entry to the prisoner's cabin. I left Griffin on guard to come check with you. Hope he can handle her. She's pretty upset that I wouldn't let her in."

"Let her in. I gave his lordship to her."

Jon-Jon winced. "Poor bugger."

"Aye."

He left to relay the order. Viktor could've just as easily communicated directly with the guard. Griffin was a member of his cadre. He shared a direct link with the fledgling vampire.

That link suddenly flared and was painfully severed. A sharp cold, so severe it burned, washed down his throat and spread through his chest, momentarily paralyzing his heart.

"Viktor?" Grimm stood over him, where he lay on the cabin deck. He offered his captain a hand up.

Viktor took the offered hand. Something was very wrong. He felt almost human weak. Reaching out with his mind, he could sense all his crew, but only five of his six vampires. He found only a void where Griffin should have been.

He could also sense Jon-Jon was both angry and very, very frightened. In all his years of sailing with the man, Viktor knew only something truly terrifying could shake his second mate like that.

"Trouble," he stated curtly. Grimm followed, as Viktor stormed out the door. He found himself having to run to keep up with the angry vampire.

It took a few moments to make sense of the scene the two came upon outside of Ferguson's cabin.

Jon-Jon crouched near Griffin's body. He'd dragged it to the far bulkhead. His eyes stayed glued to the thrashing form of the siren.

Belladonna writhed in her true form. She made piteous, gurgling noises through the gaping wound in her throat. Pain filled her golden eyes. Her shark-like tail thrashed weakly on the deck. Purplish-blue blood stained her throat and chest.

The same blood dribbled from the dead vampire's mouth.

Viktor barked, "Mr. Jon, report!"

Jon-Jon seemed to take some comfort from the captain's presence. "Just as I got back, she tried to push past Griffin. Griff attacked; tore her throat out before I could stop either of them. Then he just dropped to the deck all lifeless. She turned into that, so I dragged him over here to keep her from eating him."

Viktor turned to the siren. Belladonna reached out a taloned hand to him imploringly. His anger flared. Griffin could be replaced. The sea-witch could not.

"She's flopping like a fish out of water," Grimm observed.

Viktor realized what needed to be done to salvage the situation. He knelt and lifted the siren in his arms. The feat would have been nearly impossible, had he still been human. Her tail added a considerable amount of weight, as well as made her an awkward armful.

"You need to be in the water to heal properly, don't you?" he asked. She nodded, wrapping her arms around his shoulders and nuzzling against his chest. "Feeding would help, as well, I imagine."

He turned, about to order Jon-Jon to bring Griffin's body. What he saw stopped him in his tracks. In a matter of minutes, the corpse blackened, bloated, then, shrank in on itself. All that was left was a fanged skeleton covered by a blackened, leathery, greasy-looking skin. Clothing hung large and loosely on the mummified thing.

"Mr. Jon, get that thing off my ship, before it starts spreading disease," he ordered. "Mr. Grimm, invite his lordship to join us on deck."

Viktor stood at the railing, Belladonna still in his arms, when Grimm led Ferguson on deck. He'd had to dump the man out of his hammock in order to wake him.

His lordship was groggy and grumpy. When he spotted the vampire and siren, he stopped cold. "Is that a — mermaid?" he whispered in awe and disbelief.

Grimm chuckled nastily, "Hardly, man. That — is a siren, don't you read?"

"A siren?"

Belle lifted her head to peer over Viktor's shoulder. She was still completely in her true form. Spotting her prey, she opened her razor-toothed maw impossibly wide and emitted a hungry keen.

"Ah, dinner has arrived, pet." Vik smiled, turning to see what had drawn her attention.

The second Ferguson heard and saw the siren in all her horrific glory, he screamed like a young girl. His terror brought hungry grins to both the siren and the vampire.

"Over the side with you now, pet." He dumped her into the sea below. "Mr. Grimm, send his lordship swimming."

The pirate obeyed, dragging the struggling, terrified man to the railing and shoving him over the side.

Ferguson managed to grasp the rail. He held on, scrabbling in an attempt to regain the deck. Viktor wasn't having it. He reached over and grasped the man by the wrist. Hope blossomed in his eyes only to turn to despair, when Viktor dangled him over the water and out of reach of any part of the ship.

"Not very gentlemanly of you to keep a lady waiting, Lord Ferguson." He grinned amiably. Then he let go.

Belladonna rose to catch the victim as he reached the water. The seawater washed the blood away, revealing her throat wound already beginning to heal.

Grimm turned away from the grisly scene as she used her talons to open the man's gut and reach into his body. Viktor continued to watch, no emotion showing, as she pulled out one organ at a time and devoured it. Ferguson's screams were finally silenced by a swell that washed over them, filling his lungs with water. Soon afterward, the siren dove deep with the remains of her kill to finish the meal.

"Are you fully healed?"

Viktor knew, without turning around, that it was Belle entering his cabin without knocking. Of all on board, only she would dare be so bold — or foolish.

"Yes. I had a vision as well, but you won't like it."

"We'll get to that in a moment." He stood and pinned her against the bulkhead in a split second. "What did you do to Griffin?"

She looked up at him, unfazed. "I did nothing but try to shove him out of my way. He. Attacked. Me."

"Bilge! You had to have done something to him," he bellowed in her face. "Why else would he die and rot like that?"

"Probably because I am cold-blooded, and my blood is toxic." She shrugged. "As to why he rotted, he's been dead for close to a month. What did you expect?"

"He died just hours ago!"

She shook her head. "No, he died by your hand and Hunger, Captain Brandewyne," she corrected him. "Your power kept him able to move about and think. Human blood kept his body fueled and gave him strength. The venom in my blood severed his tie to you and killed the human blood he had consumed. Once that happened, his body reverted to its true, dead state. For some reason, they always retain the fangs. It's the only sign of their vampirism."

"They? You've seen this happen before?" He quickly caught the nuance.

Belladonna nodded. "A couple of vampires attacked one of my sisters. She couldn't get back to the sea in time to heal herself and died. Both vampires died as well. One rotted away to nothing but bones, no skin left. The other must have been dead a very long time. He just turned to dust."

"Why was your sister unable to get back to water? Could you not help her?"

Belle looked at him, bemused. "Why would I help her?"

It was Viktor's turn to be confused. "Because she was your sister," he stated, as if it should be obvious.

"She was another siren and competition for prey. Besides," she added, "considering how hard we are to kill, I figured the vampires were the only ones who could do the job for me without putting myself at risk."

He stepped back from her, his mind working rapidly to digest all the new information. It amazed him a bit to have met a creature as ruthless as, if not more so, than him.

His intense rage about Griffin, earlier, initially blinded him to the fact the siren hadn't bothered getting dressed before coming to his cabin. He noticed, however, when she walked over and sat on his feather bed, then began to finger-comb her hair. He got a bottle of his bloodied brandy and lounged in a chair; one leg draped over the armrest. He took a long pull and enjoyed the view — from a safe distance.

"Remind me never to feed on you."

"Oh, I will." She smiled, not embarrassed in the least bit.

Viktor nodded then got back to business. Although the drink heightened his senses enough to make the female very distracting, it also sharpened his mental faculties enough he could concentrate past the growing lust.

"You said that I would not like your vision. Why?"

"Because we're going to have to return to the Isle of Youth."

He frowned. "We've already established that Dorada is not there any longer. She hasn't been there for weeks."

"I didn't say she was there now. But the key to finding her is. The witch is still close enough to shield from me." The siren displayed only mild irritation. She was well fed, and her power flared. Her body emitted an enticing scent and looked ready and ripe for plundering.

Viktor shook his head to clear it. "What is the key?"

Belladonna patted the bed. "Come over here, and I'll whisper it in your ear," she purred teasingly.

He chuckled. "I don't think so, pet. I don't trust you that much. Now answer the question."

"You don't trust anyone, do you?" She pouted.

"It's what has kept me alive this long. A pirate's life is short." He refused to be distracted. "Now answer the fucking question. What is the key?"

She saw she wasn't going to be able to seduce him, for the moment, so she stopped trying. "Someone who belonged to her; find that person, and you'll have the link you need to hunt her down."

The vampire smiled. "That wench, Paella, did mention something about three old hags left behind to warn away anyone trying to find Dorada. Perhaps she can lead me to them."

"Perhaps she can." The siren's voice turned inexplicably icy. She stood abruptly and stomped out of the cabin, slamming the door behind her.

Grimm and Jon-Jon stood at the helm, watching over the ship's operations, when Viktor joined them.

"Turn the ship around, Mr. Jon."

He complied, spinning the wheel and barking orders to the riggers to adjust the sails for the course change.

"We're going back, Captain?" Grimm asked.

"Belladonna's vision implied we need someone from the island to lead us to the witch."

Grimm nodded. "You said this wouldn't be easy or simple, so I'm not surprised. Saw Belle a few minutes ago looking very angry. She mad at you again?"

Vik grinned. "Aye."

"You seem pleased about that."

"I wouldn't go to her," he replied smugly, then added, "And I don't think she likes that I intend to enlist Paella's aide again."

Grimm and Jon-Jon laughed with their captain. They had all seen how females didn't like to have their little games turned back on them.

Chapter 18

It took a few moments for Paella to figure out why she awoke. Dreams of the pirate haunted her nights. This night's vision seemed particularly vivid, and she didn't want to leave it. That he'd left her behind still stung sharply.

Her father complained that her work had fallen off ever since Viktor's visit. All she wanted to do was sleep. She couldn't bring herself to tell him it was because her lover always came back for her in her dreams. She wished it were true, instead of just a dream. She was convinced that the island truly was cursed. Nothing good had come since *Madre* Dorada had abandoned them. Even now, what looked to be a bad storm was blowing up.

She felt a compulsion to go down to the docks. Her father had repeatedly forbidden her to go there, but it was the hour before dawn, the time when even those in the brothels slept. No one was awake to stop her.

Wrapping a robe around her nightgown to protect her from the wind and night damp, she slipped out of the inn. It didn't take her long to reach the waterfront.

A shadow emerged from between a couple of warehouses. She stopped in her tracks, suddenly afraid. She had been foolish to come here. In these evil days, the docks had grown far more dangerous.

"Paella."

Viktor sensed the girl's fear. It enticed him. It also pleased him that she had come to his call. He caught her limp form, as she fainted. It wasn't that he cared about her, but she wouldn't be as useful, if she damaged herself.

A light slap brought her out of the faint. When she saw whose arms held her, her face lit up with joy.

"You came back for me! You came back for me! I knew you would! I have dreamed it every night since you left," she cried. "Why did you leave me?"

Viktor put a hand over her mouth to silence the giddy chattering. "Hush, pet; it was dangerous where I had to go. I could not take you into such peril," he lied. She wrapped her arms around him in a fierce hug. He patted her hair, giving his companions, lurking further back among the shadows, a smug look.

Grimm and Belladonna moved forward. He chuckled softly over Vik's latest conquest. Her expression, one of contemptuous disgust, bordered on open hostility.

Paella looked up at the sound of Grimm's chuckle. The look on his face didn't bother or offend her. She was used to men giving her lascivious leers. But the siren truly frightened her. Some instinct told her that was where the true danger lay. She clung a little tighter to Viktor's waist.

Gently, the vampire detached the nervous girl. "Paella, pet, do you remember telling me about some old women who were left behind to warn people?"

She looked up at him and was immediately lost in the soft glow of his eyes. Her will melted away as if it had never existed.

"*Si.*"

"Can you lead us to them?"

"*Si.*"

She turned and started walking away from the waterfront. Viktor and his companions followed.

The girl led the way through the port town and bordering farmlands. The sun rose just as they took a footpath into the jungle.

As the morning progressed, the air became steamy and oppressive. Paella and Viktor seemed oblivious to it. She didn't even notice when her nightgown and robe repeatedly caught and tore on the vegetation as they pushed through.

Grimm sweated a bit but ignored it. The most uncomfortable of the group was Belladonna. The siren seemed to grow more agitated the further they went into the jungle. She kept looking behind.

The land grew rocky and started to climb. At last, they broke out of the jungle cover for a moment. Grimm stretched a bit, enjoying the breeze they could now feel. He noticed the siren stopped and stared out over the top of the jungle. She hugged herself and seemed distracted.

"Belle?"

"It's so far away," she whispered.

"What is?"

She shivered. "The sea."

The pirate took note of her discomfort but did not comment on it. Who knew when the knowledge might come in useful?

"Come on, we need to catch up before they get out of sight," he said, turning to follow the captain.

Belladonna shook it off and rejoined the group.

"We are getting close," Paella announced in a dream-like voice.

The footpath led onto a wide, rocky ledge. Small caves riddled the cliff face next to the path. Vines draped down, masking several of them. Only occasional rock cooled drafts indicated some of the openings.

Progressing along the ledge, they noticed how some segments of vines seemed to glitter and sparkle in the sunlight. A closer look revealed a thin layer of what appeared to be gold on the stems and leaves.

Grimm reached out to break off a leaf. Belladonna put a hand on his arm to stop him.

"Don't," she said in response to his glare. "I smell a curse on them. It is old, but still powerful."

The exchange caught Viktor's attention. He stopped, Paella stopping with him. "Cursed?" The golden leaves held no temptation for him. He knew better than to meddle with unfamiliar magic. He was trying to counteract a curse, not draw down more magical malevolence on his head.

"*Si*," Paella spoke, pointing at the gold-coated vegetation. "To take that which has been blessed by *la Madre* Dorada without her personal permission is to call down evil and death."

He examined the vines without touching them. "You say these have been blessed. Do you know how it was done?"

"*Lagrimas de Oro*; tears of gold," she answered. "*La Madre* Dorada cries golden tears. When given with her blessing, they bring healing, wealth and great fortune. If they are stolen, they bring only death."

Grimm put his hands behind his back to fight the temptation to snatch a leaf anyway. He probably would have discounted a curse as a story concocted by superstitious locals, if the siren hadn't warned him, as well. He decided it was best not to take the gamble.

"Well, I think we just found out what you will have to get from this Sister," Belle stated. "I wonder what her price will be."

"We have to find her first," Vik reminded her. "Lead on, pet."

The girl obediently turned and resumed their trek.

Within an hour, they came to the end of the ledge. A large cave opened before them, but the golden vines completely blocked the entrance. The coating on these plants was the heaviest they had yet seen. Gleaming bones peeked out from the dense tendrils in stark white against the glittering gold, apparently the remains of those who had tried to force their way through and become entangled.

"How do we get past this?" Grimm asked. "Do we just hack through with our swords?"

Belladonna held her hands a few inches from the barrier, trying to feel out the magic. "I don't think that would be a good idea." She yelped and jumped back, as a tendril suddenly whipped out toward her. "I don't think her magic likes the feel of mine."

"You need a key," Paella stated. "*La Madre* Dorada is not here to welcome or expel. The only way in is to use a key."

"And do you have this key, pet?"

She shook her head then turned to Viktor. "You do. I saw it hanging around your neck."

The others looked at their captain, baffled. The vampire knew what the girl meant, however. Old Mother Celie told him it was a key, when she gave it to him.

He reached into his shirt and pulled out the silver-bound, milky crystal. It began to glow, softly at first, but brightening as he moved closer to the gold-drenched vines.

The outer tendrils went into a brief flurry of motion, as if they were going to react to the crystal the same way they had reacted to the siren. Then, they parted like a curtain, revealing the dark cave entrance.

Viktor grasped the girl by the arm and pulled her along with him. She now seemed reluctant to go any further. Whimpering, she clung tightly to the vampire. The vines snapped out for her, the leaves making an almost hissing noise, but the crystal's glow repelled them.

Belle and Grimm moved to follow, but the seemingly angry vine curtain snapped shut the second the vampire cleared the barrier and cut them off. Only lightning reflexes saved either of them from being snared by the writhing vegetation.

The siren made silent note of how Grimm had moved with an inhuman speed that almost rivaled hers or Viktor's. Sniffing the air, she could sense a faint trace of magic around him. Though vaguely familiar, she couldn't quite place where she'd encountered it before.

Grimm took no notice of her attention on him.

"Viktor!"

"I am unharmed, Hezekiah," Viktor's voice came from the other side of the vines. "I don't think you were meant to face this part with me."

Only Belladonna's touch on his arm kept Grimm from drawing his blade to hack his way to his captain.

"Let go of me, bitch!" he snarled. "I'm supposed to protect him!"

"So am I," she replied with uncharacteristic calm. "But, as I'm sure you know, since you've known him longer, he's quite capable of taking care of himself. Besides, look there."

He looked where she pointed. A small lizard wandered a little too close to the golden vines. Without warning, thin tendrils whipped out and wrapped around the creature. Some of the finer filaments pierced into it between its scales. Before their eyes, the vines reduced the lizard to a shriveled, mummified carcass.

"Damn."

"Exactly."

Viktor smiled to himself at the loyalty he heard in Grimm's voice. Hezekiah was probably the only person, other than old Celie — and Jim Rigger, he truly loved and trusted. He had never given his first mate the special rum he used to enslave his crew. Hezekiah's loyalty was the one thing he never entertained doubts of.

Using the glow of the crystal, he examined the cavern around him. Toward the side, he noticed an area the light seemed not to touch. He moved toward the crevice, dragging the girl with him.

"Now, let's find these old hags, so I can be about my business."

They followed the narrow passageway as it twisted and turned. After what seemed like forever, it opened into another cavern.

What he found there did not please him.

Two corpses lay on the cavern floor. Only their ragged calicos identified them as having once been female. A third crone, reclining against the cave wall, looked to be only a few breaths away from death.

She pointed a bony finger at Paella. "Traitor!" she croaked. "Traitor!"

The girl cowered, trembling, behind the vampire. "No!" she sobbed into the back of his shirt.

"Betrayer of Dorada!" the hag continued to accuse. "You dare bring this evil creature to this holy place!"

"I had no choice," she mumbled. "He is my master now. He told me to bring him to you. He seeks *la Madre* Dorada."

The crone opened her mouth in a toothless grin that more closely resembled a death grimace. "You'll not find her here, Dark One," she cackled. "You are too late. Dorada felt your pet witch and saw your coming. She fled long before you arrived."

"You tell me nothing I do not already know, old woman." He smiled grimly. "However, my pet witch, as you call her, informed me that one who used to belong to Dorada could lead me to the Sister."

The old woman faltered a bit, fear finally registering in her eyes. "You know of the Sisters of Power?"

"Aye." He advanced on her slowly. "And you are going to help me locate Dorada."

"Heh, I am not the one you want, Dark One. I do not know where she has gone, only that she fled. Besides, I still belong to Dorada. I have not betrayed her or sold myself to darkness." She eyed Paella pointedly.

The girl stood, staring at the ground. "I did not know. I never meant to betray *la Madre*."

"Too late for that, ungrateful little slut," the crone spat. "Dorada picked you out to teach her ways to you. You were her chosen," she began to gasp for breath, "her — favorite. Now, she will have — to choose anew, because you — you sold your soul — to darkness — for a few — moments with this Dark One — between your legs."

The old woman collapsed into a coughing fit. It ended with a rattling, strangling breath. As silence returned, it was obvious the crone had died.

Viktor looked at Paella in a new light. The old crone's words made it plain that Belladonna's vision indicated her, not the hags, as the one who could lead him to the first of the Sisters he was bound to seek out.

And she was about to attempt suicide.

"*Madre* Dorada forgive me!" she screamed. She fell to her knees and began chanting in a language Viktor did not know.

Golden vines started growing into the chamber. They soon choked the passageway. They flowed along the ground, quickly covering the remains of the three hags. Viktor stared as the vegetation's onslaught reduced the bodies to naked bones.

Paella screamed as the first of the tendrils wrapped around her lower legs and outstretched arms. The flesh of her limbs began to shrivel and blacken.

Viktor held the crystal out, letting its glow drive back the vines. He grasped her about the waist and pulled her free of the tendrils. She shrieked in pain and horror. Already, her hands and feet were no more than shriveled claws.

"Be silent, woman!" he growled in irritation. She immediately ceased her screeching. "I believe it is time we left." He hefted the crippled girl over his shoulder and turned toward the passageway. The vines literally tore themselves away from the rock in order to avoid the glow.

He forged his way through and out of the cave altogether. His companions stood several yards back down the cliff path. Both looked very relieved to see him alive and apparently unharmed.

"Let's get back to the ship," he ordered, striding past them and back the way they had come.

By the time they reached the populated areas, darkness covered the land. They kept to the shadows. No one saw them, as they made their way back to the water.

Now, back on board the *Incubus*, it both worried and angered Viktor how the wasting seemed to spread up the girl's legs. He called Belladonna to his cabin.

The siren allowed her hand to hover over the slowly dying girl. "I can stop the rot, but I cannot repair the damage she has already done to herself."

"The chanting; so, she called the vines to her."

"Yes. I smell the same magic coming from her as I sensed when the vines exploded into growth. It is very similar to the scent of Dorada's magic."

He stroked his beard, deep in thought, as he observed the siren working to heal the girl enough to keep her alive. He wondered if Paella had been destined to succeed Dorada. Did the Sisters of Power pass on their magic and mantle of power to chosen apprentices? Or did they live forever, just sharing their power in order to work it in places beyond their physical reach? Mother Celie had been an old woman all his life. Yet now that he thought about it, she had not truly aged. She appeared no older the last time he had seen her than she looked when he had been a boy.

"Ah, there is the culprit," Belle cried triumphantly, interrupting his thoughts. She took a small pair of tongs borrowed from Anvil, the ship's smith, pinched the nail of Paella's left big toe, and braced her free hand on the girl's ankle.

"This is going to hurt — a lot." She gave no other warning before yanking the toenail off the shriveled foot.

Paella grasped the feather mattress in a death grip, her eyes bugging and back arching. Her mouth opened wide, but no sound emitted. Hate, pain, and fear shone in the girl's eyes. She watched Belladonna use a small brush to remove the tiny bit of vine tendril which had been under the nail. Belle secured the fragment in a silver snuffbox.

"That's the best I can do. I'm surprised she didn't scream."

"She can't, it would seem; hasn't uttered a sound of any kind, since I ordered her silent, before escaping the cave."

"Interesting; she's in a lot of pain. I can smell it rolling off her, as I'm sure you can, too. I have heard that humans have certain potions which can dull pain. If you have something like that, it would be good to give her some. She will probably make more sense, when you ask her about Dorada."

"Point taken; that will be all, Belle," he dismissed her, as he went over to the sideboard. He was not pleased to see she had not moved by the time he retrieved a glass and bottle.

"That. Will. Be. All."

Glaring, Belladonna stalked to the door. She stared balefully at Viktor. He returned the look, making it plain that he would not tolerate disobedience.

With a disgruntled snort, the siren exited the captain's cabin, slamming the door behind her.

Viktor poured a half glass of some of the finest brandy he had on board. He sat on the bed, next to the girl. Paella scooched away from him as best as her crippled limbs would let her. Her hatred lessened as soon as Belladonna left. She still reeked of fear and pain, however.

The scent assailed Vik's vampire senses, drawing the predator in him to the forefront. That had been the main reason he had ordered Belle out. She was just as much a predator as he. The vampire did not want to share his prey. If he lost control and fed, the girl would merely turn vampire; but if the siren lost control....

"That is no way to be, pet," he chided gently. "Come over here and drink this."

She obeyed. She had no choice. Too late, she realized she had placed herself in the vampire's thrall.

Seeing the face she made at the first burn of the brandy, he advised her, "It is better to drink it quickly, if you are not accustomed to it."

The girl sobbed into the glass, as she drained it. Once finished, she held the glass out in shaking hands. He steadied the glass with his own hand and refilled it. He continued to steady it for her, as she drank deeply. Obviously, the claws her hands had shrunken into made holding the glass difficult.

Her eyes grew bleary, the pain leaching out of them. Viktor wiped away a drop of brandy from her lip with his calloused thumb. He reached around her shoulder and pulled her to nestle against his side, then licked the drop from his thumb.

"Are you feeling better now, pet?"

She nodded drowsily.

"Good," he smiled down at her. "I am going to free you to speak again, and you are going to tell me how I can find *Madre* Dorada."

A single tear slid down Paella's cheek. She called on the magic Dorada had taught her and used it to locate her former mentor for her new master.

Chapter 19

Belladonna stood by the railing, brooding. She knew the little witchling was vital to Viktor's success, but it ate at her territorial instincts to have the girl on board. The girl appeared plainly in her earlier vision, a detail she'd purposely withheld from Viktor. She had harbored the hope one of the hags would have sufficed instead.

The stench of unwashed pirate let her know she was about to be approached. The creaking of ropes and plop of mucus on the deck let her know it was Sniff.

"Go away troll."

Ignoring that, he swung down from the rigging and perched on the railing by her. "What's troubling ye, lass? Cap'n neglecting a fine wench like yourself for that little tart?" He grinned, hitting much too close to the truth for Belle's comfort.

She gave him a murderous look.

Sniff's grin widened, revealing his lack of teeth. That he currently wore his false nose hanging by its ties about his neck rather than covering his open nasal cavity only made the sight of him more unsettling.

"Y'now, I've got something that might help ye ease yer itch, until the Cap'n gets bored with that girl." He winked.

Belle scowled skeptically. "What?"

He undid the drawstring on his breeches and pulled the waistband out. "This."

Out of morbid curiosity, she peeked. One glance was enough. She took a few steps back. "That thing is grotesque!"

"It drags the deck, darlin'." Sniff cackled proudly. "Just 'cause I don't have legs or a nose, doesn't mean I can't make a wench sing like all the angels in Heaven."

The siren sneered in disgust at the thought. Turning, she stalked off, nearly colliding with Jon-Jon in her haste to leave.

The second mate watched her until she went below, then, went over to join Sniff. "Ho, Sniff! What was that all about?" he asked, pulling a flask from his vest.

"She wants me," the rigging rat replied smugly. He reached for the flask, once Jon-Jon had a swig.

"Heh, you been drinkin' seawater, man," he laughed. "Plain as day, she can't stand the sight of you."

Sniff wiped his mouth and handed the flask back. "She's just afraid she can't handle my sea serpent."

Jon-Jon laughed even harder. "You been bragging about that whale dick o' yers again? Better be careful mate. She's liable to bite it clean off."

"Not in one bite, she won't," Sniff winked.

Viktor joined Grimm at the helm. The two men stood in comfortable silence with each other. As they stood there, each understood how the other felt at that moment, even without any magical or blood bond. The smell of the salt breeze and the feel of the ship beneath their feet plowing through the waves were intoxicating.

After a seeming eternity, Viktor stepped to take the wheel from the helmsman.

"Wind's in our favor. Have the riggers set full sails. Once we're clear of these islands, we'll be heading south southeast."

Grimm strode to the railing overlooking the deck. "Riggers aloft!" he bellowed. "Look lively, ye sorry bastards! I want all sails set ten minutes ago!"

Once satisfied with the level of activity, he stepped back to rejoin Viktor at the helm. "We have a destination, Captain?"

"Aye. Bitch is making for the Islas de los Roques, probably one of the smaller islands." He nodded, making a slight adjustment of the wheel.

"That's further than the Caymans, but not too far," Grimm frowned. "She's had plenty of time to get hidden and fortified."

Vik smirked, "You would think so. But, it would seem she can't work her magic at sea like she can on land. She's also not a very good judge of vessels or seamanship."

The first mate raised an eyebrow, hoping his captain would give a very interesting tale of how he came by his knowledge of their prey. He was not disappointed.

"Little Paella has proven a wealth of information. I do believe her untrained magic may almost be as strong as the Sister's." He smiled. "Possibly, it is stronger, since she can work hers on both land and sea. She was able to pinpoint Dorada, before the witch could shut her out. As we speak, Lazarus is aboard Dorada's vessel, keeping an eye on her."

Grimm wondered at that. He did not doubt Viktor, but he couldn't see how the demon cat could have gotten onto a ship they were nowhere near. He still didn't know how the cat had gotten on the *Montcrief* for that matter. He was unaware of Lazarus' ability to take raven form, and Viktor was not inclined to share that bit of information at the moment.

Sniffing the air, the vampire sensed a sea change. What his enhanced senses told him pleased him greatly. It would speed their passage up considerably.

"Big storm brewing; it will be here by nightfall," he announced. "We can ride the winds before it and cut maybe a day off our voyage."

The only ones who did not enjoy the speeds the *Incubus* attained were Belladonna and Paella. The speed failed to impress the siren. She could swim faster. To prove it, she leapt into the sea and scouted ahead for uncharted reefs and shallows. That was the excuse she used, anyway. In truth, she found herself increasingly irritated by the kidnapped girl's presence on board.

Paella, on the other hand, felt too seasick to enjoy the ride. The storm made the sea very rough. It was more motion than she cared to experience outside of bed. She felt positively wretched. Not for the last time, she wished her pirate lover had let the vines finish her off.

Belle returned to the ship about half a day before they came in sight of the islands. She considered her news too important to waste time getting dressed. Rather, she went straight to the captain's cabin.

Her knock received no response. At first, she thought no one occupied the cabin, but then, she heard a soft, guttural moan. It irritated her to think Viktor was pleasing himself with the little barmaid, when there were much more important things to attend to.

"Viktor, I am not going to wait for you to finish with her!" she hollered through the door, as she opened it up. "This cannot wait…."

She saw no sign of the vampire in the cabin. The moans came from the crouched girl, kneeling over a chamber pot. She raised a waxen face and looked at the siren.

"Please, *señorita*, ask him to make the boat stop moving so much," she pled. "Why did he have to bring me here?"

Belladonna sneered down at the girl. "It was not my idea to bring you. If he did not need you to find the Sister, I am sure he would have left you to rot in those cursed vines."

"I wish he had," Paella moaned. "I feel *muy mal.*"

"So do I," the siren muttered, as she left the cabin.

She finally found Viktor in Grimm's cabin. The smoke from the cigars they enjoyed filled the cabin. Belle sneezed a few times before becoming acclimated to the smell. She just didn't understand why humans enjoyed burning dried plants and inhaling the smoke.

"You are not dressed, pet," Viktor stated the obvious.

"I don't mind, Vik." Grimm leered at the siren.

The vampire chuckled. "You wouldn't, Hezekiah. What is so important that it couldn't wait for clothing?"

"There is a bad reef ahead, about an hour away at the current speed."

He gave her a look that said the news was not worth such haste.

In response, the siren walked over and sat in Grimm's lap, draping her arms around him and smiling coyly at Viktor. Hezekiah froze, trying very hard to keep any expression from his face. Belladonna just put him in a very precarious position with his captain. Viktor had killed men for less.

The vampire gazed coldly at them. It infuriated him that she would so brazenly flirt with his first mate. Even though he had never bedded her, Viktor considered the siren to be his and off limits to any other male.

"Oh," she blinked in mock innocence, "did I forget to mention that the idiots Dorada has sailing for her have run their ship across the worst part of the reef? They are slowly sinking and have no hope of making the island they were headed for."

Quickly shifting his mental tack, he smiled coolly. "How fortuitous; we shall have to offer assistance."

Grimm stood and tried to disengage from the siren, but she would not let go. Plainly, she enjoyed tormenting the two pirates. She gave a musical laugh which fired both men's desire.

Grimm found himself starting to embrace her, rather than trying to get her off him. He didn't seem to be able to stop himself.

Belladonna molded herself against the pirate, reaching up to pull him in closer for a kiss. It was too much for Viktor.

He snatched her by her hair. It broke her concentration and her grip on his first mate. As Grimm stumbled back, shaking his head to clear it of the siren's spell, Viktor pinned her hands behind her back and used her hair to force her head back, exposing her throat.

"I will not have you throwing yourself at my crew," he growled, eyes and fangs flashing.

Grimm quietly backed away from the pair, grateful his captain's ire was directed at the siren rather than him. What had he been thinking, giving in to advances from one of Viktor's wenches? But then, Belladonna was no ordinary wench.

Belle arched her back, not minding the discomfort of the position Viktor held her in. She found it exciting that the vampire was physically stronger than her. It was a new experience.

"What are you going to do, my Captain?" she chuckled throatily. "You cannot feed on me."

"No," he smiled cruelly," but I can do much worse." He could smell her lust. He kissed her fiercely but used the leverage on her wrists to prevent her body from touching his.

She moaned in pleasure and frustration. It was exquisite torture being held immobile, as his lips left her mouth and trailed hot breath down her throat to her shoulder. She shuddered with a small whimper.

Without warning, Viktor flung her away from him. As she picked herself up off the deck, he told her in a voice like ice, "Go back to your cabin and put some clothes on."

Ignoring the order, she approached him with a mind to resume what they had started. He slapped her backhanded, momentarily stunning her.

"Do as you are told, woman. Mr. Grimm, come with me. We have a ship in need of our assistance. I want to get to Dorada, before she can get to land and have her magic at full strength."

A few of the newest crewmembers, taken from Lord Ferguson's ship, were familiar with the waters surrounding the islands they now approached. Grimm picked out the best seaman among them and set him to pilot them through the reefs. It didn't hurt that the tide was rising, making for better draft for their ship.

Satisfied he left the ship in capable hands, Viktor returned to his cabin to prepare for his meeting with Dorada. In his experience, charm often worked better than force when trying to get a female to cooperate. Given that *Madre* Dorada was a powerful witch, he reasoned charm would be the better route.

With that in mind, he set about picking out his best finery. He personally considered such frippery impractical for day-to-day wear and use, but there were times when appearance was more important than practicality.

While he rummaged through his trunks, he picked out a scarlet velvet dress which caught his eye a while back. He made a habit of keeping a few feminine garments on hand. They made excellent presents for whores who particularly pleased him. Keep them happy, and they would keep him happy.

Dress in hand, he approached Paella. The girl lay on the bed, on her side, facing away from the door. Dark circles under her eyes marked her pale, tear-stained face. Sweat soaked and matted her dark hair. She still wore the tattered, dirty nightgown she'd worn since he'd taken her from her home.

"Wake up, pet," he said softly. "It's time to get cleaned up and dressed."

Blinking up blearily at him, she tried to sit up. The earlier seasickness had weakened her too much, however. "Can't I just sleep a little more?" she asked.

Viktor reached around her shoulders and sat her up, then, began removing her soiled garments. "No, pet, it's time to be about business. We must go see *Madre* Dorada. Her ship is sinking, and she needs our help."

She started to struggle feebly. "No! Please, I cannot face her! I have betrayed *la Madre*!"

He shushed her but found himself having to take her will to stop her writhing. Her fear of Dorada proved almost enough to break his hold on her.

"No time for protests, pet. Be quiet and be still!"

He managed to get her washed up and dressed. Her hair, he braided then coiled about her head, fastening it with jeweled pins.

The dress made her appear even paler, almost deathly white. It matched the crimson coat and brocade vest he had picked out for himself, however. To finish out his ensemble, Viktor tied his shoulder length black hair with a velvet ribbon. He placed three ruby studs in his left earlobe and three small gold loops in his right.

Before long, the lookout spotted Dorada's ship. Jon-Jon knocked at the cabin door to alert the captain.

"Enter, Mr. Jon."

"We've found her, Cap'n. We'll have to use the boats to get to her. Tide's almost at high, but we're too deep to get close," Jon-Jon reported.

"Very well." He eyed the man's appearance. As usual, his scalp and face looked stubbly and in need of another shave. He wore no shirt under his leather vest, displaying his tattoos. "You look to be clean enough, but still intimidating. Take Paella to the boat and wait for me."

"Aye, Cap'n."

Viktor found Grimm still with the helmsman. He wore one of his better coats but had made no further efforts to gussy up. "I'm not the one who has to impress her," he reasoned. Vik ceded the point.

Grimm picked out a handful of strong crewmen to accompany their boarding party. Though not a full battle compliment, they would be able to handle matters if Dorada's crew gave them any trouble.

Belladonna soon joined them. Every man on board not occupied with ship's operations, and several who were, followed her with their eyes. She made an impressive sight. She wore a pair of leather breeches shrunken to mold to her like a second skin. She'd taken a vest similar to Jon-Jon's and cut it short, leaving her waist fully exposed. The silver snuffbox containing the golden vine fragment hung from a cord between the swell of her breasts. And, she had pulled her hair back with a strip of leather, then, separated it into four braids.

To distract himself, Grimm yelled at the crew. "Back to work, ye lazy barnacles! Get yer eyes back in yer heads and mind those lines!" His outburst had the desired effect of getting the crew back to their tasks.

Belle leaned her butt against the rail and smiled at Viktor. She was fully aware of the effect she had and enjoyed it immensely.

He stared blandly at her, refusing to show how temptingly distracting he found her. "Are you determined to provoke me, pet?"

She glanced down at the one reaction he couldn't hide. "I'm a siren; don't you read?" She chuckled throatily.

He grunted in response. "Get to the boat. It is time to meet Dorada. I'll deal with you later."

"Promise?"

Disorganized chaos greeted them aboard the wrecked vessel. People running everywhere, several trying to perform tasks that countered each other made navigating the deck treacherous. Those who saw the pirates either panicked and tried to flee or just stood and stared. No one challenged them the right to be there.

"Pathetic excuse for a crew," Grimm muttered. "They don't even try to resist."

"You sound disappointed, Hezekiah." Viktor smiled wryly.

"Disgusted is more like it, Captain."

Belladonna scanned the scurrying people. "They look and act like food."

"Aye, but they belong to the Sister," Vik reminded her. "I do not think she will be very cooperative, if we feed on her minions."

The siren sighed but did not press the matter. She had reasons of her own for not wanting to anger Dorada which had nothing to do with the vampire's quest.

Deciding he didn't want to waste time searching the ship for Dorada, he grabbed one of the frightened men running about. It took giving the man a shake just to get his attention.

"Where is the captain of this vessel?"

"No captain, *señor*, only *la Madre*," he gibbered distractedly.

"And where is she?"

"*La Madre* is locked in, *señor*. She will not come out! The storm came, and she locked the door, then we wrecked. She has forsaken us!"

Viktor gave him a light slap to stop the panicky yammering. Unfortunately, it wasn't light enough. The man's body went instantly limp, as he was knocked unconscious. He let the man drop to the deck with a disgusted sneer.

"Worthless lot; so, she's locked herself in her cabin. Just like a woman," he grumbled.

The group made their way below decks, looking for a locked door. It didn't take long to find on the relatively small vessel.

A female voice immediately answered the vampire's knock. "Go from this place, creature of darkness. Dorada has no magic for you."

"Oh, but I think you do, *Madre*," Viktor's voice was at its most charming, a tone which had always served him well with women in the past. "Besides, I have something of yours." He waved Jon-Jon to bring Paella near the door.

The voice countered, "You have nothing that belongs to me. That unclean child is yours now, body and soul. I forsake her as she forsook me."

Paella sobbed and hid her face against Jon-Jon's chest.

With a nod from Viktor, Belladonna stepped to the door. Her voice rang with power, as the slowly encroaching seawater sloshed about her bare feet. "My Captain may not hold anything that belongs to you, earth-witch, but I do; and you are in my element."

There was silence for a moment. When Dorada spoke again, they heard a trace of fear. "What do you seek, sea-witch?"

"Let us in and deal with my Captain, then we will discuss terms between ourselves. My business is different from his."

"So be it."

They heard the latch draw back, and the door swung open. The Sister sat alone in the cabin. Dead, shriveled vines draped the grand window, casting the room in gloom. Seawater swirled around on the floor.

Viktor offered Belle his arm and stepped into the room. The siren released his arm and stepped aside, leaving him to speak with the earth-witch. As the rest of their party entered, he took one step forward and bowed, but never took his eyes off the middle-aged woman. Her returning stare was closed off, revealing nothing.

"I have been looking for you for quite some time, *Madre* Dorada."

"This I know, Dark One. It is why I fled my island." She smiled at his appearance. "I am not so easily seduced as others, but I am flattered by the effort. I spoke truth, when I said I have no magic to offer you, however." She waved her hand around at the dead plants. No trace of life or glimmer of gold was to be seen.

"Would you offer, if you had it to give?"

"You have passed the first test, albeit through treachery and betrayal, and have found me. *Si*. I would be bound to aide you, but I would not wish to," she answered.

"Yes, Mother Celie told me that most of you would not want to help," Viktor remembered. "Why is that?"

To his surprise, she gave him a straight answer. "If you are the One, then you may be the end. If your quest succeeds, all will change, and nothing will be as it was. If you fail, then all is lost; if you truly are the One."

"There is that 'the One' business again," he growled. "What are you people talking about?"

Dorada gave him a malicious smile. "It does not matter. It is already too late. The salt water has killed my plants and my magic."

"If you were on dry land, you could restore your power," Belladonna stated.

"Not without a seed. I cannot grow what I do not have," the earth-witch replied in a tired tone. "All is ending. Leave me and mine to perish here."

The siren smiled slyly, fingering the silver box hanging around her neck. "You have not yet asked what it is of yours that I hold in my possession," she purred. Once sure she had Dorada's full attention, she continued, "If there was a way to regenerate your magic, would you?"

The older woman licked her lips, her eyes drawn to the snuffbox. "What do you have in that? I can feel it calling to me."

"Would you regenerate your magic?"

"*Si.*" Her eyes shone with a manic gleam. "Even if this Dark One succeeds and changes everything, I would wish to be at my full strength when the changes come."

Belle dangled the little box by its cord. "I have in here a tendril of one of your golden vines."

"Liar!" Dorada hissed. "Not even you, sea-witch, could touch my vines without bearing their mark upon your flesh."

The siren's laughter rang through the cabin, raising gooseflesh on the men present. "You think me so great a fool as to touch your cursed vines myself? Look around you, earth-witch. You will see the courier I obtained this from."

Paella still huddled in on herself. She hoped to avoid Dorada's attention. The skirt hid her ravaged feet, and her huddling made her ruined hands difficult to see.

Viktor noticed this.

"Show your hands and feet, pet."

Reluctantly, she used the blackened claws to lift the dress enough to reveal her shriveled feet. Dorada gave her a look of scathing reproach.

"You are more fool than I realized, Paella. Not only did you sell yourself to this creature of darkness, but you also risked your life to steal some of my magic for him. You took what I taught you and used it against me." As an afterthought, she laughed harshly, "You did not pay well enough attention to your lessons, though. You did not ward off my vines in time to escape their hunger. I see I chose poorly, when I selected you."

The girl just kept shaking her head no, tears streaming down her face.

Weeping women never affected Viktor. He'd usually been the cause of the tears. It came as a surprise to Grimm and Jon-Jon, when he spoke up to defend the girl.

"Leave her alone." His tone rang dangerously low. "She did not try to steal your magic for me. Even I know stolen magic is of no use to anyone. She bears the marks of your vines, because she used what you taught her to call them to her. In a bid to gain your forgiveness, she tried to kill herself! The fragment Belladonna holds was lodged under her toenail. If Paella had not acted as she did, you would not have access to a 'seed' to replenish your powers!"

Dorada sneered at him, "I do not believe you. She still lives. I know what my vines are capable of. If she had truly meant to sacrifice herself, she would not be here."

The vampire reached into his shirt and pulled out the crystal. It flared as bright as the full moon in the dim cabin. Dorada's eyes grew wide. Her voice was hushed, "You carry the Elder's Stone. None of the Sister's magic can stand against it. Please, put it away."

Satisfied with her change in attitude, he complied. Turning to Belle, he waved her on. "I believe you were negotiating."

She nodded acknowledgment and returned her attention to Dorada. "Do you now believe this is what I say it is?"

The witch nodded silently.

"Good. I will give this to you, but you have to do something for me."

"What is your price, sea-witch?"

Belladonna smiled smugly. "I want you to take your little witchling apprentice back and keep her."

The look on Dorada's face said she did not like the condition. Before she could protest, however, the vampire seized the siren by the arm and spun her around.

"You bargain with that which does not belong to you. The girl is mine!"

She didn't even flinch. "She has served her purpose to you. In her current state, she is now nothing more than a hindrance and a burden to you. You know you would eventually grow bored with her and throw her away. At least this way, you will gain something from it," she stated matter-of-fact.

He bared his fangs at her in a snarl, galled by the fact she was right. He had already tired of the girl in his bed. She was not suited for shipboard life.

The fact that he did not seem to want to part with her erstwhile apprentice appealed to Dorada. She thought the girl unsalvageable, but if it would annoy the pirate….

"I accept your terms."

Viktor and Belladonna returned their attention to the earth-witch. "I have not agreed to release her back to you," he reminded her.

"In truth, you cannot release her, at least not fully," she corrected him. "After all, she now bears your taint. However, you need my magic, which I cannot restore without the tendril your sea-witch has preserved. Although she does not say so, I can see she does not wish to share you with Paella. You must choose, Dark One. Which do you want more, the girl or my magic? It matters not to me either way."

He narrowed his eyes at her. "Fine; you can have the wench. Mr. Jon, put her down."

The second mate complied, setting her on her feet. Paella let out a small cry of pain, as her full weight went on her crippled feet. She clung to the pirate's arm to keep her balance.

"Come here, Paella," Dorada ordered. "I accept you back into my service."

The girl looked up at that, a small glimmer of hope in her eyes. She took two steps, before collapsing to her knees in the slowly deepening water. Determined not to lose this slim chance at forgiveness, she began crawling. The sodden skirt made it difficult, but she finally managed to reach her former mistress' side.

The witch finally softened a bit. Reaching down, she lifted Paella's face. "I forgive you child. You were never prepared to resist a creature like him. I can see how you would fall prey." She returned her gaze to the siren. "I have upheld my part of the agreement. Give me the tendril."

"As agreed." Belladonna removed the snuffbox and handed it by its cord to Dorada. She took great care to keep their hands from coming into contact with each other.

Chapter 20

A shiver of power rippled through the cabin as Dorada closed her hand around the snuffbox. "You did well to encase the tendril in silver, sea-witch. The magic is still strong and viable."

Turning to Viktor, she asked, "What price do you name to transport my people and me to the nearest island, Dark One? I must have arable soil to cultivate my power."

"I understand." He nodded. "Provisions for my men, any gold you have, and five of your men as blood stock for myself and my vampires. You have my word that their deaths will be swift, and I will not turn them."

Dorada considered carefully, before answering. "Provisions for your crew, the gold, three men, and I will heal Paella and give you one last night with her."

"Make it four men."

"As you wish."

Viktor nodded to Grimm. The first mate went back up on deck and gave the signal to send over the boats.

As soon as Dorada appeared on deck on Viktor's arm, the chaos among her people ceased. They practically flocked around her. Smiling benignly, she reassured them, "The Dark One and his crew have agreed to carry us to our new home. Follow their instructions."

A few did question this. "*Madre*, didn't we flee our home to escape the Dark One?"

"*Si*," she admitted. "That was a test for him. I had to know he was who he was meant to be. If he had been false, he would not have caught us."

They seemed to accept this explanation. Silently, she made note of the ones who dared question her, however. She would select the ones she would give to the vampire from among them. She preferred blind obedience in her followers.

It took a full day to make the transfer from Dorada's vessel to the *Incubus*. It was another half day's sailing south of their current position to the nearest island.

Luckily, the natural harbor proved deep enough to accommodate the large pirate ship.

It took far less time to get the earth-witch's people off the ship than it had taken to get them aboard. Most of the cargo they brought remained with the pirates.

Although small and uninhabited, the island showed signs of abandoned camps. The crewmen familiar with that area informed their captain only native fishermen or the occasional smuggler used the camps. With nothing worth trading, the island merited no permanent settlement to such folk. Lush vegetation, however, made it perfect for Dorada's purposes.

Dorada invited Viktor and Belladonna to observe the ceremony and ritual she would use to establish her power in this new place. The earth-witch only requested they watch from the edge of the clearing it would be performed in. She did not want them so close their magic could interfere with or influence hers.

It started just as the sun touched the horizon. Dorada entered the clearing from the east, facing the setting sun. Two attendants flanked her. In silence, they removed her garments. They began smearing her naked body with a pungent mud mixed with special herbs and oils. At that moment, Viktor abhorred his extra-sensitive sense of smell. He found the aroma mildly nauseating.

When she was fully coated with the stuff, another attendant handed her a silver trowel. She walked to the center of the clearing. Two posts, about four feet apart, had been set there earlier in the day. Using the trowel, she dug a hole about a foot wide and half a foot deep. Laying the trowel aside, she held out her left hand. The attendant brought her the silver snuffbox.

Dorada opened it and poured the golden tendril out into her hand. She sang to it softly. The bit of vegetation writhed in response, verifying the magic was fully preserved and viable. Smiling, she carefully placed the tendril in the center of the hole, but she did not cover it yet.

Instead, she stood and stepped back two steps. When she spoke, her voice seemed to carry the essence of the earth itself.

"The seed has been planted. Now, it must be fertilized."

On cue, two of her more muscular followers entered the clearing. They held a struggling nude man between them. Though obviously drugged, he still struggled enough they strained to drag him into the clearing. Finally, they got him to the posts.

Dorada spoke again, her voice soothing him and causing him to cease his struggles. "Peace, Tomás. You have been chosen for a great honor. Do not be afraid."

Viktor recognized the man as one of those who questioned the witch back on the ship. He had a feeling things were not going to end well for Tomás.

"You are young," she continued talking, keeping him mesmerized, while his escorts tied his wrists and ankles to the posts.

"You are virile." She ran a hand down his chest and stomach. His body reacted when she cupped him.

"And you are eager to serve *la Madre*." She chuckled, pleased with his erection.

Her attendant brought her a very wicked looking blade. With one swift stroke, she completely castrated him.

Time seemed to stand still for a moment. Then, Tomás took in a sharp breath and let out a shrill scream. He lost consciousness.

Dorada laid the severed sex organ and testicles in the hole on top of the vine tendril. Taking up the trowel again, she covered them over, as if planting flowers in a kitchen garden. Once that was done, she stood again.

"The seed is planted and fertilized," she intoned. "Now it is watered by blood."

She began chanting. Her followers joined in the chant. It reached a crescendo, and a vine sprouted from the planting.

Viktor and Belladonna realized the chanting kept rhythm with the sacrifice's heartbeat. With each pulse, blood spurted from his ruined groin onto the young shoot. As his heart slowed, so did the chant. When the sacrifice was almost dead, the full moon rose behind the witch, bathing everything in a cleansing, silver light.

The chant ceased with a triumphant cry. The green vine leapt onto the corpse, completely enveloping it in mere seconds. With dizzying speed, the vine flowered, then, developed two purplish-black fruits.

Dorada reverently plucked the fruits and held them high in the moonlight. There seemed to be a black glow about them as if they absorbed the moonlight and emitted an anti-light in response. She turned to face the vampire and the siren.

"Follow."

She turned and exited the clearing.

They joined the earth-witch in the shelter her followers had fashioned for her. The fruits rested in a basket on a table near the chair she sat in. She now wore a robe but had yet to clean off the ceremonial mud.

At a signal from her, an attendant helped the still crippled Paella in. "As I promised, you shall have one last night with my apprentice."

"You also agreed to heal her," he pointed out.

"Patience, Dark One," she chided. "I must restore my own power, before I can restore Paella."

"I don't care if you restore her or not," Belle muttered sulkily. She was not happy with the terms of Viktor's bargain.

He ignored her outburst. "I thought that whole business back in the clearing was to restore your power."

The earth-witch smiled, "That was but the first part of it. Full restoration will take at least one moon to complete." Seeing he was not pleased with that bit of information, she added, "Do not worry. I will be able to restore Paella's limbs tonight."

She stood and retrieved the fruit from the basket. She handed one to Paella.

"Eat."

"*Gracias, Madre*," the girl bowed her head, then, bit into the fruit. At the first acrid taste, she almost dropped it. She had to fight the urge to spit the bitter thing out. Seeing that Dorada busily devoured the other fruit, and that it seemed to be just as sour as hers, she forced herself to choke the whole thing down.

Viktor noticed a difference between the two fruits. Dorada's held a small pit at the center. Paella's was seedless.

Dorada put the pit in the snuffbox Belladonna had used to preserve the tendril. "I will plant this at dawn. When it sprouts in a few weeks, my tears will return. Now, you may take the girl for the night. The men you requested have already been sent to your ship."

Paella, fully healed, approached the vampire, keeping her eyes downcast. "*La Madre* has ordered a place prepared for us to spend the night."

He looked over the girl's head and gave Dorada a hard stare. "Do you not trust me to return her? I have a perfectly good bed in my cabin."

"I trust you to keep your word, Dark One. However, I will not break my bargain with the sea-witch," she explained. "Besides, if she leaves the island before my power is fully restored and has taken root, the healing spell will be reversed."

"Very well, but there is still the matter of obtaining what I need from you to continue my own business," he reminded.

"We will negotiate that on the morrow. Now take the girl and go to the place which has been prepared. I must bathe," she dismissed them.

The bower turned out quite comfortable, for something so hastily constructed; although it bore more of a feminine touch than the pirate would have preferred. The combined scent of various flowers woven into the palm frond walls nearly overwhelmed his acute senses.

Viktor suspected there might be a spell of some sort woven in, as well. On a normal basis, all his appetites were voracious, but his lust seemed to be unusually high this evening. Back on the ship, he had grown bored with Paella, just as the siren had predicted. Yet, this night, he could barely contain himself long enough to disrobe, once they entered the privacy of the bower.

Before long, he was beyond caring if there was a spell or not.

Neither of them slept that night.

It was noon, before Dorada was available to receive him. He used the morning to make sure his crew stood ready to sail at a moment's notice. He'd also bled the four victims he'd bargained for and mixed the blood with enough rum to preserve it. Paella fell into an exhausted sleep shortly after he left her bed.

He remained patient in waiting for the Sister. She had mentioned planting that fruit pit at dawn, after all. Besides, Paella's performance that night more than pleased him.

Finally, Dorada returned to her shelter. Once she was ready, her attendants granted him entry.

"You have come to me, Dark One, to seek my help, my magic. I tried to flee my fate and nearly killed my magic in the process.

You found me regardless, and the one who betrayed me to you proved to be my salvation. I am bound by honor and by the Elder's magic to give you my aide."

He pulled out the silver vial which hung about his neck. "Mother Celie gave this to me to collect and preserve the magic of the Sisters. She said she would need it to bolster her own powers. She is no longer strong enough to counter my curse by herself, but she told me it would be bad for all the Sisters to be gathered in one place."

"*Si*. The Elder has forbidden it," Dorada confirmed. "For us to be brought together would destroy the world. Put your little bottle away for now, but do not lose it."

"Yes, I remember you said it would take at least a month before your power could fully return," he said, tucking the vial back into his shirt.

"*Si*. The seed has been planted successfully."

The way she said that made him think she was talking about more than just the pit of the magic fruit. He had a fleeting, vague memory of suspecting a spell on Paella's bower. As quickly as the thought entered his mind, it vanished like so much smoke.

"Still, there are rules that bind my magic. I cannot just give some to you."

He had been expecting something like this. "No, I did not think so. I was told there would be tasks to perform. I cannot just take your magic; I have to buy it."

Dorada seemed a bit offended by his wording. "I would not say that my magic is for sale," she puffed indignantly.

"Everything is for sale," Viktor said with a chuckle. "It's just a matter of negotiating the price."

"I do not share your opinion, but, in this case, I have to admit it is accurate. I charge you to find and retrieve the Mermaid's Tear. In exchange, I will grant you one of my golden tears, once they have returned to me."

Viktor smirked. This will be all too easy, he thought.

"Agreed."

Dorada and Paella watched, as the *Incubus* sailed away from the island.

"The spell worked exactly as you knew it would, *Madre*." The girl smiled. "I think he suspected for a moment, but it did not stop him."

"*Bueno*." The older woman nodded. "Even if he truly is the One and changes everything, our power will adapt and survive. It will not be long before we have the Tear. The plan has worked perfectly. You played your role well, *mi hija*."

Chapter 21

"Did you get what you needed, Vik?" Grimm asked. They were in the captain's cabin enjoying a meal from the fresh provisions.

"Not yet, Hezekiah." The vampire shook his head. "It's going to be at least a month before the Sister will have it to give."

"I see. So, what are your plans for the interim?"

"The witch gave me a quest, but it will be easy enough, I imagine," he answered around a mouthful of food. "Figure we'll do a bit of pirating once that's out of the way.

Grimm took a long pull from his bottle then asked, "What did she set you to find?"

He chuckled, "She wants a mermaid's tear in exchange for one of her golden ones. Where's Belle gotten off to?"

"Haven't seen her since the two of you left for that ceremony, yesterday. She never came back to the ship," Grimm answered. "Judging by your good mood, I'd say you had some good sport last night. Did ye bed both of them?"

"No, I was only with Paella," he replied. "What would make you think I'd had Belladonna as well?"

It was the first mate's turn to chuckle. "I know you, Vik Brandee," he leered. "You usually aren't this happy, unless you've worn out at least three wenches. I figure Belle would count as two, given her nature."

The vampire shook his head. "I haven't seen her since I went with Paella to her shelter." He thought about it for a while and concluded. "She's probably in a jealous snit. Give her a couple of days to cool off, and she'll be back. There's no real rush."

"You thinking of getting a tear from her?" Grimm raised an eyebrow. "Good luck getting her to cry."

Viktor shook his head, "No, not from our Belle. As she is so fond of reminding us, she's a siren, not a mermaid. But she will make finding a mermaid much easier."

"You have a point there."

"The trick will be keeping her from eating it, before I can obtain a tear."

Grimm chuckled at that. "If anyone can, it's you, Vik."

Two days after they'd left the island behind, the winds died down completely. After about a week of being becalmed, the pirates became worried. The more superstitious among the crew grew frightened.

Viktor and Grimm were concerned, as well. Both knew such doldrums were not normal in these waters, especially at this time of year. When they saw a ship sail just outside of hailing distance of them, while their own sails hung limp and empty, they realized the weather was not natural.

"Do you think Dorada cast some spell to keep you from being able to fulfill your search? She didn't seem too fond of the idea of helping you," Grimm wondered. "She struck me as the kind who would try to find some sly way to avoid honoring an agreement."

Viktor disagreed, "I don't trust her either, Hezekiah, but I don't think this is her doing. Her magic is earth and plant based. No, if she could control weather, she would have been to her island and well-entrenched before we found her."

He stroked his beard, pondering their current plight. It didn't feel like Zeke's doing, either. If the old wizard wanted his attention, he would manifest Hell's Breath Island. He would not just becalm the ship.

That left just one other source who could have done this and had a motive to do so. He started stripping down, until he was clad only in breeches.

"Viktor?"

"Keep an eye on the ship and crew," he ordered. "I don't know how long I'll be gone, but I've a siren to find."

"Aye, Captain," Grimm hesitated, worried for his friend. "Are you sure going for a swim is the wisest choice? We've both seen what she can do with a man in the water. One of the small boats would be safer."

Viktor clapped him on the shoulder. "A boat would be safer, provided she didn't rip it apart, something she once threatened, when I first met her. I've a feeling she's not that far away. If I go straight into the water, it should be just the lure to draw her in."

"You've got more balls than I do, facing her in her native element," he admitted. "Here's hoping she lets you keep them." He couldn't resist the jibe.

Viktor just shook his head, chuckling. Leaving the cabin, he went topside then dove into the unnaturally calm sea.

The siren cruised around beneath the ship for days, staying deep enough to be out of sight if anyone looked over the side. She absolutely hated that Viktor had gone with Paella that night. She knew Dorada had been lying when she'd said the girl's healing would revert if she left the island.

The reason she knew it for a lie was two-fold. The earth-witch's magic had flared to hide the lie from the vampire's acute senses. Also, she had lied, herself, about being able to heal the girl. She had deliberately left her crippled in the hope Viktor would find her too repulsive to bed.

That plan failed, but the seasickness the girl had suffered had done the trick.

Then that bitch, Dorada, had offered the little slut up! Belle wanted to scream. She had bargained to get rid of the witchling, but the earth-witch had found a way around the bargain.

The siren remained at a loss, however, as to what Dorada had to gain from the coupling.

The vibration of a large object hitting the water interrupted her musing. With the sea around the ship magically becalmed, any vibration or underwater sound was easily detected. She knew the sound and feel of the chamber pots being emptied, and this was not it.

It sounded like a human swimming. The siren realized she was hungry; very hungry.

She darted toward the underside of the ship. Scanning the area, she saw legs kicking and arms sweeping back and forth, keeping the man afloat. She couldn't believe anyone would be so foolish as to jump in the water.

Her predatory instincts began to override her reasoning. She no longer cared who was in the water, or why. She just saw food.

The water felt warmish but refreshing. Viktor had almost forgotten how much he enjoyed swimming. The warmth of the water made his muscles relax. It tempted him to let his guard down, but he was sure the siren was nearby.

When he felt his legs being grabbed, just before he was jerked underwater, it confirmed his suspicion. He managed to turn and face Belladonna, just as she sank needle teeth into his shoulder.

On sheer reflex, he jerked her head back sharply by the hair. The resulting wound from her teeth tearing out a small chunk of meat burned like hell. She wrapped her arms around him, digging poisonous talons into his back and positioning her head to dart in for another bite. In the water, he lacked the leverage to keep her off.

He gritted his teeth, bracing for the attack. Mr. Grimm had been right. He should have used a boat.

The attack never came.

Belladonna's hands and face reverted to human. She wore a look of both recognition and horror. Even as the water reddened with the vampire's blood, she gave a great thrust with her tail. They were both propelled in an arc from the water to the deck of the ship. She turned them in mid-air, so that she hit first, taking the impact of the landing.

Grimm reacted quickly, helping Viktor to his feet and getting him back to his cabin. The landing left Belladonna slightly stunned. The transformation of her tail while it shrank, divided and reformed into legs forced her to remain immobile.

By the time she regained mobility, Grimm had gotten Viktor into a chair. Turning to shut the cabin door, he saw the siren approaching. With almost inhuman speed, the first mate drew one of his guns and pointed it at the center of her forehead.

"Back off, bitch!" he warned. "I've seen what you've done to him."

Belle's voice was low and deadly. "Out of my way, human. He needs my magic to help heal."

Grimm cocked the pistol, glaring at her.

Viktor came up behind him and laid a hand on his shoulder. "Let her pass, Mr. Grimm. She's right; I do need her help."

The first mate shook his head. "Captain, she just took a hunk out of your shoulder."

"And she brought me back aboard the second she realized who she'd tried to eat. She is no longer a threat, Hezekiah," he reassured. "Let her pass, then leave us. I've a few things to discuss with our Belle in private."

The almost painful pressure the vampire exerted on his shoulder told Grimm it would be wise not to argue.

"Oh, and send Mullins in about half an hour," he added. "He's been shirking his duties. The spare lines have been in a useless tangle ever since that storm we rode. He's had more than enough time to untangle and neatly stow them."

"Aye, Captain. I'll have Jon-Jon and a few others work on those lines, as well." He left the captain's cabin and closed the door behind him.

Suddenly, Belladonna didn't look so sure about wanting to be alone in the cabin with Viktor. He noticed this and believed he knew the reason why. Finally, he had some leverage that might keep the siren in line. It was time to test his theory.

"You did quite a bit of damage, pet," he spoke amiably, brushing the open wound with his thumb, as if admiring it. "I guess I shouldn't have underestimated you."

"I am a predator by nature, Viktor," she told him. "You were in the water, and I was hungry. My instincts took over."

"Then why did you stop?"

"When I realized it was you, I had to stop," she hedged.

"Hmm," he approached her slowly. "Nice to know that you are concerned for my well-being."

She didn't try to run but looked as if she wanted to. He thought she was acting like prey, and it appealed to him greatly. When he reached out to touch her face, she did flinch and try to pull back. It made him laugh.

"What is wrong, pet?" He pulled and held her body to him, his sodden breeches doing little to hide his arousal. "You, of all people, shouldn't be afraid of a little blood." He brushed his bloody thumb across her lips, gently forcing it into her mouth.

Belle's eyes fluttered closed, as she licked the fluid from his thumb and her lips. She moaned softly, bringing a lascivious smile to his face. When she opened her eyes, however, horror and anger warred with lust in her expression. It confirmed his theory.

The siren pushed him away, painfully aware he had let her do so. "You bastard," she growled angrily.

Viktor chuckled, "It's not the first time I've been called that. I'm sure it won't be the last. You should be happy, pet. You've wanted me inside you for some time now." He waved a hand at the shoulder wound. "Granted, I don't think this is what you had in mind, exactly."

"You scheming, conniving bastard. You planned for this to happen!"

"Not exactly, pet. But I am opportunistic enough to take advantage of the situation. Already, I feel a tenuous bond forming. You have swallowed both my blood and my flesh. Ah, and I can see by your expression that I misjudged earlier. It would seem your horror was not so much over what you did to me, as it was over what you did to yourself."

Her growling shriek was all the answer he needed. He smiled wryly.

"Do not think to win me so easily, Viktor Brandewyne," she hissed. "True, your blood and flesh bind me to you, but I will never be your slave. I am not like those weak-minded creatures you call a crew."

"I never said you were, pet."

"And I am not your pet!" She went to storm out the door.

He tested the strength of the new bond. "Going so soon, Belle?" He found himself able to stop her from leaving with just his will but realized he would have to choose his next words carefully. He could feel her will and magic building up to fight him. The bond was still too new and fragile to risk goading her into breaking it.

She turned to glare at him.

"I do need your help healing this bite and the holes you tore in my back."

She eyed him warily. She nearly fell, when he released the hold on her. Taking that as a sign he was not going to force his will on her, she approached him cautiously. When he still made no move toward her, she surveyed the damage she had done.

"This will sting," she warned him, before waving a hand over the scores on his back. A hissing intake of breath from him rewarded her efforts. "I've neutralized the poison. With a feeding, your body will heal the rest before morning, on its own. I believe you have already arranged for that."

She quickly moved back to the door.

"Belladonna." The fact that he didn't use his powers on her, merely spoke her name, kept her from leaving.

"I have always been free, Viktor. I answer to no creature. You frighten me. You may very well be the one to tame me. What scares me most is that I almost want you to."

Surprisingly, the vampire understood her fear. He, himself, had no desire to ever be made slave to any being's whim. The unplanned blood bond forged between them made him realize he had been in danger of just that, with the siren as the master.

"I enjoy your wildness, Belle, but I need your cooperation to succeed in my venture," he told her. "I give you my word I will not try to force my will on you, provided you do not try to force yours on me. This is not negotiable. If the issue is ever forced, I will win." He sent a rush of power through her that almost made her legs collapse.

"I accept your terms and will abide by them." Her voice held fear. Her scent could not hide her desire for him, however. For the first time, she wished she had some enveloping garment to cover herself with. If she gave in to her lust while she was still able to taste his blood in her mouth, she would seal her fate and make herself his slave. She could see he was more than ready for her. All she had to do was walk over to his bed and let him take her. It would be so easy, so simple.

Viktor spoke words that were rare for him. "Thank you."

She blinked at him. His behavior puzzled her. Everything she knew and had observed about him led to the conclusion he would force his control on all those around him. Yet, he was allowing her to escape without completing the one act that would forever seal the bond between them. Perhaps she really could take him at his word. It occurred to her that he had never really forced his will on Hezekiah, either.

A knock at the cabin door interrupted the moment.

"Go on to your cabin and dress. I'll come speak with you after I've fed." As an afterthought, he smiled and added, "You mentioned being hungry. Would you be interested in my — leftovers?"

She nodded and opened the door, deciding to leave while she still could. Passing the stocky man waiting there, she trailed a hand over the crewman's arm and chuckled to herself. He smiled and watched the nude siren as she walked off.

"Come in, Mr. Mullins," Viktor ordered, "and shut the door behind you."

Viktor had Mullins' head nailed to the main mast as a warning to anyone ducking out of work. The level of activity on board tripled for a week.

Chapter 22

Deciding it would be wiser to enlist her aide after she'd fed, Viktor put off talking to Belladonna until the next morning. He got no answer, when he knocked on her cabin door. He could sense her presence, but it felt muted. Opening the door, he was preceded by a furry black blur.

Lazarus perched himself on the shelf above the bunk and peered down at the sleeping siren. Viktor entered the cabin, closing the door quietly. It surprised him to find her asleep.

He couldn't remember the last time he'd slept. It seemed as if he no longer had the need for it. He didn't seem to get tired anymore. He had assumed the siren didn't sleep, either.

The proof of his error lay before him.

Pulling up a chair, he decided to watch her until she woke. The sight of a sleeping woman had always appealed to him, and Belladonna provided a very pleasant sight. Her auburn hair lay about her pillow in unruly, crimped tendrils, where she had undone her braids. Her face was slack, making her appear deceptively harmless. Her arm had pushed the blanket down enough that one nipple just peeked out.

It brought a wry smile to Viktor's face. The smile was echoed by Lazarus purring very loudly.

"Who asked for your opinion?" he gave the cat a mock glare.

"Meh."

It almost looked as if the cat stuck his tongue out at the vampire. Then, he leapt from the shelf to land full weight on Belladonna's stomach. He quickly bounded away, before the siren could react, or Viktor could nab him. Safely ensconced on the far side of the cabin, he began grooming himself, as if nothing had happened.

"Damn cat!" Vik growled. He turned back to find the siren blinking sleepily at him. "Good morning. I didn't know you slept."

She gave a little smile, then she stretched for a full three minutes. He groaned appreciatively.

"Normally, I don't," she said, once she'd finished stretching.

"Don't what?"

"Sleep," she giggled. "In my natural habitat, it's not safe to sleep because of other predators. But it takes a great deal of energy to maintain human form. So, I occasionally need to sleep, although I can feed more often, if sleep is not an option."

"I'm sure that my crew would prefer you sleep, rather than feed more often." He laughed.

She smiled knowingly at him, "And what about you, Captain? Why are you and the cat in my cabin? Were you going to ravish me in my sleep?"

"It was tempting, but I prefer an active wench to a sleeping one." He winked. "As for Lazarus, he just likes fish."

"Meh," the cat commented and went back to his grooming.

"I'm here, because I need your help, Belle."

She nodded and set about slipping into shirt and trousers. "I thought as much, but it's nice to hear you say it. What do you need of me?"

"I need to find and capture alive," he paused to emphasis the "alive" part, "a mermaid."

"Alive."

"Yes."

Belle sighed. She shook her head, chuckling. "That definitely will not be easy. They're hard enough to hunt, as it is. It's usually best to kill them quickly. They put up one hell of a fight, otherwise."

"Can it be done, though?"

"Yes. Just seems like a lot of trouble to go to, if you're not going to eat it."

He thought for a moment. "Is mermaid blood toxic, like siren blood?"

"No. They're a separate species. They don't have venom as a defense. Why?"

"Just wondering if my bite would have the same controlling effect on a mermaid as it does on a human."

She shrugged. "That, I can't answer. Guess you'll have to try it out; provided we catch one."

"We need to find one, otherwise I won't be able to get the magic I need from Dorada," he insisted.

"Very well, I'll do my best to find one for you," she told him. A question occurred to her. "Does it matter if it's a little damaged? It'd be easier to bring in with a paralyzed tail."

"I have no problem with that," he shrugged. "She just has to be alive."

The siren smiled, showing her true teeth. "Then I guess I better start hunting."

Grimm found Viktor in his cabin, studying several charts. The island where Dorada was located had been marked.

"We've got a good wind coming up," he informed the captain. "I've got the lads up in the rigging making ready to get underway. Do we have a heading?"

"Northeast to open water. The hunting should be good there."

Grimm grinned. "Aye. Treasure ships will be heading out to make the crossing, now that the hurricanes are done and before the winter storms hit the northern sea."

"That too," Viktor chuckled, "although, I meant mermaid hunting. But I've no objection to a bit of piracy, while we're at it."

"It'll put the lads in good humor," the first mate confirmed. "We could use some fresh provisions, as well. Belle's snit cost us a good deal of what that witch gave us."

"Tell the men a double share to the one who spots the next prize, Mr. Grimm," he ordered.

"Aye, Captain," his eyes shone with anticipation. He did love his chosen occupation.

As luck would have it, the lookout spotted sails on the horizon about an hour before Belladonna returned to the ship reporting a pod of mermaids.

"Of course," Viktor muttered, his voice dripping sarcasm. "Such perfect timing; I take it you were unable to catch one and bring it back?"

"I didn't try. You want one alive. If I caught you one when I found them, it would have spooked the rest. I want to hunt, as well."

"Won't that spook them and keep me from catching one?" he asked pointedly.

"Not if you catch one yourself, before I hunt."

"I'm getting a headache from this," Grimm muttered.

"Don't worry, Hezekiah. I think I understand what she's getting at," Viktor smirked. "What heading are they on?"

"You're heading right for them," the siren informed him.

"That's good luck, Vik," Grimm commented. "We can catch two fish with one hook, so to speak."

"Perhaps," he stroked his beard thoughtfully. "The mermaids take precedence, if it comes to it, however." He looked at Belladonna. "I thought you said they would be hard to catch."

"I did, and they will be," she answered. "We do have a slight advantage, though. They're in between you and the ship you are chasing, and this pod is made up of juveniles."

"You say that last as if it makes a difference in the hunt."

She smiled in a predacious manner. "I know my favorite prey very well, Viktor. A mature mermaid is damn near impossible to catch. The juveniles are not as wily, and they are arrogant. Their scent tells me that at least three, if not more, of the pod are coming into heat. They'll want to play with the crew of any ship that crosses their path."

"Play?" Grimm was suspicious.

"They will try to lure men overboard and have been known to lead ships onto reefs and rocks."

"I've heard the tales, lass. Is that how they hunt?"

Belle looked at the first mate as if he were dim-witted. "Hunt? Mermaids are not sirens. They don't hunt. They're kelp eaters."

"Show some respect, pet," Viktor's tone was warning. "Mr. Grimm is ignorant of our prey, as am I, but he is not stupid. Now, if it is not to hunt, then why do they behave that way?"

The siren sighed, "To mate. Mermen are exceedingly rare. It's usually easier to use a human male. The problem with that is that the human often drowns in the process."

"Thus, the rocks," the vampire made the connection. "If they can mate in the shallows, the man stands a better chance of surviving long enough to impregnate. I see." He smiled to himself.

Grimm stared hard at him. "I know that look, Vik. What are you thinking about?"

"Of going fishing."

"Dammit, Viktor! After what happened with this crazy bitch?!" He pointed at Belladonna. "You can't do it, man. How are you supposed to lift your curse, if you are dead?"

The vampire gave him a deadly stare. "You forget yourself, Hezekiah."

He blanched, aware of what his captain was capable of, but he did not back down. "Only because I'm thinking about your welfare, Viktor."

"You're worse than a mother hen," he softened. "Weren't you listening? The mermaids don't want to eat me; they want to fuck.

Plus, we might be able to use them to our advantage in taking that ship."

Belle seemed puzzled by his reasoning. "They don't cooperate with humans. They only use them to mate," she argued.

"I did not say I was going to ask for their help, pet. I said I was going to use them. If they want to — play, then they will be trying to lure sailors from the other ship. There is no place in these waters to run it aground," he pointed out.

She shook her head. "They'll also be trying to lure your crew."

"Aye, but my crew are under my command," he reminded her. "If I can keep them from giving in to your advances, then protecting them from a mermaid's embrace should not pose a problem."

"So, we attack the prize, while they're distracted and/or shorthanded dealing with the creatures," Grimm caught on. "But won't that spook them away, before you can catch one?"

"I plan on catching one, before we take the ship. I'll jump overboard with a lifeline. Mr. Jon and Anvil can pull me back aboard, once I've caught a sea-lass. When she's safely on board, you are free to hunt and feed to your heart's content, Belle."

The mermaids surfaced about a hundred yards from the ship they were pursuing. The pod split into two groups and began sporting around both vessels. The creatures leapt out of the water much like dolphins, doing tail stands and singing.

As the *Incubus* neared the other ship, a noticeable difference could be seen. The pirates kept to the task of sailing their vessel, undistracted by the spectacle. The crew of the other ship flocked to the sides and rigging. Some could be seen jumping overboard.

"Cap'n! The prize is carrying wenches and whelps!" Sniff called from the crow's nest.

Sure enough, cries and screams of women and children trying to stop their men from going to the mermaids could be heard over the waves. Some threw things at the creatures, trying to drive them away.

More of the mermaids converged on the *Incubus*, determined to lure mates. Viktor judged that the time was right. Making sure to secure his lifeline and that Jon-Jon and Anvil were standing by, he dove over the side. He was a strong enough swimmer to keep from being drawn into the hull.

It didn't take long for his prey to spot him and swarm. Three of them grabbed for him, dragging him under in the process.

Grimm gripped the railing until his knuckles were white. Zeke's magic kept him safe from the mermaids' enchantments for the most part. He still found himself sorely tempted to give in. Worry for Viktor helped him maintain self-control. Despite the siren's assurance that mermaids were not carnivorous, he feared they might tear the captain apart in their mating frenzy.

He was about to order them to haul him back aboard, when the men started pulling the ropes on their own.

"He caught one," Belle stated. "I felt him give the signal to bring him in."

The vampire was completely nude, when they got him back on deck. A mermaid with greenish-blond hair plastered herself to his front, writhing. It soon became apparent that she was trying to keep him from getting loose, rather than trying to free herself.

"You need to let go now, pet," Viktor started prying at her arms.

"Not yet, my love," the mermaid objected between kisses and wrapped her arms tighter around him. She was stronger than he had anticipated, and he really didn't have the right leverage to disengage her.

The siren growled something in a language no human could hope to reproduce. She snatched the mermaid by the hair, making sure her toothsome snarl was clearly visible. "Get off!"

Survival instinct instantly overran the mermaid's mating urges. With a terrified shriek, she released Viktor and lashed out with her tail to knock the predator away. Belladonna deftly avoided the tail but released the creature's hair. Flopping to the deck, the mermaid pulled herself along, trying to put as much distance as possible between the siren and her.

At a silent signal from Viktor, all the pirates nearby ringed her in. He did not want her getting back to the railing and escaping. That shriek was sure to have frightened the others off.

The mermaid looked crazed. She realized she was trapped. Thrashing about, she managed to knock a couple of the men off their feet. Seeing her opening, she made for the side.

Viktor reached her, just as she got to the railing. He managed to grab her around the waist, but the thrashing of her tail made it difficult to hold on.

"You don't get away that easily, pet," he grunted and slugged her. She instantly went limp.

"Mr. Jon, chain her to the main mast for the time being," he ordered. "Make sure it's a strong chain. Lads, to your stations! We've a ship to take!"

Belladonna stared at him. It was the first time she'd seen him completely naked. He still sported his arousal from the encounter with the mermaid. It galled her she was not the source of his lingering lust. It also amazed her that he apparently felt no embarrassment of his nudity in front of his crew. He made no effort to cover himself as he gave orders.

Finally, he noticed her gaze.

"You have your little sea cow," she couldn't keep the jealousy out of her voice. "I'm going to hunt, before the entire pod escapes." Without another word, she leapt over the side.

"She's in a bit of a snit again," Grimm commented.

"Her jealousy is starting to grate," Viktor replied.

Grimm raised an eyebrow. "By the way, what happened to your clothes?"

"The mermaids were quite eager and impatient. Besides, you can't expect to catch a fish, if you don't set the hook." He grinned.

They both laughed.

The ship didn't have much in the way of trade goods, although it was well provisioned. The majority of those on board were settlers *en route* to the South American coast. They planned on starting a mission deep in the mountainous jungles. The actual crew, small to begin with, was smaller now; several had answered the lure of the mermaids.

Viktor considered the missionaries to be suicidal fools. It was strongly believed among most of those who sailed these waters that the tribes they sought were cannibals and headhunters. He believed he'd done his captives a favor by taking them away from their men, although, that was not his motive for doing so.

No, the pirate did what he did for one of two reasons. Either he really enjoyed it, or he stood to make a considerable profit. If any chosen activity met both those criteria, all the better.

A slaver that both he and Grimm did occasional business with operated on an island about two weeks' sailing east of their current position. He supplied brothel workers and paid top price — in gold.

"I've no need for more crew or your ship," Viktor addressed the survivors of the brief battle.

A familiar face stepped forward among them. "Captain Brandewyne!" the man called.

"Jenkins?" he peered at the man. "What's an old smuggler like you doing with that sorry lot?"

The man could not bring himself to meet the pirate's eyes. With a bowed head, he answered, "I've seen the error of my ways, sir. I had hoped to atone for my sins by helping found this mission outpost."

"Zealous fool," Grimm muttered under his breath.

Viktor ignored it. "Don't see how getting cooked and eaten by a bunch of wild cannibals would get a man into heaven, Jenkins. It hurts to see you taking up with such an unmanly lot."

"I'm not a young man anymore, Captain Brandewyne," Jenkins told him. "I know you, and I realize I'm of no use to you, but I would ask a favor of you, for old times' sake."

"You can ask." The vampire's tone remained neutral.

"I've a wife and son among your prisoners, sir. Please, I beg of you, set them free." He dropped to his knees, tears streaming down his face. "They're all I have left."

Viktor's face hardened. "Get up, man," he growled. "You shame yourself." Turning, he faced the cowering, weeping group of women and children. "Madame Jenkins, step forward, if you are here. Bring your boy with you."

A young woman managed to work her way out of the group. A small boy of about four peeped from behind her skirts.

"You always had a good eye for the women, Jenkins." He complimented him. "She's a comely wench; would've brought a good price, too. Anvil!"

"Aye," the blacksmith stepped forward.

"Set these two free and take them to their ship."

The large man did as ordered then returned to the *Incubus*. The pirates pulled the boarding planks. A few kept muskets trained on those left on the other ship to make sure they stayed there.

As the riggers set the sails and cut the lines to the other ship, Grimm approached Viktor. "The man's a fool. He'd have done better to leave them with us. We took all their provision."

"So, we did, Mr. Grimm." He nodded. "That pathetic creature isn't even a shadow of the Jenkins I knew. Still, he deserves better than a slow death by starvation."

He watched as they pulled away from the stripped-down ship and its hapless passengers. His crew had taken all the sail cloth and lines, as well, leaving the derelict at the mercy of the currents, with no hope of survivors reaching land alive.

"Burn it."

Belladonna returned to the ship, to find Viktor in an ill mood. The mermaid hung in his cabin by wrist manacles from a hook in the ceiling. Numerous welts showed on her flesh. Blood oozed from wrists rubbed raw by her struggles against the manacles. A large spike pinned her tail to the deck. Both of her breasts bore the marks of the vampire's fangs.

The sight softened the siren towards him. "Why didn't you say you wanted to play with her?" She gave him a slightly demented smile.

"I'm glad you're back, Belle. The bitch is being uncooperative," he grunted in exasperation. "Maybe you can work it out of her."

He held a flail out to the siren. She took it with an evil grin. "This will be delicious sport, although, I don't understand what it has to do with your quest."

The mermaid, who had been moaning softly, let out a whimpering, almost-scream at the sight of the siren. She began shaking and making hiccupping sob sounds.

"I need for her to cry."

Belladonna shrugged. "She is crying."

"I can hear that," he snapped irritably. "Dry sobs won't do me any good. I have to give Dorada a mermaid's tear."

The siren blinked at him then started laughing. "If that is what she wants, she has asked for something which does not exist. You hunted down and tortured this sea cow for nothing."

"What are you babbling about?" He suddenly got in her face.

Un-intimidated, Belle replied, "Mermaids don't have tears. Their clear inner eyelids negate the need for them."

"So, the bitch thought to get rid of me with an impossible task? I'll go back to that island and…."

"And what, Viktor?" Belladonna interrupted his rant. "Her magic is still regenerating; and you know as well as I do that it will not aide you, if it is not given freely. How did she phrase her price?"

"She said to bring her the mermaid's tear."

"Not a mermaid's tear, but the Mermaid's Tear? Tricky way to buy time."

He stroked his beard, letting the siren's line of logic sink in. It made sense Dorada would make it as difficult as possible for him to fulfill his end of the bargain. She was weak right now. The longer it took him, the stronger she would be, when he returned to her.

It also gave him an indication of what he would be facing dealing with the other Sisters.

"So, we need to find out what this Mermaid's Tear is. Is it a ship, or a book, or a treasure? It has to be transportable, because she said to bring it to her, not her to it."

A weak, dry, cracked voice drew their attention to the mermaid. "I know what it is." She flinched, as much as her position would let her, when they approached her.

"You know what the Mermaid's Tear is?" Vik questioned.

She nodded. "Please, let me down."

When he moved closer, she whimpered, her eyes full of pain and fear.

"Easy, pet," he soothed. "I'm just going to remove the spike. It may hurt, but I'm not going to beat you anymore."

Her shriek broke off into a dry coughing fit. As he unlocked her wrist restraints, she lost consciousness. He had to move quickly to catch her, before she could flop to the deck.

Belle peered over his shoulder, as he laid the creature on the bed. "She's dying. Her tailfin is graying, and she's dropping scales." The siren pointed to the fish scales littering the deck.

"Damn. If she really knows what we're looking for, I need her alive."

"I can heal her wounds. Salt water and a little magic will suffice."

He went to the door and called for Jon-Jon. The second mate arrived quickly.

"Find me the largest empty cask on board and bring it to my cabin. Then I want it filled with seawater."

"Aye, Cap'n. Oh, we had to knock a few of those wenches in the head. That thing's hollering had 'em hysterical."

"If they continue to be a problem, let a few of the lads have a go at them. Not too many, mind you. I don't want the cargo damaged, just a little of the fight worn out of them," Viktor offered a solution. "Now, be quick about that keg and seawater. Our guest is drying out."

"Aye, Cap'n." Jon-Jon set about finding what his captain wanted.

"Why isn't she waking up?"

Belladonna indicated the fang marks on the mermaid's breast. They were the only wounds she had been unable to heal. "Too much blood loss; she was almost too far gone before you decided to save her. I've done all I can. You're going to have to call her the rest of the way back," she told him. The siren turned and headed toward the door.

"Where are you going?"

She stopped but did not face him. "When she wakes, she will not react well to my presence. I am her species' primary predator," she stated and opened the cabin door. "Besides, I don't want to watch."

Chapter 23

Viktor scowled at the closed door. The siren's moods puzzled him at times. He shook his head and returned his attention to the unconscious mermaid. Focusing his will, he stroked her face gently and called her.

"Wake up, pet."

Her eyelids fluttered, and she moaned softly. "Alyssa.... unmmmmm."

"Alyssa? Is that your name, pet?"

She nodded in her sleep, instinctively leaning into the caress. He could sense she was almost there. Just a little more force of his will would nudge her awake but leave her pliable. He leaned over until his lips were just above her mouth.

"Alyssa," he whispered, "it's time to wake up." He felt the magic click into place. The mermaid had no choice but to answer his call.

She wrapped her arms around him and closed the short distance between them. Viktor found himself returning the kiss with a passion. The air in the cabin seemed thick with magic. It took him a moment to realize he was the source rather than the mermaid.

Pulling back from the kiss, he took control of the wild magic and drew it back into himself. The mermaid's expression told him that she would do anything he asked of her, just to get another taste of him.

Smiling, he tucked a strand of hair behind her ear. "Alyssa, do you really know what the Mermaid's Tear is, or was that just a ploy to get me to take you down?"

"I do not understand," she frowned. "What is plo-ee?"

He blinked in surprise. For such an overtly sexual creature, she was shockingly naïve. He had to remind himself that she was not human.

"Never mind, pet," he waved the question off. "Tell me what the Mermaid's Tear is — please," he added as an afterthought.

"It is very pretty and looks like a giant pearl. But it is not a pearl. I think it is a rock. It is white with blue, green, yellow and red flashes in it when it is turned in the light. It is rounded, but wider on one end than the other, sort of like a sea gull egg," she described it. "And it hangs on a chain, like that," she pointed to the chain his crystal was suspended from, "only it's the pretty yellow so many humans favor instead of the moon's gray-white, like yours."

"I see," he smiled. What she described sounded like a large opal. "Do you know why it is called the Mermaid's Tear?"

She shook her head. "No. I do not know what tear means."

He had to accept that. She could not produce tears. It only made sense that she would not know what one was.

"Very well. Do you know where I can find this pretty stone? If I give it to a powerful witch, she will use her magic to help me," he explained to her as if she were a child.

She blinked up at him, cocking her head to one side, absorbing the new concept of trade. Finally, she responded, "Yes, I know where you may find it, but you must give me something in return."

Viktor frowned. Given her *naivete*, he hadn't expected her to be so intelligent. It seemed that Alyssa caught on to things rather quickly. Belle warned him mature mermaids were quite clever. Perhaps this one was not as much of a juvenile of her species as the siren had led him to believe.

"What do you want from me, Alyssa," he asked resignedly. It was yet another complication, but he needed the information.

"I want you to give me a child."

It was his turn to blink. "That's easy enough," he replied. "Right now, we have several on board. You can have your pick."

She shook her head. "No. I do not want a human. I want you to give me a child."

Realization of what she meant brought a slow, lascivious smile to his face. "I see." Her price was one that would be a pleasure, literally, to pay.

The sounds from the captain's cabin drove Belladonna from the ship. She swam at top speed for an hour, before her extra-sensitive hearing could no longer detect them. And yet, she could still hear the moans of Viktor's pleasure in her head. She found it maddening.

She knew it was still too soon. It would be months, or longer, before she could safely resume her efforts to seduce him without the risk of becoming completely enslaved to him. In truth, she might never be free of that particular risk.

Part of her didn't care, though. It had taken every ounce of her willpower to keep from rushing back into his cabin, when she'd been hit by the wave of magic and lust he'd released.

The frustration built in her, until she had to find some release. Rising to the surface, she let out a powerful scream.

"Stop that racket!"

Shocked by the voice, the siren fell instantly silent. No human would have been left sane enough to speak after hearing her scream, let alone be able to order her silence. Looking around, she found herself inside a small rocky cove, cut off from the sea by rocks and low tide. She had been in open sea, when she had surfaced.

"That's better. Now come dry off by the fire. We need to talk."

Turning away from the sea, she saw Uncle Zeke standing on the island's shore. She dragged herself ashore and joined him at his fire, once her legs formed.

The old man sat and poked at the fire, staring into the dancing embers he stirred up. Unlike the vampire, the siren could sit patiently. She knew the old wizard would speak when he was ready.

She'd had centuries in which to learn patience. Only humans and Viktor had ever been able to try it to the point of frustration. Humans were such short-lived creatures with too much of a need for immediacy, and Viktor — well, Viktor was just Viktor.

"Your favorite food is starting to breed out," Zeke broke the silence.

"What do you mean?"

"Your master has just created a new species."

Belladonna frowned, "I have no master."

Zeke cackled, "Deny it all you want, sea-witch, but you do have a master. The mermaid he has got with child will bear a merman unlike any that has ever been. He will resemble a siren more than a merman and will have his sire's sexual appetites. You won't be able to eat the lad or any of his future offspring without tying yourself even more tightly to Viktor Brandewyne. Killing any of this new breed may even bring the vampire's wrath down on your head."

She didn't appear to be phased by the prediction. "He will be only one merman. There are far many more mermaids, and they usually breed with humans." She shrugged.

Zeke shook his head, "All that will start to change. He will actively hunt down mermaid pods to mate. They will be drawn to him and will fight each other to the death for a chance to mate with him. There will be more sons than daughters among his get, and they will have the same allure and breeding habits as him. In a couple of centuries, it will be rare to find a purebred mermaid."

Belle did not like the sound of that. "How will I know the difference, and what do you mean that this sea whelp will resemble a siren?"

"You'll know them by their hair. This new breed will all be as raven-haired as their progenitor," he told her. "They will be like sirens in that they will be able to take human form, unlike true mermaids and mermen."

"You mean they will breed with humans, too?" Panic started to creep into her voice. It began looking like both her favorite foods would start breeding into something she could not safely eat.

The old man reached over and patted her arm reassuringly. "Don't worry, girl. They'll have an appetite for coupling with humans, but there will never be any issue from those couplings. With the addition of so many males, there will no longer be a need for humans as breeders."

He went back to stirring the fire while the siren digested the information he had given her.

"Then, I'll just have to kill that little sea cow as soon as he's through with her," she decided.

"You don't want to be doing that right away," he warned. "This child was meant to be. But the sooner you hunt down and destroy his dam after his birth, the better. That fool boy went and bit her. She'll eventually turn, just like a human would. That was not meant to be."

It didn't take long for the siren to grasp the implications of all Zeke told her. There would be a new breed of predator to compete with as well as the new breed of merfolk. At least she was free to destroy that particular nuisance. However, even if she had not attacked Viktor, the introduction of his bloodline to the mermaid population would have eventually led to her enthrallment to the vampire pirate. The Sisters had woven a web so fine; she would never have seen it.

She was about to ask Zeke why he had told her all this, when a dense fog enveloped her.

"It's time for you to go now."

Once again, she found herself in open water. In the distance, she saw the *Incubus'* sails approaching.

Alyssa proved more useful than anticipated. Mermaids held a fondness for gossip, it seemed. Their main sources of information were dolphins and the occasional whale.

"Whales aren't too helpful, though," she explained. "They're too stuffy to play, and they usually run away from ships. They fear humans. Dolphins are more fun. They'll dance all around ships and hear all the talk. Humans do and say some silly things."

Viktor had to agree with that last statement, excluding himself, of course. "And you say that some dolphins heard about the Mermaid's Tear?" he prompted.

"Yes. There was a ship crossing the Great Sea to the east. They were taking the pretty stone as a present to some ruler of the humans. They also said they had a lot of the yellow metal. Do humans use it for ballast? It is very heavy," she rambled.

"It would be a bit too expensive to use for that," he laughed. "How long ago was this ship spotted, and was it east or west of the Windward Islands?"

She thought about it for a moment. "The pod I heard it from passed us a couple of weeks ago," she answered. "They had seen the ship a few days before that. They saw it just this side of the islands. They said there was much talk on board about a fear of pirate attack when they were to pass through the islands into the Great Sea."

Viktor smiled to himself. He would have to see if Belladonna could aide in harnessing this dolphin gossip network. Their information would likely be much more accurate than his usual sources, when it came to locating potential prizes. Humans tended to lie, if they thought there was some gold in it for them.

Doing the math in his head and coupling it with his knowledge of the seas in that area, he concluded his prey should be a little less than halfway through the crossing, provided they had made it through the islands safely. The gold weight would slow them down, so he should have no trouble catching up with them. Selling off his human cargo would have to wait, however. Putting into port would cost him too much time.

"Thank you for your aid, pet. Now, I best get you back into the sea, before Belladonna returns."

"Who is Belladonna?"

"She is the siren you saw earlier."

Alyssa instantly grew agitated. "Please, do not let her eat me!"

"You carry my child, pet. She will not dare harm you," he assured her. "I will not permit it."

Having felt his power, she believed he was able to control the siren. Seeing she had calmed, he hefted her in his arms and soon delivered her back into the waters he had drawn her from. She wasted no time in heading back west in search of the remainder of her pod.

Chapter 24

Grimm hadn't been happy about postponing the off-loading and sale of their "cargo." The longer they delayed, the more they had to feed the captives, which cut the profit to be made. But he understood the necessity for the delay. He had Viktor's approval to strip the prize ship, once they had the bauble in hand.

Belladonna's aide with the wind and weather cut travel time to the Windward Islands in half. In one week, they covered a distance which normally took two to sail. They navigated the reefs with caution, keeping an eye out for sails. Viktor didn't expect to find their prey there, but he knew these waters were rife with the Brethren. He didn't have time to waste with rival pirates.

The lookout spotted smoke on the horizon about four days after they cleared the islands.

"Lazarus, come forth," Vik summoned. The cat seemed to materialize from nowhere. "Show me what we're dealing with." He nodded toward the smoke. In the blink of an eye, the cat was gone, and a raven winged its way to investigate.

Grimm suppressed a shudder. The demon cat still unnerved him a bit. His practical side, however, appreciated the advance information Viktor got from his use. They were still sailing dangerous waters, and Viktor and old Billy Black were not the only pirates known to use the ship-in-distress ploy.

"Damn," Viktor muttered after a while.

"What?"

"If this was our prize, then, someone has beaten us to it," he grumbled. "Lazarus is checking to see if any logbooks were left behind. There don't appear to be any survivors. All speed for the wreckage."

Grimm relayed the order. Within the hour, they pulled up alongside the smoldering hulk. He ordered a boarding party over to scout the vessel out.

After thoroughly looking the derelict over, Jon-Jon reported their findings to the captain. "We found the logbooks and a wagoner of maps, Cap'n. Don't think much of a pirate fool enough to leave good charts behind." He deposited said items on the captain's table.

"Hmm, that does seem odd," Vik agreed. "Was anything else of value left aboard?"

He shook his head, "No, Cap'n. All we found were a few charred bolts of cloth and a few spare sails." His contempt of the obviously amateur pirate showed in his voice.

"Very well, I'll look these over to see if this was the ship we were looking for," he took the logs. "Why don't you go below and pick out a wench to spend a couple of hours with, provided you can last that long."

"Well, two hours doesn't really seem long enough, Cap'n, but I understand ye don't want me wearing out the cargo." He left the cabin with Viktor's laughter following him.

The temperature seemed to drop, when Viktor came on deck. Clearly something displeased him.

"Mr. Grimm!"

"Aye?"

"Those bloody sons-of-bitches are going to pay for taking my prize," he growled.

Grimm relaxed just a little, relieved it wasn't anyone on board who had drawn the captain's ire. "Shall we run up a bait flag and set a spiral course?" he asked, suggesting a tried-and-true method for finding a particular ship that hadn't gone far. "This wreckage is still relatively fresh; maybe a couple of days old, if that."

"Normally, I'd agree with that ploy, Hezekiah," Viktor conceded, "but I'm not feeling that patient. Go ahead and run up a French flag; that should draw the bastards in close when we find them. Have the lads mask all but ten of the guns. We want to look like a harmless merchantman. Where is Belle?"

The siren dropped to the deck from a spar, landing gracefully. "What do you want?"

"You sound a little miffed, lass," Grimm teased. "Did we interrupt a dalliance with Sniff?"

She glared disdainfully at the first mate. "If that disgusting little troll was on duty, I wouldn't have been aloft."

"Enough of this," Viktor's tone reminded them there were more important matters to attend to. "Belladonna, I need you to locate the closest ships. One of them is bound to be the fool who dared try to steal my prize. Do not take action when you find them. Merely let me know where they are."

"Well, that's no fun," she grumbled. The vampire gripped her jaw, making sure he had her undivided attention. "You will obey the order." He flexed his will. "The fun will come later. You have my word."

The siren's heart sped up. She was unused to being dominated and unsure of whether or not she liked it.

"Very well," she finally responded.

Grimm thought of something to add to her instructions. "Didn't the mermaid say that this ship was carrying a good deal of gold?"

"Aye; The logs confirmed it." Viktor saw where his first mate was going with this. "The ship we're looking for will be riding low in the water from the extra weight."

Belle smiled. "That will make it much easier to locate. It should slow them down considerably, as well."

"That it will, lass," Grimm grinned. He saw the gold as a bonus for capturing the Mermaid's Tear.

The siren returned with a report of only one other ship in the area, and it fit the expected description. She gave Viktor the heading and sang up a wind to help speed their way.

Soon, sails appeared on the horizon.

"Let the wind return to normal, Belle," the vampire ordered. "We don't want to approach so quickly that we appear aggressive. I want them to come to us."

"As you wish." She changed one note in her song before ending it. The wind calmed, but not completely. Gradually, the *Incubus* lost some of her forward momentum.

"They're taking the bait," Grimm observed, watching the other ship turn in their direction.

Viktor narrowed his eyes at the ship. Grimm used the glass. "What do you make of her, Mr. Grimm?"

"She's smaller than us; an older build than I usually see," he answered. "Probably some rag-tag local operation. Can't make out her name at this distance."

"I can." Viktor allowed an almost demented evil grin to split his face. He could see more than just the ship's name. He saw the scarred, patched hull, which he recognized instantly. He'd made some of those scars over the years. "It's the *Georgia Belle*."

Grimm peered through the glass again, still unable to focus in on the approaching ship. "We need a better glass," he muttered. "Are you sure, Captain? It's Harris? I didn't think that little bastard would still be afloat."

"Oh, it's Harris, all right," he half laughed. "I can see that ridiculous red feather bouncing all over the deck. He must think he's actually giving orders. And the little shit has my Mermaid's Tear."

He started chuckling to himself. Grimm had a good idea what was on his captain's mind.

"Harris doesn't know this ship, and, by most accounts, you are believed to be dead."

"Aye," he grinned. "Don't do anything to rouse his suspicions. Get all but a skeleton crew below decks, ready to spring out. Bring a few of the wenches and brats topside, as well. The exercise will do them good, and they'll provide the illusion we're a packet ship, carrying passengers and goods."

"Aye, Captain. That'll get Harris' greedy attention."

Viktor turned and headed for his cabin. "I think I shall adorn myself to make my grand entrance."

Grimm shook his head, laughing. "I almost feel sorry for the bastard, when he sees he's tried to pirate your ship again. How many times can a man piss himself?"

"Let's find out."

"Mr. Jon!" Grimm bellowed.

"Aye!" Jon-Jon called back.

"Get most of the lads below and bring the brats and bitches topside. We're to look like a Frenchie packet."

"Aye, sir. Who's the poor bastard we're after?"

"Harris."

"Shit!" Jon-Jon grinned and gave an astonished whistle. "Small damn ocean. Reckon he'll piss himself this time?"

"More than likely," Grimm nodded. "Now hop to it and see that the Captain's orders are carried out."

"Aye!" Jon-Jon went about his tasks, giggling like a mad man.

Belladonna had been listening to the exchange and approached Grimm about it. "Everyone seems amused all of a sudden. I take it there is an interesting history with this pirate?"

"That there is, lass. Let's get below, and I'll tell you about it over a glass of gin."

"You can have the gin. I don't care much for the smell of it."

"More for me, then."

In late summer of 1765, Viktor put in at Savannah to resupply and pay his respects to Mother Celie. By then, the twenty-six-year-old pirate had already built quite a reputation for himself.

He, his first mate, Jim Rigger, and second mate, Hezekiah Grimm, were overseeing the loading of provisions. They stopped their conversation as one, when a young man in an outlandish outfit approached the ship.

He dressed in gaudy, bright silks, dripping with brocade. Tons of lace festooned his blouse. A sword and pistol swung awkwardly from a bright red sash. A large hat with a crimson plume topped off the ensemble. The lad tried to swagger, but his floppy-topped boots made it difficult to do so without tripping. He ended up having to settle for a mincing step.

The pirates sniggered among themselves, as they watched his progress. When the little peacock started up the gangplank, Viktor stepped out onto it and blocked his way.

"Can I help you, lass?"

"I beg your pardon! I am not a woman!" the lad sputtered indignantly.

"Are you sure?" The pirate said with a leer.

"Of course, I am sure!"

Viktor smirked. "My mistake; never seen such frippery on a man before. You look like a French whore's dressmaker used you for a mannequin." He gave one of the lace cuffs a calculated flick. It gratified him to see the boy puff up and redden. "So, who are ye, and what's your business here?"

The young man pulled himself up to his full, unimpressive height. He stood about five inches shorter than Viktor's six-foot-three. The fact that he stood lower down the gangplank than the pirate only exaggerated their difference in height.

"I am Chadwick Harris, and I am looking for Captain Brandewyne."

Vik sneered at that. "What is it you want, man? The Captain is a busy man."

"Well at least you finally recognize my gender," Harris said with an offended sniff. "But I and my family are much too important to discuss business with an underling, such as you."

The pirates behind Vik didn't bother to hide their amusement. He ignored them and laid a heavy hand on Harris' shoulder. "Well, that's too bad, Chadwick. No one gets to talk to the Captain, unless they go through me."

He gulped visibly, his Adam's apple bobbing. "I — I s-see. Very well, I have heard of Captain Brandewyne; that he is a great pirate; that he was raised and aided by the Thunderbolt Witch; and that he learned his trade from the famous pirate, Billy Black."

"All true, but you still haven't said what you want with the Captain."

"I want him to teach me how to be a pirate." The lad jutted his jaw out, trying to hide how intimidated he felt.

Viktor blinked at him then smiled. "Well, why didn't you say so man? Mr. Grimm, do you think there'd be a place on board for Mr. Harris?"

"Oh, I imagine there are a few among the crew who'd appreciate having the lad along," he played along.

"Aye," Rigger chimed in. "He's a pretty one. The lads get lonely, when they've been too long at sea."

Harris glanced at the pirates nervously. "You mean that they turn to — to — sodomy?"

"Oh, aye," Vik nodded. "I've even seen men working the deck clad in dresses taken from some prize ship. Some sailors just can't handle celibacy, and if there's been poor hunting, there's no gold for whores in port."

Several crewmen had joined behind Viktor to watch the show. Morris, a large, hairy man with liver-lips and only one eye, piped in, "Let him join us!" He made kissy faces at Harris and rubbed his belly suggestively. "Aye. Mmmm. I get some of that! I get all up in that! Mm-mm uh-hmmm!"

Harris recoiled in disgust. "You're all mad!"

Viktor gave him a light shove, causing him to stumble down the gangplank. "Go on and get out of here, boy. There's no place for you on a pirate crew."

He scrambled to his feet and managed to run clumsily back up the dock. Loud hoots and guffaws from the pirates followed him back to shore. Angrily, but from a safe distance, he turned and shook his fist at them. "Just wait until my father hears about this!"

Vik had to shout over the increased laughter from his men, "That's right, Chadwick, run back to daddy. Maybe he'll buy you a boat, so you can hunt down the big bad pirates who made you cry like a little girl!"

Three months passed without Chadwick Harris even crossing Vik Brandee's mind. The hunting had been fair, but there had been no great profit on the prizes taken.

At sunrise the lookout spotted sails approaching rapidly. Practiced eyes among the crew pegged it as a merchantman, but well-armed. Viktor had no intention of running from the vessel's aggressive approach, not even when the spotters reported it had struck colors and run up the black flag.

Rather, he looked through the glass to see if he could spot who would be fool enough to think to pirate him. He spied a vaguely familiar black hat with a crimson plume bobbing around on the deck frenetically. It took him a few moments to place it.

"Harris?"

He held the glass out for Rigger, whose eyes saw better than his, to look and confirm his suspicion.

"Aye, Captain. Looks like the little peacock was able to acquire a ship and crew after all. Seems he's determined to be a pirate."

Viktor chuckled, "Have the lads prepare to greet our guests. This should be entertaining."

They allowed the interloper to catch up with them, rather than running. That alone might have served as warning to more experienced pirates. Indeed, Vik suspected it had dawned on at least one of Harris' crew. He could see through the glass a large man with a shaved head arguing with the bobbing feather. Yet, the ship still approached. He saw the man shake his head but turn to the crew and bark some orders. The ship turned and released a light volley. One shot pierced a sail, but the rest fell well short, plunging harmlessly into the water.

"Did they just fire on us?" Rigger asked incredulously.

"It would appear so," Vik confirmed. "Looks like they're reloading. Hold your fire, for the moment."

"Aye, Captain."

As predicted, the interloper released a second volley. Once again, all the shots fell short. The ship was close enough to make out Harris having a near-apoplectic fit directed at the larger man.

"I see someone on board has a sense of self-preservation. They deliberately missed us. Take out their foremast, Mr. Rigger. One shot only. Let's see if we can push them to mutiny."

The order was followed to the letter, but it didn't have the effect he'd hoped for. Rather, it served to unite Harris' crew.

With only two masts remaining, they knew they had no chance of escape. Instead, they moved closer to Viktor's ship, determined to go down fighting. That earned them a grudging respect from Viktor and his crew, but it didn't gain them any leniency when the actual combat started.

Harris' crew quickly surrendered, however; so, casualties remained low. Wanting to savor the effect on Harris, Viktor and his mates retired to the captain's cabin. He gave orders to assemble all the prisoners on deck, with Harris in the front.

The would-be pirate could be heard yelling all over the ship. He alternately ranted at his crew for failing to follow orders and raged at his captors to release him or face the wrath of his family.

"Oh, be quiet, you little ninny!" Vik ordered, as he emerged on deck, flanked by Grimm and Rigger.

Harris' face grew even more livid. "You!"

Vik gave him a mock bow. "Aye, Chadwick Harris, me; although, I believe I failed to properly introduce myself, when last we met. Viktor Brandewyne, captain of this fine vessel and your humble host." Chuckles from the pirate crew greeted the final part of his statement.

The color rushed out of Harris' face, and a dark, damp spot grew rapidly on his breeches.

The pirate captain gave a lop-sided smile and clasped his prisoner on the shoulder. "I'm in a good humor today, Chadwick. I'll let you live. After all, you're still new to our trade. You had no idea it is not wise to try to pirate other pirates, unless you are certain you have the strength and skill to best them," he added as a disclaimer.

He moved to put his arm around the frightened man's shoulders. "I know one of your men tried to warn you off, but you didn't listen to him. The shots you fired deliberately missed us."

"The man is an insubordinate bastard," Harris fumed. "I plan to have him flogged."

"You've much to learn about our trade, Chadwick." Vik made a tsking sound and shook his head. "Always weigh carefully advice given you by those with more experience. If your man had followed your orders explicitly, we would have slaughtered your entire crew."

Harris trembled, as the realization of the extent of the cold-bloodedness of the man next to him sank in. He only then began to understand piracy was not a game.

"Point the man out to me," Vik ordered, even though he was already aware of where the man stood.

Harris obeyed, indicating a tall, well-muscled man with a stubbly shaved head and the shadow of a beard.

"Step forward and give me your name."

"Name's Willoby Jon. Those as know me call me Jon-Jon, Cap'n," the prisoner answered, standing defiantly straight.

Viktor smiled. "I'm impressed with how well you held your crewmates together. I can use a man like you, Mr. Jon." He returned his attention to Harris. "I'm going to give you a choice, Mr. Harris. I'm going to let you keep your ship and enough provisions to reach the nearest port. You can either spend an hour with Morris in exchange for keeping your entire crew; or you can forego that pleasure and leave with just enough men to sail your vessel."

Morris blew him a kiss and leered, just for effect. Harris whimpered a bit. "What does he plan on?"

"Oh, he fancies pretty boys like you," Vik told him matter-of-factly. "I imagine he wants to bugger you in the ass, but I could be wrong. He may want you to bugger him."

Harris tried to back away, shaking his head, his eyes wild with fear.

"Too bad, Morris; looks like this fish is going to slip the hook." He chuckled, never releasing his grip on his victim. "Mr. Jon, your first duty is to pick out which of your men are best suited to see little Chadwick here is safely returned to his daddy; skeleton crew only."

"Aye, Cap'n," Jon-Jon nodded. "Begging your pardon, Cap'n, but what is to become of the rest of the lads?"

"A fair question. They are welcome to join my crew, but I'll personally slit the throat of any that challenge my orders or fail to pull their own weight aboard my ship."

One of the captives foolishly asked, "What if some of us don't want to join up with you?"

In answer, Viktor slicked his hair back with one hand, then, flicked that hand forward. The hapless sailor stared down at the dagger that had suddenly blossomed from his chest. The blade quivered for three heartbeats, before the man fell to the deck, dead.

"Anymore questions? I didn't think so."

"Why did Viktor let this idiot go free?" Belladonna asked, genuinely curious.

Grimm shrugged, but answered, "I can think of two reasons, although I never asked. Savannah is an important port to him, and Harris' family wields enough power and money to possibly make things uncomfortable for him there. But, the real reason, I believe, is that Vik enjoys tormenting the little bastard."

Chapter 25

To keep up the deception they were a packet ship, any of the pirates Harris was sure to recognize went below for the ambush. The crew remaining topside even made a show of trying to run from the *Georgia Belle*. As they hoped, Harris fell for the bait.

The topside crew pretended to surrender, when a warning shot was fired at them. The *Georgia Belle* secured to the *Incubus*, and Harris led the boarders himself. The women and children reacted hysterically, knowing the newcomers were no better a lot to fall prey to than their current captors.

Oddly, neither Harris nor his men seemed to notice how calm and unafraid the men of the *Incubus* remained. It gave further proof that six, nearly seven years at sea had taught the man very little about his chosen profession.

"Butterick, get those biddies rounded up and silenced. I can't hear myself think over their squawking," he ordered. "Timmons, you and a few of the men check this vessel over. I like the looks of her."

The two men set about to follow his orders. Viktor's men knew their trade far better than his. Timmons and the sailors with him died before they even knew they'd walked into an ambush, when they went below. No one heard a thing.

"You there," Harris accosted one of the captives. "Lead the way to your captain's quarters, since the man seems too craven to face me here."

The man obliged, convinced he was leading a dead man.

As per Viktor's orders, the way to his cabin held no hidden crewmen, only a large black cat that glared at Harris before turning to lope down the corridor.

Harris smiled to himself, looking around at the excellent construction of the vessel. "I'm looking forward to sailing this ship. She'll make a fine pirate." His guide opened the cabin door and stepped aside for him to enter. The splendor of his assumed prize so distracted him, he got three steps into the cabin before he realized who awaited him.

"She already is a fine pirate vessel," Viktor assured him smugly from his favorite chair. Grimm stood behind and to the side of him. Belladonna lay ensconced on the bed on her belly, chin in hands to watch the show. Jon-Jon stepped from behind the door, shutting it.

"Were you planning on taking my ship from me, Chadwick?"

Harris stood, face ashen, mouth opening and closing several times, before he could say anything. "I-I already have," he stammered.

"Really? You don't sound so sure." Vik pulled the cork from a bottle of bloodied rum that was more blood than rum and took a swig. "How can you say you've taken a ship, when the ship has taken you?"

Harris grew a little bolder. "I knew one day you would get overconfident. Then, I'd have my revenge for all the humiliations you've dealt me. Finally, that day has come. My men currently hold your ship. You know, I'm surprised at you, hiding in your cabin like this. And to think, I thought you could teach me how to be a pirate. I've done quite well without your help. Soon, I'll set you and your men adrift, then, pleasure myself with your bed wench."

"I could just eat you up," Belle said sweetly.

"You'd get indigestion," Grimm muttered to her.

Viktor didn't seem perturbed. "You seem awfully sure of yourself, Harris. You've turned into quite a ballsy bastard since our first meeting. I'm impressed."

He frowned at him, irritated that his efforts at intimidation didn't seem to be working on the older pirate. "That reminds me, going by the scuttlebutt, you're supposed to be dead, aren't you?"

In a blink, the vampire stood right in his face, holding him aloft by the nape of his neck effortlessly, so he wouldn't have to bend over. "Not so as you would notice." He bared his fangs in a wicked grin.

Not only did Harris piss himself, but he also screamed like a little girl, his voice shrill and thin. "Unholy demon! I know you've never liked me, but please have mercy!"

"Be still." Vik's voice breathed power. Harris' eyes darted about in terror, as he found his body paralyzed by the vampire's will. Viktor set him down and looked at Jon-Jon. "Grab him a chair, before he falls down."

The vampire suddenly reappeared in his own seat, as if he'd never moved. "I'm hurt, Chadwick. How can you say I've never liked you?"

"You've always rejected me." Fear made his voice sound thin and weak.

"I was doing you a favor. You would never have survived on my crew. If I really didn't like you, I'd have gutted your father, fucked your mother and sisters in every square in Savannah, and used you for crab bait."

"Why waste good meat on a bunch of crabs?" the siren asked.

"Easy, pet," Vik chuckled. He stood and walked over to where his victim sat. The man reeked of fear and urine. His heartbeat pounded in Viktor's head. It would be so very easy to just drain the man. He understood quite well Belladonna wasn't really joking with her barbs about eating Harris. The man smelled like food.

He found himself caressing the man's neck, instinctively searching out his pulse with his fingertips, before he brought his bloodlust under firm control. Harris, still unable to move, sat pouring sweat, staring mesmerized and terrified at Viktor's glowing emerald eyes. The sight of the tips of the vampire's fangs peeking between his slightly parted lips caused Harris to whimper.

Viktor's fingertip brushed against the links of a golden chain. An odd tingle of power traveled up his arm. A slow smile curved his lips, as he pulled the pendant out of Harris' shirt. A luminous white opal about the size and shape of a bird egg set in gold wire filigree hung from the chain.

"Very pretty; Alyssa described it perfectly. Thank you for delivering the Mermaid's Tear to me, Harris."

Belle spoke up, when she saw his arm tense to snatch the bauble. "Don't break the chain. It is an object of power, and it might be dangerous to damage any part of the whole."

"Point taken, Belladonna." He slid the chain through his fingers, until he located the clasp, then, carefully unfastened it. He toyed with the thought of placing it around his own neck but decided against it. The stone's latent magic tried to interact with his, and it made him itch. He refastened the clasp and locked the necklace in a small chest.

"What are you going to do with me?"

"I don't see how you keep a crew, man," Grimm commented. "You've never once asked what will be done with your crew on any of the occasions we've taken you."

"They've always failed me, by allowing you to take my ship." He spat in open disgust.

Vik laughed. "True to form; you bollux things up for yourself, but it's never your fault, is it, Harris? Still, you did bring me a wonderful prize as well as this lovely stone. I think it's only fair that you receive some compensation. Unfortunately, Morris is no longer with us. Perhaps an hour with Belle would suffice?"

The man blinked in amazement at his good fortune. His leering grin indicated that he would be very pleased with that offer. "You really mean it, Brandewyne? You'd grant me an hour with that beauty there on your bed?"

"Aye."

"You really do like me!"

Belle was about to protest being offered up without so much as a by your leave. A thought from the vampire stopped her. Silently, he let her know he was only toying with the idiot of a pirate. He truly enjoyed tormenting the man, just as Grimm had told her.

She rolled off the bed and sashayed over to Harris. Placing a hand on either shoulder, she straddled his lap. He, in turn, ran his hands up her thighs to her waist and further, until he cupped her breasts through her shirt.

"Oooh, very nice," she purred throatily. Lowering her head, she kissed him full on the mouth, tasting him thoroughly. The display affected every man in the cabin.

She pulled back from the kiss, stretching her head back and pressing herself more firmly into his hands. "This is going to be delicious." She gave her most natural smile. Her mouth spread almost ear to ear, revealing her needle-like teeth. Her golden eyes shone amber.

Harris let out a small squeak just before losing consciousness.

"Pooh, I should've realized he wouldn't last long," Belle pouted.

"It's Harris." Vik grinned smugly, as if that explained everything. And, in a way, it did.

They returned an unconscious Harris to the *Georgia Belle* and allowed a token crew to go free with him. The gold, they kept.

Viktor took full advantage of the extra strength of his five remaining vampires. They enabled him to transfer the heavy ingots and coins over to the *Incubus* in a fraction of the time it would have taken a full human crew. Plus, he didn't have to worry about any of his cadre pocketing some of the gold during the transfer.

He didn't need any extra crewmen, which proved unfortunate for the remaining prisoners. He decided they would be considered part of the provisions. He ordered three men hung by their ankles, and their throats slit to feed the cadre. Belle and Lazarus disposed of the remains. He locked the rest of the prisoners in one of the smaller holds.

"Things are a bit crowded below decks, Vik," Grimm informed him. "Think we'll have time to sell off the live cargo, before we return to Dorada?"

"I don't see why not. But the business needs to be conducted as swiftly as possible. I've no time for dallying."

Grimm would have liked to ask for some port time for the crew, but he'd seen Viktor in a similar mood several times. He just hoped none of the lads made the mistake of complaining. It wouldn't end well for them.

"I'd like to give the lads a ration of the special rum. It'll keep them out of the gold," he suggested.

The vampire looked at him for a while without speaking. Now that he'd brought it to his attention, he could feel the link with his crew growing weak.

"A prudent suggestion, Hezekiah," he finally spoke. "See to it none of the men are left out."

"Aye, Captain." He left to carry out the order, relieved at Viktor's reasonableness. He seemed to be more obsessive lately than was usual for him. As first mate, Grimm saw it as part of his duty to prevent mutiny before some fool on the crew had the chance to even contemplate it in passing.

Had the captain not been so engrossed in completing his quest, he would've given the crew their shares of such a rich prize and the time and port to enjoy them in. At least the tainted rum Vik had prepared would keep the lads in line for a good while.

Grimm had Jon-Jon assemble the men on deck to dole out the rum. "We'll be stopping in at Delacroix's to off-load the wenches and brats," he announced. A happy roar greeted the news. "Captain's orders; no sporting time in port. Only those selected to guard the cargo will be going ashore."

There were a few grumbles. Jon-Jon made a mental note of the dissenters. He and Grimm expected there would be a few. Grimm instructed him to give a double portion to any disgruntled pirates. Jon-Jon thought it was to buy their silence. He had no idea it was to ensure their obedience. As Grimm understood Viktor's explanation of how the magic worked, the first ones to start rebelling would be the most resistant to the vampire's blood and will. They would require a stronger dose to keep them under control.

Even though he believed Uncle Zeke's magic would protect him, Grimm did not join the men in their drink. He was more loyal to Vik Brandee than any of that lot would ever be, blood bond or no.

Chapter 26

It took them almost a week to reach the slave trader's island. Pursuing the Mermaid's Tear then having to hunt down Harris to retrieve it had taken them several leagues out of their way. They posted extra watches, while they sailed through pirate-infested waters. Although few would be so reckless as to take on a ship like the *Incubus* when she was showing her full armament, there was still a risk of some trying to board by night to poach their prize. Viktor didn't fear any other pirate. He just didn't want to waste time with any of them.

Belladonna had gone hunting, which prevented her from singing up favorable winds to speed them along. It was just as well. If she had aided, the ride would have been a rough one. They needed the captives as healthy as possible, if they hoped for a good price on them.

Delacroix, the result of the union of an escaped slave and a Carib brothel cook, had skin the color of coffee and eyes and hair a distinct blue-black hue; the latter, he wore shoulder-length and kept oiled into shiny ringlets. He favored bright blues and reds for his clothing and wore an abundance of gold.

Although both Viktor and Grimm did repeated business with him, neither man cared to spend much time in his presence. The slaver's trade of supplying brothels did not bother them. It was his penchant for children that they found both puzzling and repugnant. They just didn't understand the appeal. Still, being true pirates, they would never let that qualm get in the way of making a profit.

Grimm and a select few herded the captives ashore. Viktor's Hunger began to grow again, so he felt it wiser to remain in his cabin and leave the negotiations to his more than capable first mate. He sent Lazarus along to act as courier, if any problems arose.

The women grouped around the children. They were all frightened, but grateful to be off the ship. The way they clung to each other told Grimm it would be a difficult task to separate the lot of them. He wasn't too concerned about it, however. As far as he cared, that was Delacroix's problem not his.

Knowing the man's tastes, he figured the presence of children would allow him to push the price up considerably.

"*Mon ami!*" Delacroix came out to greet them himself. Grimm figured word must have reached him quickly as to who had "cargo" to offer. The slaver strode over and embraced the pirate.

He was quick to push the man off him, but not so roughly as to bugger the deal. "I'm not your friend, Delacroix, nor one of your catamites. I'll thank ye to keep your hands to yourself," he growled.

Delacroix laughed it off but didn't try to touch him again. The Grimm Reaper's reputation was well deserved, and the slaver had no desire to shorten his life span.

"So, what have you brought me today?" he asked the pirate, opting to stick to business.

Grimm signaled for the captives to be brought forward. The women still clustered tightly around the children, making them difficult to see. Delacroix circled the group, inspecting.

"They appear to be in good condition, but clothing can hide a multitude of flaws," he commented. "Let us see them stripped. I know how rough you sea dogs can be. I'll not pay top price if they're damaged — or pregnant. Brooding whores don't make me money. I also want a better look at the little ones."

The pirate nodded and turned to the captives. "You, women, separate and strip down."

"Are you mad?" "How dare you!" These and various sobs, cries and pleas for mercy greeted the order.

"Have it your way; makes no never mind to me," he said with a shrug. "Lads, if they won't do it on their own, cut the clothes off them."

A few tried to run but soon tripped up in the hobbles Viktor had ordered put on them. He and Grimm had done this often enough to know what to anticipate. There were always a few runners, the ones who would blindly try to escape, never taking into consideration that there was nowhere to run to on an island.

After a great deal of screaming and struggling, the women stood huddled and naked. A few stood erect, however, refusing to be shamed. They were the ones who had recognized the inevitability of their fate and, resigned to it, had voluntarily disrobed. Grimm admired that. They were fine, healthy young women, and stood a good chance of surviving long enough to buy their freedom.

The children had been separated from their mothers during the melee. They now stood in a small group, clinging to each other. Some were crying, but most were frightened into silence. As one, they stared toward their mothers. Knowing that they faced a fate worse than the brothels, Grimm hadn't seen fit to force them to disrobe, as well.

Delacroix resumed his inspection of the merchandise. A few of the women bore bruises, but nothing serious. There were no cuts, broken bones or major scars visible on any of the women. None appeared to be with child, either. On the whole, they looked to be in good enough condition. Plainly, the slave trader stood to make a handsome profit on them.

He turned his attention to the children. Crouching down to be at eye level, he smiled reassuringly at them. "Do not be afraid, *mes belles petites*," he cooed. "If you come here to me, I will give you cakes and sweets."

One child stepped timidly toward the slaver's outstretched hand. "That's right, *chere*."

"Get back with the others!" Grimm barked. The child jumped and returned to the relative safety of the group. Delacroix stood and snarled at him. "You haven't paid for them yet, Del," Grimm reminded.

"You know I like to sample the goods, Reaper." The slaver spoke French, so his intended victims wouldn't understand him.

Grimm replied in the same language. He didn't have time for hysterics from the cargo. *"I do not have time for that. You will have to take my word that they are untouched. I don't have a taste for brats and won't tolerate it on my watch; nor does my captain."*

"Your captain?" Delacroix returned to English. "You are joking, *mon ami*. Everyone knows that the Grimm Reaper serves under no man but himself."

Grimm did not smile. "I have already told you, I am not your friend, Delacroix, and I don't like you well enough to joke with you. My captain has pressing business elsewhere and has ordered that I expedite this sale. Now, shall we tend to our business?"

The slaver narrowed his eyes at the pirate. He still didn't believe Grimm was not the captain but didn't really care. Regardless of the reason for it, the pirate seemed in an unusual hurry. The fact that only the guards for the prisoners had come ashore, rather than a larger portion of the crew looking for sport, confirmed it. This led Delacroix to believe he had the advantage in bargaining.

Grimm's refusal to let him try out one of the little ones irritated him, as well. He toyed with the idea of dragging out price negotiations as retaliation. Only the pirate's deadly reputation deterred him from doing so.

"I can offer twenty gold apiece for the bitches; as for the little ones, hmm." He shrugged and made a show of thinking about it. "They look a little underfed. Ten silver a head."

"That is nowhere near your regular rate," Grimm stated flatly. "They're worth twice that, and I'm insulted that you dare mention silver. Any craft master would pay double your offer on the brats as apprentices. And I'm not some wet-behind-the-ears pup who doesn't know the value of a fresh, healthy whore who hasn't been wallowed out wide enough to dock a dinghy." He nodded toward the women. "Try again, Delacroix."

He noticed Lazarus slip off and head back to the ship. He doubted the slaver had even taken notice of the cat. In short order, he felt sure the man would regret having offered any kind of delay.

Delacroix got a stubborn set to his jaw. "Fine, I'll make it gold on the children, but the price stays the same. You want to rush negotiations and get out of port; then you accept my offer."

"Mr. Grimm! I gave order that this business be concluded in a timely manner." The icy voice of doom carried down the dock to the two men.

The pirate and the slave trader both turned to see Viktor Brandewyne stalking up the dock toward them.

"Aye, Captain. Mr. Delacroix has taken that as license to offer substandard prices for prime cargo."

"They've been saying you were dead," Delacroix whispered, stunned. "I thought the Reaper was lying about not being the Captain."

The vampire fixed him with a chilly stare. "They were wrong, and it is never wise to doubt the word of the Grimm Reaper."

"No, I can see it is not."

"What was the offer, Mr. Grimm?"

"Twenty gold a head for the wenches; ten gold a head for the brats. He offered silver at first for the little ones."

"Silver? Indeed." Viktor pulled out one of his daggers and began cleaning the dirt from under his fingernails. "I know I have a good deal of time and provisions invested in this cargo, but I think I would sooner slit the throats of the whole lot, before I would sell them so cheaply."

He moved over to the group of children and singled out the one that had caught the slaver's eye earlier. Grabbing the boy by the hair, he forced the child's head back, baring his throat. Deliberately, he held the blade against the tender flesh.

"I think I may do the brats, regardless," he stated coolly, as if announcing he thought he might take a walk in the garden. "It would be more of a kindness to them than to let you have them to fulfill your pederastic fantasies."

Delacroix's eyes widened, as he saw he was about to lose the very part of the cargo he desired the most. He wanted the women, so he could make a profit and for pleasure. But the children; he desired them for his personal gratification. Only a very few of his clients had tastes along the same line as his.

"No, wait!" he cried desperately. "I will triple the offer, only, please, do not harm *les petites*!"

"You see, Mr. Grimm," Viktor smiled. "It's just a matter of knowing how to negotiate. Collect our fee and return to the ship as soon as possible."

He released the terrified boy and strode back down the dock.

As Grimm collected the payment from Delacroix, the siren rejoined the company. The first mate noticed the slaver seemed to be distracted in the middle of counting out the gold. He turned to see what had drawn his attention. Looking out the window, he could see Belladonna approaching the prisoners.

At least she's dressed, he thought. He wasn't worried about the guards he'd brought, but he hated to think what chaos she would have wreaked among the slaver's men, had she been naked.

"It's not fair to hide the best away until last," Delacroix complained. "It forces me to open a new round of negotiations. I thought you and Brandee were in a hurry."

"She's not for sale. Let's finish the accounting."

"Everything is for sale. I'll quadruple the offer, if you will throw her in."

"Tempting, but no deal, Del. She's not for sale. She belongs to the Captain," Grimm shook his head.

Belladonna looked in the direction of the hut, as if she'd heard their conversation. Looking less than pleased, she started stalking over.

The slaver seemed to be entranced by the very sight of her. "*Alors*, man. At least see if he will sell me one night with her."

Grimm placed a hand on his shoulder to get his attention. "Trust me on this, Delacroix. You would never survive the experience. I've seen what she can do to a man. It is not pretty."

Delacroix grinned, "She's that good?"

"I'm better," the siren stated, arms crossed over her chest. 'Mr. Grimm is correct that I am not for sale, but I do not belong to the Captain. I belong to myself."

The slave trader laughed at that. "Of course you do, *cherie*. Very well, you say that you are not for sale. Surely there is something I can offer that would entice you to spend some time with me."

She looked him over and half-sneered, "I doubt it. I prefer my meat a little less oily. All that stuff in your hair would just get all over the place and ruin the flavor."

"I can wash my hair, *Cherie*." He leered.

"Del, she wasn't making an *entendre*," Grimm informed him. "Belle, I'll ask ye not to maim or eat the man until after he's finished paying for the cargo."

The siren gave a toothsome snarl, which was sufficient to cool the slave trader's ardor. "Your cautions are not necessary, human. I have already fed today, and, as I said, this one is not to my tastes. I'm going back to the ship."

She turned and stalked back out.

Delacroix showed just a bit too much white around the eyes. "She is cannibal?"

That made the pirate chuckle. "Hardly; cannibals eat their own kind. She *is* a man-eater, but what just walked out that door is in no way human. You have just met your first, and, if you are lucky, your last siren."

"A mermaid?"

"No; a siren. Believe me, there is a huge difference. Now, how about we finish this transaction?" he prompted. "The Captain is wanting to get on about his business and is not a patient man."

"Point taken, Reaper."

☠

Lazarus sat on a shelf, tail twitching, watching his master brood. Viktor sat, drumming his fingers. A nearly empty bottle of his blood-rum mixture sat close by. The diluted beverage did nothing to sate his Hunger. His senses were heightened to the point of nearly driving him mad. He could hear every heartbeat on board the ship. Worse, he could smell everything, and his crew was rather — fragrant. Interestingly, however, the odors actually fueled his Hunger rather than suppressed it. Even during his brief foray on shore to speed things along, his bloodlust had threatened to overtake him. He'd wanted nothing more than to give in to his urge to slit that child's throat and drink his fill. If he had done that, he knew there would have been a good chance not even his own men would have escaped alive. His Hunger remained insatiable and constantly waiting just below the surface. Giving in to it in that situation would have resulted in a feeding frenzy like the one that overtook him shortly before he caught up with Grimm's captors.

He caught the scent of the siren the instant she came back on board. He could even smell that she was irritated. Belladonna's scent affected him differently than the odors of his crew. He became painfully aware that another appetite was growing.

Before long, Belle stormed into his cabin with only a perfunctory knock. "You need to straighten out that first mate of yours," she fumed.

Viktor sat, unmoving, staring at her. "Indeed?"

"That smelly, oily, flesh peddler you came here to see tried to buy me!" The outrage rang clear in her voice.

He couldn't quite keep the smile from edging onto his face. "I take it that Mr. Grimm's response to Del upset you. Did he try getting more money out of the pederast using you?"

"No," she glared. "He told the creature I was not for sale."

"Then what is the problem?"

"He said I belong to you!"

Her scent so provoked him he could barely stand it. He stood and moved toward her. She soon found herself gazing up at him, as he loomed over her. He reached out and ran a tress of her hair through his fingers.

"Don't you?"

Viktor smiled, his senses telling him he affected the siren in much the same way she affected him. Her pulse and breathing increased in speed at his proximity and touch. He could also smell lust quickly replacing her anger.

Belladonna had not expected this sort of behavior from the vampire. She'd fully expected him to either get irritated at her or just dismiss her complaint. His seductive mood caught her completely off guard.

"No, I don't," she protested, but it came out breathy. She found it hard to concentrate.

He chuckled and dipped his face to her hair to better catch her scent, which he found intoxicating. "You don't sound very sure about that, Belle," he whispered, his lips brushing her ear.

She gave a soft moaning sigh. Would it really be so horrible to let herself be mastered by the pirate? It would be so very, very easy to give in, and part of her really wanted to.

Viktor could sense her defenses weakening. Even without the accidental bond between them, her reaction to him and her body language told him she was close to surrendering to him.

Gooseflesh broke out on her skin, as he gently gripped her shoulders and began kissing down her throat. It pleasantly amazed him at how soft her skin felt under his fingertips. Her body grew yielding, and her breathing grew faster, when the kisses turned open-mouthed. The sensation of his tongue on her skin caused her to shudder with pleasure.

She was so caught up in the sensuality, that she didn't realize he was about to bite her, until his fangs pierced her throat.

"No!" she screamed and pushed him off of her. The damage was already done, however.

A look of realization and horror crossed Viktor's face. He dropped to the deck, lifeless, the siren's blood still glistening on his lips.

Chapter 27

A human woman might have stood there in shock, or she might have panicked and become hysterical. Belladonna was not human. She knew a slim chance of Viktor surviving existed, but it would require swift action on her part and an obscene amount of luck for the vampire.

She knelt beside his body and crouched over him. Ignoring Lazarus, who had jumped down and padded over to see what she was doing, she began kissing and licking Viktor's mouth. A small adjustment to his head opened his mouth for better access. The siren slipped her tongue into his mouth, careful not to nick it on his fangs.

In her effort to remove all her blood from his mouth, the last thing she wanted to do was put more in it.

Once she was sure she had gotten all of it, she sat back and watched him for some kind of response. Lazarus stretched toward his face, sniffing, his whiskers brushing the man's beard. He sat up, blinked at the siren, sneezed, and began grooming himself, purring.

Viktor took a breath and blinked. "You didn't have to hit me that hard, pet."

"Good, you didn't swallow any," she sighed.

"What are you talking about, woman?"

She blinked at him. Could it be he really didn't remember? "You bit me."

He sat up. "Don't be daft, Belle," he argued. "Your blood is poisonous to me. I would die, if I bit you."

"Viktor, you did die." She pulled her hair back to show him the fang marks. They were still bleeding a little bit.

His Hunger took over, and he lunged for her. She was ready this time, and he was human slow for the moment. That small edge allowed her to move back and away from him, before he could grab her. She held out one hand at him, talons extended, to warn him off.

"No, Viktor. You need human blood. The only reason I was able to revive you is that you hadn't actually swallowed any of my blood. I don't think you would survive a second round," she tried to reason with him.

He stood and started stalking toward her.

"Didn't you hear what I just said?" she half-yelled at him. "You need human blood, not mine!"

"Blood isn't the only thing I'm hungry for, pet." His voice held a seductive purr.

The bond they shared made it hard to resist him. His near poisoning had weakened his powers, but she felt him really exerting his will. She had to draw on her own magic to fight his compulsion. It chilled her to realize she would not be able to fight him off, once he returned to full strength.

Then she scented it. It was subtle and well hidden, but just around the edges of their warring magicks was an alien magic, some sort of spell.

She tasted the air. Under the normal flavors of salt, tobacco, and male were essences that should not occur naturally on board a ship: flowers, growing green things, and earthy loam.

"Viktor, stop." She put as much magical force behind the order as she could; sending it back along the bond they shared.

The vampire snarled, recoiling from the psychic blow. He had not recovered enough to retaliate, or he might well have knocked the siren unconscious out of pure reflex. Once past his initial impulse, he focused on her.

"Why are you resisting, pet? I know you want me. You've made that plain on several occasions. If you are afraid I will try to feed from you, I will have one of the prisoners sent up." He misunderstood her reluctance.

"You need to do that anyway, Viktor," she sighed. "But I still cannot give in to our mutual lust. Either the earth-witch or her witchling apprentice has cast some sort of spell on you. When magical beings couple their powers and magic mingle. Not knowing how this third magic will interact, neither of us can afford to indulge ourselves."

"Damn!" he swore in frustration, slamming his fist on the table. Belladonna huddled in on herself, looking miserable.

A knock came at the cabin door.

"Enter," he snarled.

Grimm came in and quickly assessed that the captain was in an ill mood. "We just cleared the dock. It'll take the lads about an hour to tow us out of the harbor, then, we can set sail. Winds are favorable for getting us back to Dorada's island."

Viktor composed himself, somewhat. As a result of his sexual frustration, his Bloodlust was growing stronger. "Very good, Hezekiah. Send me a couple of the men we took from Harris. Now get out and take her with you."

Grimm looked at the siren, narrowing his eyes. "What have you done now?" he asked accusingly.

The vampire was suddenly just there in his face, snarling, fangs bared, one hand nearly crushing his throat. "Get out now, Mr. Grimm."

Viktor thrust him back and away from him with bruising force.

His first mate needed no further prompting. Grabbing Belladonna by the arm, he hurried them both out of the cabin.

"I protect what is mine," Viktor growled softly. "Even if it is from myself." He drained what was left of the blood-rum mixture. Unsatisfied, he roared and flung the bottle against the door, where it shattered.

"Jon-Jon!" Grimm bellowed.

"Aye, Mr. Grimm?" the second mate responded.

"Pick out two of Harris' men and send them to the Captain."

"Aye."

"And Mr. Jon," he added, "don't go in with them. He's in a foul temper."

"Understood."

Jon-Jon appreciated the warning. He was well aware of the fact that Viktor could be unpredictably deadly, when riled. He'd been that way since long before Jon-Jon had joined his crew.

Once the man left to carry out the order, Grimm forcibly dragged the siren back to his cabin. "Now answer my question, bitch. What did you do to get Vik so angry?" he shook her roughly.

She pulled free of the angry pirate, but only with some difficulty. That surprised her. A normal human shouldn't have been that strong.

"I did nothing to anger him."

He backhanded her. "Don't lie to me. If he wasn't angry with you, he would not have specifically said to bring you with me, when he ordered me out."

"He wanted me out, because it is not safe to feed from me," she told him. "Or to fuck me," came the added whisper. She rubbed her arms and gazed down and off to the side, letting her hair fall over her face.

Hezekiah stood back, absorbing and processing the information she just gave him. The Hunger being on Viktor would explain his foul mood, but not that last comment from the siren. Her body language spoke of someone genuinely hurt and feeling rejected, rather than the self-confident seductress he knew her to be, pouting over not getting what she wanted. If he didn't know better, he would swear that his friend had never actually bedded her.

He reached out and brushed the hair back from her face. She flinched and tried to pull away but had no easy means of escape.

"Easy, lass," he said softly, peering thoughtfully at her. Her expression was tormented. "My God," he whispered. "You're in love with him."

Belladonna snarled, but even her vicious teeth and golden eyes couldn't hide the truth Grimm had just learned. She felt trapped, not so much by the man before her, but by her own emotions. Until he'd spoken it aloud, she had not recognized the unfamiliar emotion. It was so — human.

The pity she saw on the pirate's face proved more than she could take, however. A rush of anger flooded over her. "Let go of me, human!" she growled. "I don't need your pity."

He smiled. "That's more like it, lass. Never could stand having a moping female around. I've seen 'em moon over Vik before. You're too strong-willed to deserve being counted in with that pathetic lot."

She shot him a murderous look. He remained unfazed. He felt reasonably sure she would not attack him for knowing how she felt toward Viktor. She'd been aboard long enough to know what the Captain's reaction would be to anything like that. Only Viktor was allowed to kill or maim any of Viktor's people.

"How about you put some of that angry energy to work, lass," He made the request half suggestion, half order. "I'm sure you could get us out of this harbor safely much faster than the lads towing us right now."

The crews of the three towboats didn't notice immediately when the towlines started going slack. Once they did, however, the chiefs of the rowers started barking at their men to quit being lazy and put their backs into it. They were still a long way from the barrier reef they were supposed to guide the ship through.

The rowers doubled their speed, but the lines grew even slacker. In a matter of minutes, the prow of the *Incubus* started to pass the smaller boats. The chief of the lead boat was about to yell up at the pirate crew that it was too soon to use the sails. To his amazement, the few sails that were unfurled hung flapping and limp, rather than being full of wind.

"What manner of witchcraft is this?" he whispered fearfully.

Jon-Jon hailed over the side, "Get back on board and raise the boats, Mr. Bland."

"We haven't cleared the reef yet, man! Are ye daft?" he answered back.

"Don't worry about the damn reef; get back on board the ship," Jon-Jon barked at him. "Siren in the water!"

"You heard the man, get back to the ship!" He needed no more prompting. Not one man among them had any desire to be that close to the water, when Belladonna was in it.

They had to scramble to secure the boats to their davits and climb aboard. The ship was picking up speed. They'd barely hoisted the boats out of the water, when they reached the reef. The spotters on the fo'c'sle started screaming back to the helm that the tide wasn't in enough to clear the reef. Already up to ten knots, there was no way the helmsman would be able to avoid a collision in time. The crew braced for impact.

The impact never came.

A wave surged beneath the ship, lifting it safely over the reef. This terrified the superstitious pirates. The wave traveled away from shore rather than toward it. Looking aft, they could plainly see the lagoon had half emptied, pushing out to open water.

A few of those with sharp hearing swore they could hear singing coming from beneath the waves.

In the middle of draining the second of the prisoners Jon-Jon brought to him, Viktor detected an overwhelming sense of panic from his crew through his link with them. He closed his eyes, reaching out with other senses to discover what crisis could grip his entire crew like this.

He saw the reef and the ship approaching it too rapidly. He saw the small boats being hoisted aboard instead of towing the ship.

Reaching along a different link, he found the source of the propulsion.

We need more water to clear the reef, pet, he thought at the siren pushing the ship.

He got a sense of irritation from her for pointing out the obvious. Then, his heightened senses picked up how her song sounded underwater. He'd never heard anything like it. Even the mermaids' songs couldn't match it.

The power from the spell song resonated with his. He could feel her magic feeding his. He realized she had been wrong about one thing. He had swallowed a minute amount of her blood. He didn't doubt that ingesting a larger amount would have killed him, but that one tiny taste melded their powers to a small extent. Perhaps the fact she'd consumed both flesh and blood from him had rendered her toxins less potent against him.

The thought of strengthening the blending appealed to him. This new sensation felt positively intoxicating. His survival instinct prevented him from actively pursuing it, however. The risks were just too high.

Still caught up in the power rush, he quickly finished off his second victim. His Hunger rested, slaked for the moment. He could have easily gone through a few more just for the blood intoxication. He felt even more aware of everything than he had before he fed.

He caught an alien scent, yet it was familiar. It reminded him of the bower in which he'd bedded Paella. Just the thought of the girl's name sent a wave of lust through him. A deadly cold anger quickly followed and quelled the lust. Belladonna had been right. Either Dorada or her apprentice had placed a spell on him. Yes, he had enjoyed his dalliance with her, but he'd had better. It just hadn't been good enough to warrant such an intense lust.

He would take the Mermaid's Tear back to the Sister and obtain her golden tear. But then, he would get this spell lifted and make her and the little tavern slut pay for their presumption.

He set about beheading the two bodies. He had no need or desire to add to his cadre of vampires at the present.

Belladonna knocked hesitantly on Viktor's door. She felt his call, but really didn't think it a good idea for the two of them to be alone together.

"Enter."

She did as she was bidden. She almost exited immediately.

The vampire had his back to the door. He stood clad only in breeches. A washbasin with used water sat nestled in its stand close to him. He gazed intently into the small mirror with a straight razor in his hand, tidying his goatee. The muscles in his back flexed with each stroke of the blade. She found it entrancing to watch.

Finally, he turned to face her. She felt like a bird charmed by a snake.

"…are you listening, pet?" Viktor frowned at her. He'd been talking for over a minute, before she realized that he'd even spoken.

She blinked a few times before speaking. "Please put on a shirt." Her voice came out breathy and low, with a little bit of a shake to it.

He grunted with minor irritation but did as she requested. Obviously, his state of undress distracted the siren too much. Since both knew the inherent danger for them if they gave in to their natural inclinations, he saw no point in tempting fate.

"Better?" he asked curtly. She nodded. "Good. Now, as I was saying, do you think you can divine the nature of the spell that bitch put on me?"

"I will try. This will be easier, if you are seated."

He took a chair, and she moved to stand behind him. Fingers splayed, she held her hands to either side of his head, being careful not to actually touch him. Gradually opening her senses, she gently probed the spell.

Without warning, the earth magic sent out tendrils and drew her in.

His hair felt thick, soft, and incredibly warm beneath her fingers. The scent of the shaving soap mingled with his masculine muskiness in a tantalizing combination of aromas. She soon found the latent strength she felt in the muscles of his shoulders and arms demonstrated to her, when he stood and wrapped them around her, clasping her to him fiercely. She offered no resistance to his kiss, his lips and tongue masterful and eliciting a soft moan of pleasure and surrender from her. Their bodies were soon entwined on the bed. His entry caused her to cry out.

All these sensory images passed through her mind in less than a minute. Viktor was still seated before her. She had not actually touched him.

With lightning speed, Belladonna fled to the door.

"Belle?" Viktor sensed something had frightened the siren but had not experienced the hallucination with her.

"Do not come near me or touch me." Her voice was flat and emotionless, although lust and terror both shone in her eyes. "Dorada has cast a love and fertility spell and a spell of binding on you. I believe she sought to use her little witchling to control you and bind you to her service. However, it seems your own powers twisted the spell. As long as it is in place, any female you bed will be irrevocably bound to your will, rather than you being bound to hers."

"I see. I could make that work to my advantage," he mused. "But I've a feeling it would be more of a burden than a boon in the long run, especially if it is going to interfere with our ability to work together. I'll use Hezekiah as a go-between until I can get the spell removed."

"I appreciate that, Viktor," she replied. "With your leave, I'll sing up swift winds to speed us back to the earth-witch's island."

He nodded his approval. "I agree. The sooner I'm done with her, the better."

She exited the cabin as quickly as possible.

Chapter 28

Even with the gale force winds the siren summoned to push the ship along, it took nearly three weeks to reach Dorada's island. At first sight, Viktor and Grimm thought they had misread or incorrectly marked the charts. A dense jungle now completely obscured the rocky outcroppings. The island had exhibited nowhere near this level of lushness, when they'd left it. If not for a faint glimmer of gold seen through the vegetation, Viktor would have sailed on past it. Worried about this rapid change, he sent Grimm to Belle's cabin to get the siren's input.

"The earth-witch has been busy," she observed. "Almost too busy. Tell him to be on guard, Hezekiah. She has already tried to bespell him once. Do not trust Dorada."

"Never have, lass," he snorted. "I'll keep my eyes open, though. Vik already said he expects her to try to renege on her part of the trade."

"Does he know she lied to him about Paella being able to leave the island?"

The pirate looked at her blankly. "I don't know, since he never mentioned it to me. How is it that you know this little tidbit of scuttlebutt?"

"I have known since the lie was uttered. The earth-witch used magic to mask it from Viktor. I do not believe he detected it."

"And why is that?" Grimm did not like where this was going.

"Because he never detected the lie I told him. I told him I could not heal the little witchling's shriveled limbs."

He blinked. "You wanted to be rid of her," he stated. "You thought he would immediately discard her as if she were a broken toy. Did you use magic to mask your lie?"

"Yes, a very low level. It is easy to sense — if you know what to look for and are capable of detecting such things," she nodded.

He rubbed his face thoughtfully. Several minutes passed before he spoke again. "I realize you are giving up an advantage by telling me this. I'll let Vik know he has a blind spot." He gave her a hard look, before opening the door to report to the Captain. "Never, ever lie to Viktor again, lass. You won't be able to hide it anymore. I won't tell him about the lie you already told him. He's been in a dangerously ill mood for over a week, and he's going to be angry enough you kept this secret from him this long."

"Perhaps I should make myself scarce for a while."

"I suggest you stay put," he ordered coldly. "Vik is going to need your help dealing with this bitch." He stepped through the door, but added before closing it, "Besides, if you run, it will only be that much worse when he finds you."

Belladonna spent several minutes staring at the closed door. She wondered why the pirate was trying to protect her and what it was going to cost.

Viktor took the information Grimm brought him, as well as the tacit knowledge the siren had kept it secret for well over two months, rather calmly.

Hezekiah blinked in surprise at Viktor's lack of explosive rage. He hadn't exaggerated to the siren about the captain's mood during their return trip. Viktor had been feeding daily, nearly depleting their supply of prisoners. But the corpses he'd sent to the sharks as a result were viciously mangled, rather than merely beheaded. Clearly, his frustration made him rip his victims apart.

This new calm worried Grimm. Anyone who did not know Viktor would take it as a sign that he was no longer angry. Grimm knew better. Vik was his deadliest when he was calm and smiling, like he was at the moment.

The vampire felt grateful he finally had the opportunity to take action. His frustration and rage had been born of his impatience to get back to the island. Now that he had arrived, he could conclude his business with the first of the Sisters.

"Thank you for this helpful information, Mr. Grimm. Once we drop anchor tonight, be prepared to take on a passenger. We will proceed to harbor in the morning. Inform Belle and Mr. Jon to be ready to go ashore at that time." He smiled, a cold and terrible thing.

"Aye, Captain. A passenger?"

"Yes. You will understand when they arrive, Hezekiah. I want them brought directly to my cabin, and they are to remain unmolested."

"It will be as you say, Vik."

Grimm left the Captain's cabin wondering who could be coming out to greet the ship and how Viktor knew about it.

Paella sat up with a start. She'd been dreaming about the vampire pirate again. The fact both excited and frightened her. She had only dreamed of him once before, since he'd left her with her mistress.

It had been about a week earlier. She'd awakened from it to find herself standing in a shallow cove over an hour's walk from the settlement. Hidden in the nearby jungle lay an old, half-rotted pirogue. She remembered spotting it on earlier walks and assumed it a leftover from some smuggler or fisherman's camp. There had been several such caches found around the previously uninhabited island.

Something made her take note of the small craft and its location at that time. Now she felt a driving need to go see if it was still there. *Madre's* followers had been sending out clean-up crew to dispose of such debris.

She slipped out of her shelter and away from the settlement as quietly as possible. Something told her it was best if she were not seen by anyone. When she finally reached the cove, relief filled her to find the boat still there. But she must move it, she felt. Surely it wouldn't be long before others found and destroyed it, if she left it here.

Struggling to drag it to the water, Paella alternately tugged and pushed the pirogue. It was heavier than she expected. Finally, she got it afloat. Climbing in, she found a small oar that had been left with it. She set about paddling further down the coast, away from the settlement and portage.

After about thirty minutes, she started thinking she must have been mad. She couldn't, for the life of her, think what could have prompted her to want to move the stupid boat. Her shoulders and back ached from rowing. Her knees ached from the rough, hard bottom of the boat, and her feet felt numb from her kneeling position.

Clouds gathered to obscure what little moonlight fell from the waning crescent. This, of course, made it even more difficult to judge what kind of headway she was making along the shoreline.

Taking another stroke with her oar, she was nearly thrown from the small craft when the oar stuck, either in the sandy bottom or a hidden coral or rock. Struggling to free it, she nearly capsized. In a panic, she grabbed the side of the boat, trying to maintain balance, releasing the oar in the process. Once she steadied the boat, she reached for the oar.

Her hand closed on empty air. In that short time, the retreating tide had drawn her away from it and the island. Terrified, she used her hands to try to paddle back to the oar, but the tide kept pulling in the opposite direction. Eventually, exhaustion overtook her.

The pirogue carried no anchor. She found herself at the mercy of the tide and current. Let them take her where they would.

A jarring thud woke her. Had the waves carried her back to shore? No. Looking up, she saw a ship towering over her. Recognizing it for the one chance she had, Paella cried out, "Help! *Por favor*, help me!"

On deck, several heard the thud of the impact. The *Incubus* lay at anchor, so something had drifted into it, rather than being run down. A female voice crying for help really got the pirates' attention.

"There's a castaway wench over the side, Mr. Grimm," one of the pirates reported.

"Bring her aboard."

"Haul her up, lads," he relayed, leering. "There'll be some fine sport tonight!"

Grimm slugged the man hard enough to knock him to the deck. "Belay that talk, Crubs, and that goes for the rest of you sorry lot! Captain's been expecting her. He gave explicit order she be brought to him unmolested. Is that understood?"

Several cowed "ayes" answered him.

In short order, they had Paella aboard. She looked tired and frightened. Grimm quickly approached her, seeing the predatory looks on some of the men's faces. The fact she flinched from him let him know to proceed gently.

"Easy, lass," he soothed. "None of these sea dogs will harm you. The Captain is waiting for you. I don't know what you are doing out here, but he seemed to know you'd be coming."

The nervous girl looked both frightened and hopeful at that news. "*Madre* will not be pleased with me. If only I had not lost my oar."

The comment made little sense to the pirate, so he did not respond to it. Instead, he turned to the sullen, bloody-nosed crewman and ordered, "Escort this lass to the Captain's cabin, Crubs; and if he asks what happened to your nose, you best give him the reason for it."

Crubs blanched but obeyed. His eyes held the look of the damned.

☠

"Hello, pet," Viktor smiled. "What took you so long?"

Paella's voice came out small. "I lost my oar." She seemed frozen in place. She realized he had called her to him, and it frightened her. *Madre* Dorada told her that the magic bower would free her of his power and bind him to their service, instead. Obviously, something had gone wrong with the spell.

The vampire turned his attention to her escort. He smiled at the man, but it held neither friendliness nor warmth. "Have Stitches look to that nose, Crubs. And remember to keep a civil tongue in your head around a lady."

"H-how did you…?" the hapless man never got to finish the question. Viktor's hand cut off his air.

"This is my ship and my crew, Crubs. I know everything that happens on board. Now get out, or I'll let Belle give you a swimming lesson!"

The pirate couldn't get out of the cabin fast enough.

Once he was gone, Viktor turned back to Paella. He began stalking toward her like the predator that he was. She backed nervously away from him, until she came up against the edge of the bed.

"I am glad you could make it, pet. I've been without for a time, and you are just what I need to satisfy that appetite." He chuckled.

"What are your intentions?" she asked timidly.

He stood in front of her, placing his hands on her arms. "I am going to take my pleasure from you in full, pet." He suddenly lifted her and tossed her back on the bed. "And then, we are going to have a long talk."

Not all the screams and moans which emanated from the cabin were ones of pleasure. Viktor was not gentle. He had been greatly frustrated by not being able to have Belladonna, and he partially blamed Paella for it.

The siren answered the knock on her door to find Grimm on the other side. He did not look happy to be there.

"Your healing services are needed, lass."

"What has he done?" she asked flatly.

He tried to give her an innocent look. "I don't know what you mean, Belle. We've just got a man with a broken nose what needs fixin'," he lied.

"Everyone on board heard the screams, and I can smell recent sex on the air, Hezekiah." She looked bored. "Try again."

He grabbed her arm to urge her along. "Just come to Vik's cabin. You'll see for yourself."

What she saw was not pleasant.

Examination revealed Paella had suffered multiple bruises, a dislocated hip, a broken pelvis, and a broken arm. The only thing that surprised Belladonna was that Viktor had not fed on the girl, at least not recently. She only found old fang scars on the girl's inner thigh.

"You rode her too hard." There was no judgment in her voice, merely a statement of fact. She carefully kept any emotions clamped down. It was the first time in weeks she had been in his presence.

"Can you repair the damage?" The vampire's voice was equally devoid of emotions.

The siren nodded. "Good thing she is unconscious. This will be painful." The first thing she did was to jerk the girl's leg back into place, properly reseating the hip joint. That really required no magic.

The rest wasn't so easy. Belle shooed the men out, while she worked her spells. Mending the arm wasn't too hard. The break was a clean one and simple to set. The broken pelvis was the tricky part. It was broken in two places, which made it difficult to set correctly. She could just work the healing spell, but the bones would knit wrong and leave her permanently crippled.

Belladonna didn't really care one way or the other, but she was sure Viktor would not be happy, if she did a slipshod healing. A damaged witchling could anger the earth-witch enough to give her reason to make Viktor's quest even more difficult.

"It is done," the siren informed Viktor and Grimm. "Her body is healed, but she is still fragile."

"Is she still unconscious?" the vampire asked.

"No, she is awake."

Belle turned without waiting for a dismissal from him and walked off in the direction of her cabin.

"Don't leave the ship," he ordered. "You'll be joining us on shore later."

She stopped but did not turn around. The air seemed to grow a little cooler. Then, she continued to her cabin.

"Select a landing party, Hezekiah. We'll raise anchor at dawn and round the island to the harbor."

"Aye, Vik. Everything will be in order when you're ready to go ashore."

"Good. That will be all for now." He went back into his cabin, shutting the door behind him. Grimm left to inform the crew of the new orders. He already knew who he wanted watching their backs when they went to face Dorada.

Viktor did not let his dismay show, when he saw Paella flinch at his return. He honestly had not intended to be as rough with her as he had been. He had taken all his pent-up lust and anger out on her, and her body had not been able to stand up to it.

As he approached her, she cowered away from him, huddled against the bulkhead on the far side of the bed. He sat down on the edge and spoke gently to her. "I am not going to hurt you anymore, Paella. Come here." He patted a spot beside him.

She eased closer to him, but her eyes were bright with fear. She whimpered, her body tense and rigid, when he placed an arm around her and gently pulled her to him.

He softly stroked her hair and kissed her forehead in an effort to soothe her. Finally, she relaxed against his side, but could not keep from trembling. He realized that was the best he was going to get.

"That's better, pet. Now, you are going to tell me everything you know about this spell that you and your *Madre* Dorada have put on me. Why you did it, and how to remove it."

Chapter 29

"So, you have returned to my island, Dark One." Dorada greeted Viktor and his landing party. "Did you find what you sought, then?"

"You sent me on a fool's errand, earth-witch," the vampire answered. "Mermaids cannot cry tears."

She smirked at him. "So, you fail the test and return empty-handed. Perhaps you are not the One after all."

He crossed his arms and smirked back. "Since I don't know what this 'One' you people keep talking about is, I don't care if I am it or not. As for returning empty-handed, I wouldn't say that. Mr. Grimm."

He held out his hand, and Hezekiah placed a small jewelry casket in it. Viktor opened it to reveal the opal pendant on its golden chain.

"The Mermaid's Tear," Dorada whispered in awe and greed. "So, you were able to find it after all." She reached out to take it, but he held it back out of her reach and closed the casket.

"Not so fast, *Madre* Dorada," he chided, handing the prize back to his first mate. "I believe you agreed to grant me one of your golden tears in exchange. Just as I cannot take that from you, you cannot take this from me. Each must be given freely."

She scowled but nodded. "You speak truth, Dark One. Your sea-witch has counseled you well. I wonder that she is not here with you now."

"Belladonna will be along shortly." He brushed off the siren's absence. He had decided to set both her and Lazarus to watch over Paella.

"That is good. I was afraid she might have abandoned you because of your dealings with my apprentice." Dorada's concern was patently false. Viktor recognized it as an attempt to fish for information, as well as a stalling tactic.

"Belle knows her place. But, speaking of Paella, I see she is not present, either."

He was rewarded with seeing Dorada's temper flare, before she masked it. The emotion crossed her face so quickly, that only he and Grimm caught it.

"She has gone into the jungle to meditate and prepare herself for a very important ceremony," she lied, her magic flaring to hide it from his heightened senses. It confirmed that she had no idea where the girl had gotten off to.

"Pity," Vik shrugged, "I was hoping to see her again. But I am sure her presence is not necessary for our transaction."

Dorada shook her head, "No, it is not necessary, but it would have been better if she were here. In truth, we were not expecting your return to us so soon. My followers are still busy purifying the island of any detritus from those who previously made use of it. Perhaps you and your companions would be our guests this night. I shall send out runners to retrieve my apprentice from her meditation."

This aroused Viktor's curiosity. He knew the Sister was lying about knowing where Paella was, but he wondered why she wanted, or perhaps needed the girl present, before she would do the exchange. If she thought he would hand over the opal before she relinquished her magical tear, she was sorely mistaken.

"I thank you for your offer of hospitality," he smiled, half-bowing. "I will accept, to show my good faith, but I think it would be best if my men and my first mate returned to the ship for the night. We are pirates, after all, and the lads tend to get a bit boisterous after a long stretch at sea."

"Aye, and the Captain'll be needing me to keep 'em in line on board, while he's ashore," Grimm added.

"Very well," Dorada nodded, accepting their reasoning.

Of course, Viktor's real reason for sending the others back to the ship was to protect them from her magic. He felt sure that she would not try any further spells on him, since she already thought him in her thrall. There was, however, other business he could attend to while waiting for the earth-witch to make her play.

"*Madre*, while we are waiting for the lovely Paella's return, perhaps some arrangements for provisions could be made. My crew would do well to have some fresh bread and vegetables. Salt meat grows tedious after a steady diet of it," he requested.

"Understandable, Dark One," she ceded. "My new home is proving very fertile, as I'm sure you've noticed. Our current harvest is bountiful. I will give you food enough to fill your holds, but I have a boon to ask in return."

"I expected no less."

"I am glad we understand each other," she smiled. "Since my island has grown so lush, it will doubtless draw many of your ilk to strip its bounty. My people here are few, as yet. I want you to spread word that the island is cursed."

The vampire chuckled. "A clever ploy; fear of a curse will protect your island and people from outsiders far better than force, which you are ill prepared to provide at present. Agreed; Mr. Grimm, see to the transporting of provisions. Mr. Jon, you're fond of sea tales. See what manner of cautionary you can come up with. Something that will grow more horrific with each telling would be grand."

Both men nodded acknowledgement of their orders and set about fulfilling them.

Viktor made sure he kept the crystal Mother Celie had given him close to his skin that night. Since it had repelled Dorada's golden vines on the Isle of Youth, and the earth-witch seemed to recognize and fear the magic of the crystal, he reasoned it would protect him from further enchantments while in her domain.

While feigning sleep, he stretched his senses, listening for the return of the runners sent to look for Paella. As he knew would be the case, none could locate the girl. Only one tracker even found evidence of her passage but was confused and more than a little frightened that her footprints vanished in the middle of a patch of soft dry sand.

Viktor smiled to himself. He would have to reward Lazarus for doing such a fine job of obliterating the trail. It would not have been good for Dorada to learn her apprentice had taken to the water. She would've quickly deduced where the girl had ended up, which would have negated one of the pirate's bargaining chips.

He found it satisfying to listen to Dorada's growing agitation, as each searcher returned with little to nothing to report. It seemed the earth-witch muttered to herself when she was upset or displeased. Paella's unexplained absence vexed her greatly. He heard her grumble, "Drat the ungrateful little bitch. With her or no, I'll have to make the exchange in the morning. I'll just have to select another apprentice to use to complete the spell."

So, he thought, she did need the girl, despite her lies to the contrary.

The next morning, as arranged, Grimm, Jon-Jon and the select landing party returned to shore. Once again, Belladonna was absent from the group.

Grimm brought with him the jewelry casket holding the Mermaid's Tear. He and Viktor had agreed that it would be best to keep it on the ship overnight. Amazingly, Dorada had not objected to the idea.

She delayed until late morning to receive them. Escorts led the pirates to a green bower, woven from living saplings and vines. The structure resembled a lodge or longhouse similar to those of the eastern tribes that had been driven out long ago by colonists. A curtain of gold-coated vines separated the larger antechamber from a smaller private area in the rear.

The vines parted, allowing Dorada to pass through to greet them. Viktor had to admit, she knew how to make an entrance. She wore her hair unbound, with flowers woven through it. She wore nothing else. Her body was not youthful, but neither was it old and saggy. She looked the part of a mother, breasts and hips full, and belly slightly pooched; a woman who had plainly birthed and nursed several children. She was the embodiment of fertility.

Viktor bowed with a flourish, but never took his eyes off her. "Greetings once again, *Madre* Dorada. I take it that we are to conclude our transaction today."

"Yes, Dark One. It would be foolish to wait for my apprentice to return," she answered. "My messenger has informed me that she will not be able to return from her meditation for another week. Her moon time must run its course."

"I see," he nodded sagely. "I had heard that blood uncalled for could have adverse effects on magic."

"You were well taught, it seems. Very well, you have brought a vessel for the tear?"

"I have." He removed the chain holding the silver vial he'd been given for the purpose. He was about to hand it to her, when she held up her hand to stop him.

"You must not be near me during the exchange," she warned. "Have someone with no personal magic bring it to me. My tear must be untainted by a male's magic." She closed her eyes and waved her palm out at his men. Stopping and pointing, she declared, "This one may approach safely."

Viktor handed the vial to Jon-Jon, who delivered it to Dorada. He then went back and got the casket containing the Mermaid's Tear from Grimm and waited to make the exchange.

She opened the silver vial Blond held it to her cheek. She blinked her eyes rapidly, as if something was in them. Slowly, a tear welled up in the corner of her eye, glittering gold. It seemed to tremble, suspended for an eternity, before a blink dislodged it to glide down her cheek.

Once the tear slid into the vial, the earth-witch resealed it. "Take this tear, which carries the blessing of *la Madre* Dorada," she intoned, as she returned the vial to Jon-Jon and took the jewelry casket from him. She smiled at the sight of the opal pendant within.

Jon-Jon handed the vial back to Viktor, who hung it about his neck. "It has been a pleasure doing business with you, *Madre*," the vampire gave a mock bow. He watched carefully, as Dorada placed the Mermaid's Tear over her head by its chain. Her smile of avarice and anticipated power turned to a frown of puzzlement and frustration. She cupped the stone in her hand, peering sharply at it.

"You have dealt me false, Dark One," she accused, glaring up at him. "This is not the Mermaid's Tear."

"I assure you, madam, that it is indeed the object you charged me to bring to you," he countered.

"It can't be!" Her voice grew shrill. "If this truly were the Tear, I would be able to feel and use its power!"

"That is the Mermaid's Tear," he insisted. "I went to great pains to find it for you. Perhaps something blocks its power from you."

"Impossible. The only way I could be blocked from its magic would be for someone with great personal power to have put it on and bonded with it, before you gave it to me."

"Do not think to accuse me of doing so," he warned coldly. "I would not have risked losing your magical aid. Even if I had been so foolish as to entertain the thought of doing so, you saw to it that I would not."

She looked at him, pretending to not understand what he meant.

He smirked at that. "I know that you put a spell on me to keep me from donning that stone. Just holding it in my hand made me itch."

Dorada relaxed a bit, thinking that was the only aspect of the bewitchment he knew about. "You are a pirate, Dark One. You could not expect me to trust you completely where treasure was involved."

"True. In that you were wise, *Madre* Dorada," he ceded, then added, "but, just because I could not wear your little bauble, does not mean someone else of power would be prevented from doing so. Your spell of deterrence was placed on me, not on the stone itself."

She narrowed her eyes at him. "You let the sea-witch wear it?"

Viktor laughed heartily, "If you think that, you know nothing of sirens, especially one like Belladonna. If she had bonded the Tear to her power, I seriously doubt she would allow even me to remove it from her, let alone hand it over to another female."

"Then who wore it? The poor creature you took it from?"

"Harris did wear it, but I do not believe he is the source of your consternation. He is a weak-minded fool who fancies himself a pirate captain," he chuckled, a laugh that was echoed by his crewmen.

The earth-witch responded by sending her gold vines writhing toward the pirates. "Give it back!" she hissed. "The Tear is ruined for me. I cannot use it. Give back my golden tear!"

Viktor pulled out the crystal, holding it high enough that its glow surrounded him and his men. "Call off your weeds, witch," he commanded. "Our bargain was that I bring you the Mermaid's Tear to exchange for one of your golden ones, no more, no less. Nothing was agreed to as to whether the bauble was usable to you. You have no authority to demand this tear's return."

"Who wore the Mermaid's Tear, then? Can any of you tell me?" She shrieked in frustration, as the vines shrank back to their original dimensions, driven back by the crystal's glow.

"I believe I can answer that," a voice proclaimed from behind the pirates.

They turned and parted to allow Belladonna and Paella to pass. The women stopped to flank Viktor. The shock and nearly apoplectic rage on Dorada's face was priceless. She was so infuriated, she could only sputter incoherently.

"It seems that the pretty rock was too tempting for your apprentice," Belle stated. She deliberately omitted that she'd made sure the opal found its way to the girl. Paella kept her eyes downcast, refusing to look at her mistress.

Dorada glared at the girl. "Is that true, child? Have you worn the Mermaid's Tear?"

"*Si, Madre*."

The earth-witch calmed considerably. Smiling, she held her arms open. "I forgive you, my daughter. I do not know why this Dark One saw fit to abduct you, but you are home now."

Paella looked surprised at that. "I was not abducted, *Madre*."

Dorada gave Viktor a hard look. "What game is this you play, Dark One? It is cruel enough that you fly off with my apprentice and let me think some ill has befallen her, but you block the memory of it from her mind!"

He smiled wryly. "I have done nothing of the sort, other than keeping her presence on my ship a secret. Amusing to think that you believe I literally flew off with the wench."

"Do not toy with me, Dark One. You may be able to walk by daylight, through some unknown sorcery, but I know what you are, blood drinker. One of the gifts of your kind is that of flight. Now I understand the vanishing footprints."

"Indeed. Mother Celie neglected to inform me of that," he stroked his beard. "I shall have to try that sometime. However, I repeat, I did not abduct the girl. She came to my call."

"Impossible. Our original bargain was binding. The rejuvenating ceremony severed your bond to her."

He nodded. "Yes, it did, but, when you so foolishly used that damn bower to ensorcell me, you gave her back to me." He twirled the crystal. "You forgot to take into consideration that I wore this. Apparently, it twisted your fertility and bondage spells back on themselves. Rather than binding me to you through Paella, you irrevocably bound her to me. Not even death will free her."

Dorada paced furiously, desperately trying to see some course of action that would salvage all the plans ruined by this turn of events. This pirate had the devil's own luck at evading her snares.

"Will you allow her to remain here? I need her to wield the power of the Mermaid's Tear." She sighed resignedly.

"On one condition." His tone made it plain that it would not be negotiable. "Paella can remain with you and serve you, if she so chooses, only if you remove all the spells you placed on me completely."

Belladonna spoke up, "Do not leave any of your magic on him, earth-witch. I will know, and so will my Captain. He knows if any of our kind lies to him. I told him what to look for."

"Why would you give up such an advantage, sea-witch?" Dorada was puzzled.

"I have my reasons."

"Very well, I agree to your condition, Dark One. I have no other choice." She approached the vampire cautiously. He waited patiently but watched her every move unwaveringly. She placed a hand on his chest, humming. She moved her hand to his groin. Belladonna growled, but Viktor's body did not respond to Dorada's touch.

Finally, the earth-witch wet one finger in her mouth. She had to stand on tiptoe to reach his forehead.

Once she was flat-footed, she stepped back from him. "The spells are removed. Your eyes are so cold, Dark One." She shuddered. "Never has a man resisted my touch so easily. You must leave this place before nightfall. If I cannot control your magic, I cannot allow you to stay on my island."

"She fears you, Captain," Paella looked at him in awe. "*La Madre* fears no man. She tried to use me to enslave you, but her spell went awry. I will stay, but I do know if I wish to serve her any longer."

"Do not think me weak, child, just because of this creature of darkness," Dorada warned. "When your son is born, you will see how powerful I can be. Serve me, and that power will pass to you. I am sure you do not wish to see all the training you have received go to waste."

Paella held protective hands over her belly. "It is many months before my child will come. I will not sacrifice him up for your power."

"You are bound to the Tear now, child. Its power will compel you to offer up your firstborn boy child."

Belladonna started giggling uncontrollably. Everyone turned to stare at her with expressions ranging from puzzled, to irritated, to angry.

"You find it amusing that they are talking about murdering my son?" Viktor raised an eyebrow, his voice chilly.

"I find it positively hilarious," the siren chuckled. "Oh, I'm sure that the little witchling will find it in her to kill her first male whelp, but it won't be your son or the child she is carrying right now."

Dorada rounded on her angrily, "You speak nonsense, sea-witch! My spells ensured that the Dark One would sire a male child. The power to be gained from such a sacrifice, will double the power I will pass on."

"The brat in this bitch's womb is female, earth-witch," Belle grinned. "She was pregnant by the Captain before we even found you. But your spell did work. He has sired a son, and that child will be powerful indeed."

"Alyssa." Viktor grinned wryly. The siren nodded confirmation.

"Who is Alyssa?" Paella demanded waspishly.

"The mermaid I caught while trying to find that damn trinket."

That got Dorada's attention. "You actually captured a mermaid? No, no, no, this is all wrong. This was not supposed to happen."

"Actually, yes, it was," Belladonna countered. "This child was meant to be. You saw to it, when you were deliberately obscure about what you wanted the Captain to fetch for you."

"And how would you know?" she sneered derisively. "I never intended for him to mate with a mermaid. He shouldn't have been able to catch one, even. It was just meant to be a diversion to buy more time for my power to rebuild."

The siren shrugged, "I only know what the old man told me."

"What old man?"

It was Grimm who answered. As was his habit, he'd been following the conversation very closely, a skill that had aided Viktor and himself in the past for devising strategies. "I believe she is talking about Uncle Zeke."

"I know no one by that name."

"You once referred to him as the Elder," Vik clarified.

Dorada's face lost all color. "You truly are the One foretold," she whispered. "All the more reason for you to leave my island. You have what you came for."

Paella grasped his arm. "Take me with you," she pled. "If I stay here, I will never see you again!"

He removed her hand from his arm effortlessly and pushed her into Dorada's grasp. "I don't need a breeding female tagging along. Before long, you'll be sick and miserable. The sea is no place for a pregnant woman."

Turning, he gave a nod to his men. They left the woven lodge and made their way back to the ship. Not one of them, especially not Viktor, turned to look back or acknowledge the cries and pleas of the distraught girl.

As soon as the tide was favorable, the *Incubus* took to the open sea.

There were still six Sisters to track down.

Chapter 30

Celie watched the sparks rising from her fire. She gave it another poke and muttered to herself.

"You were lucky, boy. Ol' Zeke was wise sending that wild gal with you. I just hope you keep your wits about you. Dorada was the weakest and youngest of our kind. My other Sisters won't be so easy to find or deal with."

The sparks danced wildly, swirling into the gloom of the moss-laden oaks.

"Yep, and you've got other troubles building. Them as what hunt your kind are gathering."

The woman burst into the captain's cabin. "I was to be informed when we reached the Western seas!"

The captain rounded on her. "I did not give you leave to enter, woman."

"You serve my Master, as do I," she reminded him. "I have been charged to find Viktor Brandewyne, and you were ordered to aid me."

He got right in her face. "I don't need you reminding me of what I am to do. I am well aware of my duties. However, this is my ship, not yours. You will show respect due me as master of this vessel, and if you ever barge into my cabin again or speak to me as if I were merely a servant, I will confine you to your cabin."

"You wouldn't dare."

"Not only would I dare, but I know exactly how to make you stay in there."

She was sufficiently cowed by the threat, but clearly not happy about the situation. "I don't know why the Master chose to send me with you," she grumbled. "Why couldn't he have chosen someone more tractable?"

The captain chuckled. "Because you need me, lass; I know these waters and islands, and I know the best way to get the information we need."

"I am quite capable of extracting information from people," she replied, haughtily.

"Aye, but you'll find few willing to give up news of the whereabouts of Bloody Vik Brandee. People in these parts don't know or fear you. They fear him. He is the most feared and ruthless pirate to sail these waters since Captain Billy Black. The only other pirate that can hold a candle to Brandee is the Grimm Reaper, Hezekiah Grimm." He shook his head. "I don't understand the Master's desire to seek out such a man. Brandee is a clever, cruel bastard. He's been known to hunt down his pursuers, once he's gotten wind of them, rather than run."

"Good. That should make him easier to catch."

"If you had any sense, lass, you'd hope to never cross his path."

She peered at him closely. "You speak as if you had first-hand knowledge of this pirate."

He gave her a lop-sided smile. "Let's just say he owes me a boat and some crabs."

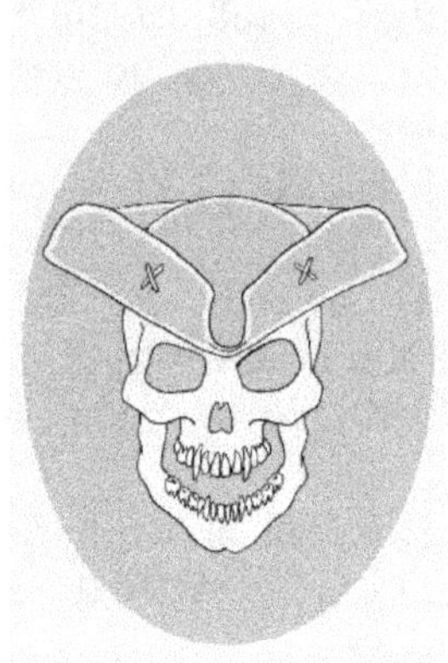

About the Author

Tamara A. Lowery, who once considered herself close to becoming a Crazy Cat Lady is now down to three cats. She lives with them and her husband in Tennessee and builds cars to pay the bills when not writing. She's been writing since the early 1980s but only published since 2011.

In addition to the Waves of Darkness series, she is the author of a steampunk episodic serial, The Adventures of Pigg & Woolfe.

She hopes to release a short story collection sometime in the near future, as well.

Website: talowery.wordpress.com
Facebook: facebook.com/Waves.of.Darkness
Plurk: plurk.com/Viksbelle
YouTube: youtube.com/user/Viksbelle

Waves of Darkness

Sisters of Power arc
Blood Curse
Demon Bayou (coming soon)
Silent Fathoms (coming soon)
Black Venom (coming soon)
Hell's Dodo (coming soon)

Blood Curse

The Daedalus Enigma (coming soon)
Maelstrom of Fate (coming soon)

Daughters of the Dragon arc
Hunting the Dragon (still in draft)

The Adventures of Pigg & Woolfe

Season 1
The Girl Who Fell from the Sky (S.1 omnibus)
Episodes
A Chance Encounter
The Truce
In the Woolfe's Den
Chase the Lightning
Peril in the Philippines
Rendezvous in Hong Kong
Double Jeopardy
Chance and Fortune
The Italian Connection
Rescue at Sea
Ghost Riders in the Sky
Castle in the Clouds

Season 2 coming soon

Tamara A. Lowery